# Brotherly

## A Wilson and Phillips-Lehman

## Mystery

### By

### Ross Lowen

www.publishnation.co.uk

**FRONT COVER ARTWORK**
**Front cover artwork by Joe Wilson**
mail@jwilsonillustration.co.uk

# DEDICATION

For Orla

## ABOUT THE AUTHOR

Ross Lowen lives in Oxford and works part time at a modern art gallery. Contact details: r.lowen@btopenworld.com

Follow Ross On Facebook:
https://www.facebook.com/profile.php?id=10006921
9184120

## ACKNOWLEDGEMENTS

I would like to thank everyone who helped me write this book. My wife Fereshteh, Alexander and Julie for their encouragement and love, Gloria for her guidance on Colombia, everyone at PublishNation, Joe Wilson for another superb cover design and my friends at Modern Art Oxford who are always supportive. Thanks to all of you.

Also available by Ross Lowen


Photographic Memory


It is 1973 and Peter Wilson, a young reporter working in Oxford, is in hospital recovering from a car accident. During his stay, he becomes friendly with a young Persian nurse, who tells him a mysterious story, casting doubt upon the true parentage of the child of a wealthy young couple.

Forty years later, whilst attending a dinner party in Hampstead, Wilson unexpectedly comes across a photograph of the nurse. Remembering the story she told him in Oxford, he decides to investigate along with his old friend Mathew Phillips-Lehman. A sometimes tragic story unfolds involving a Tory grandee, his elegant wife and a beautiful Swedish accountant. The action switches between London, Oxford and Italy, climaxing in a dramatic race against time to avoid further tragedy.

The first book, in a series of Wilson and Phillips-Lehman mysteries.

# CHAPTER ONE

# LOCH MORAR, SCOTLAND - NOVEMBER 2015

John checked that all the windows in the Lodge were closed and the back door was locked. He slipped his old wooden police truncheon into the large inside pocket of his *Barbour* jacket and his torch into one of the outside pockets. He hoped that he wouldn't have to use the truncheon but he knew from past experience that you could never be too careful.

He closed the solid oak front door to the Lodge behind him and made his way down the path to the driveway that led to the beautiful Victorian country house. It was a bitterly cold November evening and when John reached the driveway he looked to his left and although it was already dark, because there was a clear sky he could see the outline and lights of the Sound of Sleat Country House Hotel in the distance. Since he had moved to Scotland from London more than ten years ago it had always puzzled him why the hotel was named after the Sound of Sleat, the narrow sea channel which divides the nearby Sleat Peninsula, rather than Loch Morar, on the shore of which the hotel was situated. He made a mental note to find out the reason behind the anomaly.

John had spent most of the day logged on to the internet researching a criminal trial that had taken place at Woolwich Crown Court twelve years ago. He had thought that he'd put police work behind him when he retired from the force ten years ago. However, on this occasion, he didn't mind particularly because it was for a friend who he cared a lot about and wanted to help. Unfortunately, the findings of his research were almost certainly not what his friend would want to hear, but there would be little point in him hiding the truth. He had lost all sense of time whilst he was online and because he had ended up rushing to get ready to go out, he had left the letter and newspaper cuttings relating to the court case on the kitchen table where he had been working. Anyway, he would be back home later in the evening he thought to himself and he would lock them away in the safe then.

John crossed the driveway and using his torch to guide him, made his way along the track, through the woodland, down towards the loch. As he approached the small concrete jetty protruding from the shore into the loch he felt a sudden shortness of breath and nausea. He stopped for a moment, looking out beyond the jetty to the loch and the island on which the Tower stood and tried to compose himself, but the anxiety he was experiencing was becoming overwhelming. He thought he could hear footsteps behind him and as he turned to see who it was he felt a sharp blow on his forehead, just above his right eye, but it was nothing compared to the crushing pain he could feel in his chest, which seemed to be spreading to his neck and back.

Dropping to his knees on the concrete jetty, John desperately tried to find his mobile phone in the pockets of his jacket. Momentarily, he heard the footsteps again, faster this time, but now it sounded as if they were running away from him back towards the woodland, leading to the driveway. He suddenly remembered the aspirin he kept in his wallet and the advice an old friend, a doctor, had given him to always keep some handy in case you have a heart attack. The pain in his chest was becoming unbearable and together with the shortness of breath he was experiencing, he knew that he must act quickly. Fumbling in his inside pockets he found his wallet and his mobile phone and placed them both in front of him on the jetty. He managed

2

to release one of the aspirin tablets from its packet and started to chew on it, whilst trying to send a message on his phone. It was the last thing he remembered as he slumped forward on to the concrete.

# CHAPTER TWO

# MATHEW CALLS

At home in Marylebone, Peter Wilson logged off his desktop computer and switched off the light in the spare bedroom, which had been converted into an office. It was five o'clock in the afternoon and already beginning to get dark outside. He had been busy all afternoon preparing a presentation on the United Kingdom's defence capabilities during the nineteen-eighties, which he would be giving to a group of university students early next year.

Peter poured himself a glass of Irish whiskey and went downstairs to the kitchen to decide what to make for his evening meal. It was now more than three years since his wife, Gloria, died unexpectedly and this part of the day was always his least favourite time. Too many memories. Immediately following her death, he had thought about selling the Victorian terraced house, situated just off Marylebone High Street. However, as time passed, he was finding that the memories mostly tended to be happy ones and he now felt inclined to stay put, at least for the time being. When Gloria had been working, she was also a journalist, and they were both at home they would normally meet in the kitchen at about this time of day and enjoy a drink together. Whilst the depression he had experienced throughout the first year or so following her death had now lifted, he still missed her company terribly.

Peter could remember his mood changing for the better when he started to take on some part-time work about two years ago. He had spent a very successful career as a defence correspondent and investigative journalist and returning to his occupation on an ad hoc basis, particularly the investigative aspect of it had, without a doubt, helped with his recovery. The recent investigation that he had undertaken with his oldest friend, Mathew Phillips-Lehman, which had become known in the media as the "Coleville affair", named after the former MP, Sir Robert Coleville and his wife Margaret, had a cathartic effect on him and thankfully, he hadn't looked back since then.

The brief relationship he'd had during the investigation with Isabella Dolores Ruiz, a Spanish TV reporter, had ended amicably when she returned from London to Madrid to take up a new position with a Spanish television company. Peter looked back on their relationship happily and although he realised at the time, for various reasons, that it was unlikely to last, he had enjoyed being with female company again for the first time since Gloria had died. He still kept in touch with Isabella by email.

Another unexpected but pleasant event had been his re-acquaintance with Taraneh Saderzadeh, an old friend from his days as a young newspaper reporter in Oxford. She had nursed him following a nasty car accident in the early nineteen-seventies and coincidentally, they had literally bumped into each other one rainy day in Kensington forty years later. It was an unusual story Taraneh had told him all those years ago in Oxford that had led to the investigation and eventual disclosure of the Coleville's crimes. Taraneh now spent most of her time caring for her nonagenarian father in Tehran, although she visited London, where her father still owned a flat in Kensington, three or four times a year. She was due back in London before Christmas and they had agreed to meet for dinner on her return. Both of them were now in their sixties and Peter still felt attracted to Taraneh and he had a suspicion that she felt the same about him. He was looking forward to their dinner date.

Peter had prepared himself an asparagus risotto for his evening meal and afterwards watched a TV documentary about the American media artist and musician *Laurie Anderson*. It was whilst he was getting ready for bed, at about eleven o'clock, that his mobile phone rang and he was surprised to see that it was his old friend Mathew Phillips-Lehman calling him at such a late hour.

"Hello Matt, to what do I owe this unexpected pleasure?" Peter asked cheerily.

Although as soon as Mathew answered, Peter realised all was not well, he had known his friend for too long not to detect that something was seriously wrong.

"I'm driving down to my parents' house in Surrey Peter, I hope I haven't woken you it's quite late." Mathew said.

"Are they alright Matt?" Peter asked, suddenly concerned. Mathew's parents were now both in their nineties and quite frail and it wouldn't have come as a great surprise to him if either of them was unwell.

"Yes, they're both fine thanks Peter, it's John I'm afraid, Judith rang me earlier and he's in hospital near his home in Scotland, apparently, he's had a heart attack. Judith's in New Zealand at the moment, but told me she has a key to the Lodge in Scotland where John lives and it's at mum and dad's. I'm going to collect the key and then drive to Scotland first thing in the morning and I just wanted to let you know that I won't be able to meet for lunch tomorrow." Mathew explained.

Mathew's older brother John had lived alone in the Highlands of Scotland for at least ten years after retiring from the Police force, where he had risen to the rank of Chief Inspector. Their sister Judith lived with her husband Colin in the family home in Surrey, where they also cared for their elderly parents.

"I'm so sorry to hear that Matt, do you know any more about John's condition?" Peter asked, feeling sorry for his old friend.

6

"It doesn't sound too good, I rang the hospital before I set off for Surrey and he's in intensive care I'm afraid." Mathew said sadly.

"Well, if anyone can survive this it'll be John, he's as strong as an ox," Peter replied, trying his best to sound positive, "do you want some company in Scotland Matt? I could share the driving with you, it must take eight or nine hours to dive up there and motorways can be very tiring and boring as well."

"That's not why I rang you Peter, you know that don't you? I expect you're too busy to come all that way at such short notice."

"I know you didn't Matt, I'm not that busy at the moment and I'd like to join you on the trip, if that's alright with you, what time are you leaving in the morning?" Peter asked.

"Well, that's very kind of you Peter, it'll be early, I could pick you up at about seven o'clock, I want to miss the traffic by getting out of London as early as possible." Mathew replied.

"That's fine Matt, I'll pack a few things tonight and I'll be ready at seven, see you then and send my love to your parents."

Following the call, Peter sat quietly for a few minutes. He thought to himself that it was the least he could do to travel with his old friend up to Scotland. He would never forget the kindness Mathew and his family had shown him when Gloria died and after all, he had known them all for more than forty years. He had always got on well with Judith and her two sons, Archie and Tom, who both worked for the Civil Service in London and looked upon him as an uncle. Colin, Judith's husband, had become a good friend over the years as well and the two of them would occasionally go and see bands play in London, they were both rock music fans, so there was always plenty of choice. Probably because John was a few years older than Mathew,

Peter didn't know him quite as well as he knew Judith, or Judy as he had always called her, who he'd always been quite fond of, in fact, there had been a time when they were both in their twenties that he thought they may even have ended up together.

John was an interesting character, a big strong man who had played rugby at a good level when he was younger. Quiet and studious by nature, he would often be described by those that didn't know him so well as a bit of a loner, but he had a steely determination about him which had clearly helped with his rise through the ranks of the Police force. Those attributes, together with his good looks, made him extremely attractive to women and although he had never married, Mathew had often spoken about a number of intense and sometimes volatile relationships his brother had been involved in over the years.

Peter made a start on packing a few things for the trip to Scotland, all the time thinking about John hoping that he would pull through.

# CHAPTER THREE

# THE LONG DRIVE

Angus Mackenzie was in the kitchen of the Sound of Sleat Country House Hotel with Morag Campbell, who was clearing up after preparing the guests' breakfast. At this time of year, during the run up to Christmas, the hotel was fairly quiet and only seven guests were currently staying, a German couple who had also stayed earlier in the year for the excellent wild trout and salmon fishing, a young couple from London enjoying their first visit to Scotland, two Italian men who were visiting the area for the red deer hind stalking and Lady Caroline Hemsworth. Caroline, a regular guest at the hotel, was actually a Viscountess and had previously been married to Viscount Brigton, better known as Anthony Hemsworth, the wealthy newspaper proprietor.

Angus and his wife Kirsty had owned the luxury hotel and estate, known locally as 'The Sound', for nearly ten years and had built up a profitable business during this time. When they bought the hotel it was in some state of disrepair and although it was still open to guests at the time, it was making a loss. They had spent a considerable sum renovating the buildings and the substantial grounds, which covered fifty-six acres on the banks of Loch Morar. The costs of the renovation had largely been offset by the relatively cheap price they had paid for the beautiful Victorian property.

The hotel was ideally situated for visitors touring the Highlands and particularly the islands, Skye being a favourite destination. The hunting and fishing attracted visitors from all over the world, especially between March and October. The hotel had ten double bedrooms, six of them with stunning views over the loch. Morag came in on weekdays to prepare breakfast for the guests and two chefs and a small kitchen staff provided lunch and dinner seven days a week. A full-time gardener looked after the grounds, with specialist help on a part-time basis from John Phillips-Lehman who owned the Lodge and it was John's health that was worrying everyone at The Sound, as Kirsty Mackenzie joined Angus and Morag in the large kitchen. The kitchen had been modernised within the last few years and Morag had helped Angus and Kirsty with the plans. It was very much Morag's domain and she took personal responsibility to ensure it met all the necessary hygiene standards.

"I've just phoned the hospital and he's still in intensive care." Kirsty told them, helping Morag stack the dishwasher.

"Well, thank God you found him, if you hadn't taken the dogs out for a walk when you did he probably wouldn't even be with us now." Angus replied gloomily.

"It was just lucky there was an ambulance and paramedics in Mallaig at the time or I don't know what would have happened," Kirsty said sadly, "his sister Judith sent me a text message this morning after I'd rung her last night, to say their brother Mathew is travelling from London today with a family friend and they should be arriving sometime this evening."

"Did you tell me that John's sister is in New Zealand?" Angus asked.

"Yes, on holiday, luckily I had a mobile number for her, John named her as his next of kin when I updated the staff records earlier in the year." Kirsty replied.

"All that administration work does come in handy sometimes I suppose." Angus commented.

Kirsty had noticed that Morag looked a bit tearful and she put her arm around her.

"Can't believe it, he's such a big strong healthy guy and such a nice man." Morag said, reaching for a tissue in her handbag.

"He's helped transform the grounds here over the years, he'd be sorely missed I know that much." Angus said ruefully.

"Perhaps we should ask his brother and friend to stay at the hotel here with us, at least until we know what plans the two of them have?" Kirsty suggested.

"That's a nice idea, I'll arrange for a couple of the bedrooms to be made up, it's the least we can do, who's cleaning the rooms this morning, is it Elen?" Angus asked.

"No, she's away in Glasgow for a few days, her sister, Maria is covering for her whilst she's away." Morag replied, looking a bit more cheerful.

"I'll get on with that now," Angus said, "and Morag, you get off home, we'll finish off here."

\*\*\*\*\*\*\*\*\*\*\*\*\*\*\*\*\*\*\*\*

Mathew arrived at Peter's house in Marylebone just after seven o'clock on the Wednesday morning and joined Peter in the kitchen for a cup of coffee before they set off for Scotland.

"Any news from the hospital Matt?" Peter asked, whilst he poured the coffee.

"He's still in intensive care I'm afraid, I told the Sister at the hospital that we are driving up today and she said that we were welcome to come to the hospital, but because of his condition she couldn't guarantee that we will be able to see him, which is fair enough I suppose." Mathew said.

"I've packed a flask of coffee and some sandwiches for us to have on the way." Peter said as they finished their coffee and then made their way out to the car.

11

"It's very kind of you to join me on the trip old boy, it's a long old journey up there, have you ever been to Loch Morar before?" Mathew asked as they set off.

"No, I haven't Matt, but I had a quick look online earlier this morning and it looks wonderful, hunting and fishing country by the look of it, John certainly found a beautiful spot to live. How were your parents when you saw them last night?" Peter asked.

"They were fine thanks, they're just very old, I deliberately didn't tell them about John, it would only upset them. I spoke with Judith in New Zealand and we agreed that we should wait and see what happens over the next few days before we say anything to them. Archie and Tom are taking it in turns to stay over with them whilst Judith and Colin are away. She talked to me about flying back early, but she's due back next week anyway so I persuaded her that there was little point in coming home earlier until we know more about John's condition." Mathew replied

The two old friends stopped every two hours or so during the journey and switched drivers. Mathew was quiet for long periods, obviously worried about his older brother, but the long silences didn't feel uncomfortable for two friends that had known each other for so long. They would normally have played some of their favourite CD's on such a long journey, but on this occasion it didn't feel right and wasn't mentioned.

It was around midday when they started driving through the Lake District and the traffic was notably lighter than it had been earlier that Peter asked Mathew to tell him a bit more about John and his life since he had left the Police force.

"I suppose he must have been in his mid-fifties when he retired from the force. He'd reached Chief Inspector rank so he had a good pension to fall back on, but what really surprised the family was when he got a job working at Kew Gardens." Mathew said.

"Oh yes, I'd forgotten all about that, of course, didn't he go on to do a degree in horticulture or something." Peter asked.

"Forestry, he spent a year or two at Kew and then took a degree in Forestry at Bangor University, in North Wales. I remember speaking with Judith about it at the time and we were both really impressed. When he graduated, he must have been sixty by then, he moved to Scotland and bought the Lodge on the banks of Loch Morar. Years before, it had been the lodge for the big house at the end of the drive, which became the Sound of Sleat Country House Hotel. He works part-time for the Mackenzies, who own the hotel and estate. John looks after the woodland and helps out with some of the gardening, he loves it. Judith met Angus and Kirsty Mackenzie when she went up to stay with John in the Lodge. She speaks very highly of them and told me they've done a remarkable job turning around the fortunes of the hotel. Apparently, it was losing money hand over fist when they bought the place. I remember John telling me that neither of them had a background in hospitality, Angus had worked in London in the City and Kirsty had once been a model." Mathew explained.

"I suppose after the stress and strain of being a senior copper in the Met, it must be a wonderful life for him and very different to living in Clapham I would imagine. Judy told me he was like a different man when he left the Police force." Peter said.

"He never used to speak much about his job with the Met, but occasionally he'd tell me about some of the dangerous bastards who he would have to deal with day in, day out, it sounded nightmarish to be honest Peter. I don't know how he put up with it for so long and now this goes and happens, it seems so unfair." Mathew sighed.

"Yes, life can be cruel Matt." Peter said quietly, thinking of Gloria.

They arrived at the hospital in Fort William just before six o'clock and Mathew decided that he would try and speak with the doctor and if possible, go and see John. During one of the several stops they had made on the journey, Mathew had called the hotel where John worked and spoke to Kirsty Mackenzie, telling her that they had a key to the Lodge and would be there later in the evening. However, Kirsty had insisted that they both stay the night at the hotel and that two rooms had been prepared and a table in the restaurant reserved for them for dinner, at no cost.

# CHAPTER FOUR

## ANGUS AND ALEX MACKENZIE

Angus Hector Mackenzie was born in Inverness in June 1965, the eldest son of Cameron and Mary Mackenzie, landowners from Inverness-shire. Cameron was the fourth generation of Mackenzies to inherit land in the Scottish Highlands and was immensely proud of his heritage. In the late nineteenth-century his grandfather went into business with the London based banker and financier, Samuel Blount and formed the Mackenzie and Blount Steamship Company. Cameron's grandfather, Fergus Mackenzie, had a nautical background serving as an officer in the navy and he met Samuel Blount at The East India Club in London. Initially, they specialised in the River Plate meat trade. In the second half of the nineteenth century the number of city dwellers in Britain was far higher than those living in any cities in the United States of America and there wasn't enough beef and lamb being produced on British soil to satisfy their appetites. At the time, imported meat was significantly eroded by the time it arrived in Britain from America and part of the solution to the problem involved the importation of chilled prime beef from Argentina.

Fergus Mackenzie, Samuel Blount and their heirs capitalised on the solution throughout the late nineteenth and early twentieth centuries, building up a formidable shipping company. By the nineteen-eighties, Mackenzie, Blount, as the company had become known, was successfully shipping both commercial and personal cargo between the UK and Latin America, with offices in London, Sao Paulo in Brazil and Cartagena in Colombia.

Unlike his forebears, Cameron Mackenzie had shown little interest in the family shipping business, part of which he inherited in his father's will, merely attending board meetings when required.

His son Angus, on the other hand, was fascinated by the sea and all things nautical. He was sent to boarding school in England at a very early age and was delighted when he discovered that the school was in Hampshire, situated between Portsmouth and Southampton. At weekends, he could either be found taking sailing lessons near Southampton or, visiting Portsmouth's historic dockyard. Angus loved boarding school and was popular with the other boarders, excelling at rowing and eventually becoming head boy. Although he was one of the only boys at the school from Scotland, unless you knew his name, it was difficult to detect that he came from north of the border because he spoke with an English accent.

Angus's only sibling, his younger brother Alex, attended the same boarding school as him but found it difficult to settle and returned home to Scotland when he was only eight years old. Alex was a very different child compared to his brother. He was shy and sensitive and struggled academically. These differences created tension between the brothers and Alex also experienced difficulties at home, mainly with his father. Mary Mackenzie was a loving mother but their father Cameron could be short tempered and seemed to have little interest in his children's wellbeing, particularly where Alex was concerned. This led to tensions arising when Angus returned home during the school holidays and the situation worsened when he reached his teens, to such an extent that on some occasions he would stay at school during the holidays rather than returning to Scotland. There were always a few children, whose parents perhaps lived overseas, that stayed at school during the holidays so Angus wasn't alone on these occasions.

As he grew older, whenever Angus did return home it upset him when he saw how withdrawn his younger brother had become. He also felt upset when their father bullied Alex and guilty that he didn't intervene to help his brother. On one occasion, when Angus had just turned sixteen, he remembered returning home for a long weekend only to find that Alex, who was only a year younger than him, was sporting a black eye. When he asked his brother how it had happened, Alex refused to answer, but it was obvious to Angus that his father had caused the injury. Alex was clearly upset, but Angus shut out the shame of what was happening at home by spending the whole weekend with his friends and ignoring his younger brother.

The guilt that he felt over his insensitive and hurtful behaviour towards Alex would resurface in later years causing him further anguish, resulting in a series of unforeseen consequences. The contrast between life at the boarding school, where Angus was so happy and his life at home in the Highlands of Scotland couldn't have been greater. If the truth be told, Angus was embarrassed by his younger brother, which only added to the self-loathing which would re-emerge, from time to time, throughout his adult life.

\*\*\*\*\*\*\*\*\*\*\*\*\*\*\*\*\*\*\*

Despite Alex's difficulties, there was one interest in which he excelled, photography and it would ultimately have a huge impact on his life. He was just twelve when his mother's cousin, Finlay, came to stay for a week at their large Victorian home near Inverness. Finlay was a wedding photographer and a few years earlier had setup a successful business which specialised in large, often society weddings throughout Scotland and occasionally south of the border as well. He was a tall, handsome man in his mid-forties and

17

thanks to his striving business, he had recently bought a beautiful property in Edinburgh with his partner, Arthur.

Finlay always took a camera with him when he visited the Highlands because of the beautiful scenery and when Alex first saw the camera in the kitchen during breakfast one morning, he unusually showed an interest in it and asked Finlay if he would teach him to take a photograph. Finlay was only too pleased to help the young boy, whom he knew was struggling through his early life and passed on some rudimentary knowledge of how photography works. Before he returned to his home in Edinburgh, he gave Alex the camera as a gift. He also recommended a book on photography that Alex should read and told his cousin, Mary, where she could buy the book for her son in Inverness, the shop also sold and developed film.

Over the next few years, Alex became an accomplished photographer, particularly portrait photography. Each week, he would take the bus into Inverness with his pocket money and buy the most recent photography magazines he could find and collect any film which had been developed for him. He would also visit the beautiful Inverness Library and lend various books on photography and on one occasion found a book about fashion photography that he would read again and again. His mother was delighted that her son had found a hobby which interested him and in which he excelled and even his father seemed grudgingly pleased. On his fourteenth birthday, his parents had a dark room installed in the basement of the house, where Alex could develop his own film. By this time, Alex had won several photography competitions and was making quite a name for himself in the world of amateur photography.

Angus was surprised and slightly put out by his younger brother's relative success. It was the first time that he had been overshadowed by Alex and on a recent return home from school, he noticed that photography was one of the main topics of conversations when friends of the family visited. Alex appeared to become a different person from the normally shy, reserved boy when photography was mentioned and he would happily discuss the techniques he had used to take some of his best photographs.

Even at school, where Alex had previously struggled academically and socially, he had become very popular. The headmaster and art teacher arranged for the school to put on a small exhibition of his photography in the main hall, which was open to the public on Saturday mornings and it was covered in the local paper and on the local television news.

Naturally, Mary was proud of her son's achievements and had a number of his winning photographs framed and hung throughout the house. Alex would regularly write to Finlay asking for advice and Finlay was delighted when the young teenager even started passing on some of his own tips.

*********************

In 1984, Angus was accepted at Cambridge University to study History. He had already made up his mind that his future lay in the family shipping business, working at its head offices in Bishopsgate, London. Consequently, following completion of his degree at Cambridge, he had decided he would undertake a Master's Degree in Shipping, Trade and Finance. His father was delighted with his eldest son's progress and plans and told Angus that on the successful completion of his Master's degree, he would buy his son a flat in the City near to the Mackenzie, Blount offices.

It was during Angus's time at Cambridge that, without warning, his brother suddenly left home. On his eighteenth birthday, Alex withdrew the funds of a trust that had been setup for him and travelled by train to London. Over the next few weeks and months, he made no attempt to contact his father or brother and sent only the occasional letter to his mother telling her that he was alright and for her not to worry about him. The family had no idea where he was, although his mother had noted the London postmark on his letters. Neither did they know how he was making a living. The trust fund that Alex had withdrawn was a reasonable amount of money, but not substantial and eventually, he would have to find work to support himself. Cameron and Angus were furious with Alex, for what they called his selfish behaviour. His father said he would soon be in touch when the money ran out and he even threatened to write him out of his will, but for once Mary put her foot down and told Cameron that if he did, she would leave him. He quickly told her that he had dropped the idea. His mother was just sad, it was as if her son had just disappeared and as time passed, his name was mentioned less and less whenever the family met.

\*\*\*\*\*\*\*\*\*\*\*\*\*\*\*\*\*\*\*

Angus started work at Mackenzie, Blount in September 1990, following the successful completion of his Master's Degree. As promised, his father had purchased a flat for his son in one of the new developments in Bishopsgate. Angus could walk from his flat to the office in a matter of minutes and he spent his first twelve months there gaining full-time, hands-on experience of the shipping industry, after which he would take on a senior position within the company.

Within eighteen months, he had been appointed as a senior manager reporting directly to the Operations Director and given responsibility for all commercial trade between the UK and Colombia. As well as gaining invaluable experience of the shipping industry, Angus had also been taking Spanish lessons for the past twelve months. With a large part of the company's business conducted between the UK and South America, his knowledge of the language would be useful and Mackenzie, Blount arranged for a Spanish teacher to come into the offices in Bishopsgate to provide private lessons for him three times a week.

Angus was just twenty-seven years old, tall with fair hair, rugged good looks, unlike his younger brother whose looks were more refined, owned a flat in the City of London just a stone's throw from the offices of the family business, where he held a senior position. Money had never been a problem for the young Angus Mackenzie. His parents owned a substantial property and land in the Highlands of Scotland, as well as a significant share in Mackenzie, Blount. He had enjoyed a first-class private education and been financially supported by his father throughout his time at Cambridge and later, when studying for his Master's degree. However, this was all about to change one rainy April afternoon in 1992, when his father rang and told him he would be arriving at the London office the following morning and they needed to meet first thing.

Angus hadn't seen his father since Christmas and it was clear as soon as Cameron Mackenzie arrived at the offices that all was not well. Although he was only in his early seventies, he suddenly looked ten years older, he had lost weight and his face looked gaunt.

Angus had read about the *Lloyd's of London* insurance losses over the past few years, particularly following the Piper Alpha oil rig explosion in 1988, the San Francisco earthquake and storms in northern Europe. It was a constant subject of discussion in the office, mainly because of *Lloyd's* connection with shipping. There were rumours circulating that *Lloyd's* overall losses may have reached £8 billion and that the world's oldest insurance market was on the brink of insolvency. What Angus didn't know until that April morning was that his father was known as a *Lloyd's Name*, had invested large amounts of money with the insurance market and now faced unlimited losses. Like a number of other *Lloyd's Names* now facing insolvency, Cameron had invested heavily in a market which he believed would provide tax benefits and substantial returns. In fact, for many years it had done just that. Like many others, he had been encouraged to invest in the nineteen-seventies following the introduction, by the Labour Government, of a super tax of up to 98%, but by the early nineteen-nineties the bubble had burst.

Cameron told his son that his debts were so large that he was now forced to sell not only the family's property and land in Scotland, but its share in Mackenzie, Blount. The sale of these major assets would cover most, but not all of the debt. The meeting took less than an hour and his father showed no emotion throughout the encounter. By midday, he was at Heathrow Airport waiting for the flight back to Scotland.

Angus was shocked by the news and upset at how his father's health had clearly deteriorated in such a short space of time. He took the rest of the day off, phoning his mother as soon as he returned to his flat. Typically, she was much more concerned about her husband's poor health than the financial ruin that the family faced. She had good reason to be concerned, Cameron was to die within twelve months of selling the family's share in the company. Mary moved to live with her sister, before going into a nursing home, where she died in 2002 after suffering from dementia.

From the morning that his father had visited him in the office, Angus knew that his world had changed and from now on he would have to provide for himself in life. Unbeknown to him, his father had already spoken to the Board of Directors about his plight and although in the future the Mackenzie family would no longer own a share in the company, the directors were concerned that the brand should not be adversely affected. Consequently, an agreement was reached so that the name Mackenzie, Blount would be retained.

Within a few days, the Operations Director had spoken with Angus and told him that he saw no reason why he shouldn't remain with the company and reassured him that he would be treated fairly, like any other employee, should he wish to stay on. Angus was mightily relieved, he had to earn a living for himself from now on and he figured that there would be opportunities for him to prosper at Mackenzie, Blount. What he didn't know at the time was that when those opportunities did arise, they would come from unexpected quarters and would change his life dramatically.

# CHAPTER FIVE

# DINNER AT 'THE SOUND'

Sister Anne McGregor invited Mathew into her small office near to the intensive care unit where his brother John was being looked after.

"You've had a long journey Mr. Phillips-Lehman, you must be tired." Sister McGregor said, inviting Mathew to take a seat. Mathew noted that she was extremely tall with long red hair and a kindly manner.

"Please, call me Mathew, yes I'm a bit tired but I wanted to drive so that I have the use of the car whilst I'm staying up here. My friend Peter shared the driving, so that helped." Mathew replied.

"Are you sure he doesn't want to come in and join you?" Sister McGregor asked.

"No, thank you, Peter wanted to stretch his legs and we thought it best that I came to see you alone at first, can you tell me how John is?" Mathew asked, anxiously.

"Well, I can assure you he's being well looked after Mathew and I've asked Doctor Ansari to come and see you, he's just finishing his rounds and should be here any moment. Whilst we are waiting, perhaps you could just complete this form, we need some details of John's next of kin, it's purely procedural. I understand your sister is in New Zealand Mathew, she rang earlier today." Sister McGregor said.

"Yes of course Sister, let me complete it now." Mathew agreed and by the time he had completed the form Doctor Ansari had joined them and pulled up a chair. The young doctor introduced himself and started to update Mathew on his brother's condition.

"John has suffered what is commonly known as a heart attack, basically, the supply of blood to the heart is blocked. He is in our intensive care unit and needs to stay here for a day or two until his condition stabilizes. He fell and suffered a nasty head injury before he was found and we are also having to treat him for concussion." The doctor explained.

As an investigative journalist for more than forty years, occasionally coming across grief, anger and pain were all part of the job, but when hearing about his own brother's illness Mathew found it much more difficult to digest. To a certain extent, he had become used to suppressing his emotions throughout his career when confronting grief, but this was totally different and he was suddenly aware that he felt quite tearful.

"Can I see him doctor?" he asked.

"Not this evening I'm afraid but perhaps tomorrow, the head injury seems to have caused John some confusion and he needs compete rest for the next twenty-four hours. I've spoken to my colleagues this afternoon and we are currently thinking that a coronary artery bypass graft will be necessary, we can divert blood around the clogged parts of the artery." Doctor Ansari explained.

"Would you do this here doctor?" Mathew asked.

"No, we would take John to Inverness, it is one of the reasons he needs complete rest ahead of the journey, they have excellent facilities there. He would need to stay in hospital there for at least seven days following the operation. John is very poorly Mathew, but we are fairly confident he has a reasonable chance of making a full recovery after surgery." Doctor Ansari was on his feet and shook hands with Mathew. "Is there anything else you would like to ask me Mathew?"

"No, thank you so much doctor." Mathew replied.

25

"Oh, there is one thing puzzling us, when John arrived in the ambulance yesterday the paramedics found an old-fashioned police truncheon inside his jacket." The doctor said before leaving.

*********************

"A truncheon?" Peter asked, with some surprise as Mathew drove them to the Sound of Sleat Country House Hotel.

"Yes, apparently the paramedics found it in his jacket pocket once they'd got him settled inside the ambulance." Mathew had already explained to Peter what the doctor had told him about his brother's condition and had suddenly remembered being told about the truncheon. "The doctor also said that John had suffered a nasty head injury, probably due to a fall, just before he was found and they've been treating him for concussion. It just seems a bit odd to me that he goes for a walk down by the loch on a cold, dark, November evening with a truncheon in his pocket."

"You think he might have been expecting trouble, possibly meeting someone?" Peter asked.

"Well, it's certainly strange behaviour, even in my brothers unusual world, don't you think old boy?" Mathew replied.

"I wouldn't say John's world is that unusual Matt, it's certainly a far cry from Clapham, London and the Metropolitan Police Force, but he's made a new life for himself up here." Peter said trying to cheer up his old friend.

"What, you mean an ex Chief Inspector living alone in a lodge at the back of beyond, working as an occasional gardener, wondering around in the dark with a truncheon?" Mathew replied and Peter noticed him smiling.

"I'm sure there'll be a perfectly rational explanation when we get to speak with him Matt." Peter said, trying to keep a straight face.

\*\*\*\*\*\*\*\*\*\*\*\*\*\*\*\*\*\*\*\*

Angus and Kirsty Mackenzie were waiting to welcome Peter and Mathew when they arrived at the beautiful old hotel.

"The two of you must be exhausted." Kirsty said as Angus helped them in with their luggage. Peter couldn't help noticing what a handsome couple they made. Kirsty looked to be in her early forties and was dressed casually, but extremely stylishly, in a pair of designer jeans and a simple blue cashmere sweater. Her blonde hair was tied back and she had the most wonderful bone structure and a slim figure. She wore little make up. Peter thought to himself that she was the kind of person who would look good regardless of what she was wearing, a very beautiful woman. Angus was also good looking, Peter noted, tall and well-built with blonde hair, he was dressed in a smart dark blue suit, with an open neck white shirt.

"Yes it has been a long day," Mathew replied, admiring the staircase leading to the bedrooms, "and it's so kind of you to ask us to stay tonight, what a lovely hotel you have."

"Thank you and you're more than welcome, it's the least we can do," Angus said, "your brother is a very important part of the setup here and has become a good friend over the years, you've been to the hospital I understand, how is he?"

Mathew briefly recounted what the doctor had told him earlier and said he would be returning in the morning to get a further update.

"Well, if you get to see him tomorrow you must send him our love, from all of us at the hotel," Kirsty said, "now, I expect you two would like to freshen up before dinner, we've reserved a table in the dining room for you overlooking the loch, we only have five other guests dining with us this evening so it will be quiet."

Whilst Angus showed Peter and Mathew to their rooms, Kirsty and a young waitress welcomed some of the other guests into the splendid dining room. Peter noticed that Angus had an easy charm and confidence when he spoke. His wife Kirsty had what sounded like a Glaswegian accent, whereas Angus spoke with an English accent, probably the result of a private education south of the border, Peter thought to himself. He looked as if he was probably a few years older than his wife and as well as the confident manner, he had an air of authority about him and Peter could easily see why Kirsty had been attracted to him.

Both Peter's and Mathew's rooms were situated above the dining room with spectacular views across the loch, which had been partly floodlit so they could see the small island about one hundred meters from the shore. Interestingly, in the centre of the island stood a stone built, three story tower and because of the floodlight, Peter could just about detect from his bedroom window that it had been renovated at some point. Surprisingly, the St. George's flag was flying above the tower on the rooftop.

\*\*\*\*\*\*\*\*\*\*\*\*\*\*\*\*\*\*\*\*

Before going into the dining room, Peter and Mathew joined Angus and Kirsty for a pre-dinner drink in the small bar adjacent to the reception area. A roaring fire lit up the lovely oak-paneled walls and the Mackenzie tartan carpet only added to the warmth of the room. Kirsty handed them both a menu and suggested that they place their orders because it was already getting quite late and she was sure they must both be hungry after such a long day.

Whilst the Mackenzies certainly looked a handsome, well-matched couple, Peter couldn't help noticing a certain coolness between them. It wasn't anything specific, just an overall first impression he got from their general behaviour.

"I spent the best part of fifteen years working in the shipping industry in London and we've been here at The Sound for about ten years now." Angus explained, in answer to a question from Mathew.

"So, were you already here when John bought the Lodge?" Peter asked.

"Aye, John moved into the Lodge just a few months after we'd taken over the hotel and within twelve months he started doing some work for us on the estate, a wee number of hours at first, but we soon realised that his knowledge of forestry was invaluable and eventually we persuaded him to work two days a week, sometimes three at certain times of the year." Kirsty explained.

"You've probably already noticed the woodland we have on the estate and John has some very good ideas on how to manage the woods, whilst promoting biodiversity, we have long conversations about it believe it or not." Angus added, with a smile.

"I understand that it was you that found John after he'd collapsed Kirsty, my sister Judith told me when she called from New Zealand earlier, we are so grateful to you, I hate to think what would have happened if you hadn't found him." Mathew said.

"Well, you've partly the dogs to thank for that," Angus explained, "Kirsty takes the Labradors out for a walk in the evenings and she found poor old John down by the jetty by the loch, the paramedics were nearby in Mallaig which was a stroke of luck as well."

As Angus went into more detail concerning the dog walking arrangements, Peter got the distinct impression that Kirsty was feeling slightly uncomfortable, he could almost detect a slightly sheepish look on her face and she certainly looked relieved when the young waitress arrived and told Peter and Mathew that their table was ready, if they would like to follow her into the dining room.

\*\*\*\*\*\*\*\*\*\*\*\*\*\*\*\*\*\*\*\*

The five other diners, all residents, were already in the large dining room when Peter and Mathew sat down at one of the tables by the large window, that stretched along the whole length of the room, giving them a superb view of the floodlit loch with its small island and tower. The other diners, a German couple, two Italian men and an elegant woman sat on her own were spread throughout the dining room.

The two old friends had both ordered the cock-a-leekie soup, just what they needed on such a cold day Peter had suggested, followed by the salmon trout and Mathew had chosen a bottle of Italian Verdicchio to compliment the fish. Over dinner they discussed their plans and agreed that in the morning after breakfast, Mathew would drop Peter off at the Lodge and then drive to the hospital to check on John's progress.

The food and wine were excellent and Kirsty came into the dining room from time to time to check that everything was well and the guests were happy. Peter couldn't help noticing that she even walked stylishly as she moved across the dining room. Embarrassingly, he found it quite difficult to take his eyes off her, even though he suspected that she was almost certainly used to attracting attention.

By the time their coffee was being served, the dining room was nearly empty apart from the woman sat alone at the table at the opposite end of the room.

"You're not going to believe this old boy, but I think the woman sat over there is the Countess." Mathew whispered and Peter discretely turned around in his chair to get a better look.

"Indeed, it is, Lady Caroline Hemsworth, what on earth is she doing here?" Peter replied, looking surprised.

"Well, we'd better ask her to join us for coffee and we'll find out." Mathew replied, but before he could get out of his chair, she was walking towards their table with a smile on her face. Although she was now in her sixties, Caroline Hemsworth looked as elegant as she had done thirty years earlier, when Peter and Mathew had both worked for the broadsheet newspaper owned by her ex-husband Viscount Brigton, better known as Anthony Hemsworth. She had become known throughout Fleet Street and later Wapping as the Countess and had enjoyed the attention she had been given in those days as the wife of the famous newspaper proprietor.

Anthony Hemsworth had always been a great supporter of investigative journalism and took a personal interest in Peter's and Mathew's work for the newspaper, often to the dismay of whoever was the editor at the time.

"Good evening gentlemen, I heard from Kirsty that you were driving up from London today Mathew, but I had no idea you were bringing your partner in crime with you, how are you Peter?" Caroline asked, smiling at the two of them.

"All the better for seeing you Caroline." Peter replied, he'd always had a soft spot for Lady Hemsworth.

"Mmm…and I can hear you haven't lost that Brummie accent, even after all these years." Caroline teased.

Even though Peter had left his home town in his teens, he had retained a strong Birmingham or Brummie accent as it is known and although he had lived in London for most of his life, he still enjoyed visiting Birmingham. His parents, Stanley and Dorothy, had now passed away but he had fond memories of them during his childhood, growing up in Selly Oak in the south-west of the city. Stanley had spent his working life on the railways and had met Dorothy whilst she was working as a waitress, just after the war. Peter's old friend Mathew came from a very different background, his father had been a stockbroker and he grew up in the family home, a large Victorian property set in five acres of land near Guildford in Surrey. Interestingly, Stanley had struck up an unlikely friendship with Mathew's father when they first met at Peter and Gloria's wedding, partly due to the stockbroker being a railway enthusiast and the two of them would go on to meet socially at steam railway conventions.

"I'm very sorry to hear about your brother Mathew, let's hope for a speedy recovery. Kirsty mentioned to me that you visited him earlier." Caroline said, looking genuinely sorry.

"Thank you Caroline, I did and it looks like he may need surgery, hopefully I'll know more when I revisit the hospital in the morning. So, whatever are you doing up here?" Mathew asked as Peter pulled up a chair for her.

"Well, to cut a long story short darling, when Anthony and I went our separate ways he asked me whether I would like to keep the house on Skye, so I spend most of my time between my London home in Belgravia and Scotland. It gets a bit lonely on Skye after a while, the house is quite isolated, so I come and stay with Angus and Kirsty at this beautiful hotel three or four times a year. Strangely, it was only recently that I discovered that John is your brother Mathew and I've known him for three or four years, stupid of me really, there can't be that many Phillips-Lehmans around for goodness sake. Anyway, he's a wonderful man and over the past few months or so we've become good friends." Caroline said, warmly.

"Did you meet John here at the hotel?" Mathew asked, it seemed quite strange to be sat talking to Caroline, who he hadn't seen for donkey's years until this evening and here they were discussing his brother, with whom she'd become good friends.

"When I started coming up to Skye after the divorce, it took me a while to realise I needed some help with the gardens and Angus introduced me to John, he's a brilliant horticulturist, like gold dust darling. He comes across to Skye a couple of days a week when I'm up here and helps me. When it's not raining, we spend hours together in the gardens, absolute bliss. Anyway, enough about me, I hear that you two rascals have been up to your old tricks again, I've read all about the Robert Coleville affair, you've lost none of your flair Peter Wilson by the sound of things or, your good looks." Caroline teased.

"It was certainly a remarkable story Caroline, reminded us a bit of the old days working for the comic, didn't it Matt." Peter said.

"It did indeed, except we didn't have your old man breathing down our necks Caroline, like he used to in the old days." Mathew added, smiling.

"Anthony used to say that he would either end up broke or in prison because of you two and sometimes he wasn't joking." Caroline was clearly enjoying herself by now. "He couldn't resist the excitement though, that and hearing about some crooked politician being caught with his fingers in the till or, with his trousers down. When he heard that you'd discovered Sir Stephen Ambrose was taking backhanders for defence contracts he was overjoyed and then when you found out he also had gambling debts and a penchant for call girls, the old devil was beside himself. After all, it's not every day you've got the scoop of the decade and it turns out to be the Secretary of State for Defence in the dock."

The three of them happily reminisced for a few minutes more about the good old days in Fleet Street and Wapping when Peter, never being one to miss an opportunity, asked Caroline whether she knew of any reason why John would go for a walk down by the loch armed with his old police truncheon. Caroline was quiet for a moment and then sat back in her chair considering the two old friends.

"Shall we have a nightcap boys? Angus has a very reasonably twenty-year-old single malt Talisker."

Mathew ordered the drinks and Caroline continued. "I'm very fond of my life up here and anything I say to you two is in the strictest confidence." Caroline said with a serious

33

look on her face and Peter and Mathew both nodded in agreement as their drinks arrived.

"So, I've heard through the grapevine that John would often go for an evening stroll and would occasionally bump into Kirsty down by the loch. John might be approaching seventy, but he's still a very handsome man you know." Caroline said.

Peter was sure he could detect Caroline blushing, perhaps she had strong feelings for John herself and was actually jealous of Kirsty. He remembered from all those years working for the paper that she could be a terrible flirt.

"Kirsty had a troubled upbringing you know and perhaps a father figure like John may seem very attractive to her," Caroline continued. "there's another thing too, from what I've heard her marriage is going through a rocky patch. I can't say I'm particularly surprised, Angus can be very short tempered at times and he's not the most sensitive man in the world. Regarding the truncheon darling, I suggest you have a word with a certain Scotty Perry."

"Scotty Perry, who's he when he's at home then?" Mathew asked.

"Perry worked here at The Sound as a part-time gardener and handyman for years until John discovered he'd been stealing from the Mackenzies. Nothing serious, gardening and building tools, he'd sell them on to fund his drinking. John, being the kind of man he is, gave him a chance and told him to hand in his notice or he'd tell Angus and Kirsty and then it would be a police matter. Perry resigned and that should have been the end of the matter, but John told me a few weeks ago that he'd received some threatening phone calls, although he did go on to say that he didn't know who they were from. But putting two and two together, perhaps it was Perry.

"Do you know where we might find this Mr. Perry?" Peter asked.

"Oh yes, I'm told he can be found most evenings propping up the losers' bar in the Roebuck Inn in Mallaig, you two go careful though, you're not in South Kensington up here you know." Caroline said smiling.

"The losers' bar?" Peter asked, looking puzzled.

"You'll see why it's called that if you visit the place." Caroline replied.

# CHAPTER SIX

# KIRSTY

Kirsty Blair was born in Glasgow in June 1970 and spent the first two years of her life with her single mother in a tenement building in Maryhill, one of the poorest districts of the city. She never knew her father. Her mother, Annie, died in a road accident in 1972 and Kirsty moved across the city to the West End, where she was brought up by her mother's sister Moira and her husband Kelvin.

Aunty Moira and Kelvin lived quite a bohemian lifestyle, by the standards of nineteen-seventies Glasgow. They rented a three-bedroomed mews not far from the Great Western Road. Moira was an artist and had created a small studio in the mews where she painted, she was also involved in women's rights issues in the city. Domestic violence against women was a particular problem at the time, not just in Glasgow, but also in many communities across the United Kingdom and on occasions, Moira and Kelvin would provide temporary refuge for woman who had suffered violence, until they got back on their feet. Aggrieved husbands would sometimes turn up at the Mews, as their home had become known, demanding, often backed-up with threats of violence, that their wives return home. Invariably, they were no match for Moira and Kelvin, who had been brought up in the nineteen-thirties and forties in the Gorbals, then a densely populated poor district of Glasgow. The callers would usually be sent packing after a severe dressing down.

Kelvin was actually an accomplished musician, who played in a local folk band and to supplement the meagre income he made from playing guitar he also did some painting and decorating. Moira and Kelvin, who were both in their late thirties by the time Kirsty came to live with them, had given up any hope of having children of their own and were only too happy to look after Kirsty as if she was their own daughter.

She was certainly growing up in a very different environment to the one in which she had spent the first two years of her life with her mother in the tenement block in Maryhill. Whilst her mother was caring and loved her daughter, she was constantly struggling to make ends meet. Kirsty's father had disappeared the moment he had found out that Annie was pregnant and provided no financial support for his daughter whatsoever. For a short while after Kirsty was born, Annie had even considered giving her daughter up for adoption, but had been persuaded by her sister Moira as well as friends and neighbours to keep her and it was one of these friends who was looking after Kirsty when Annie was hit by a car whilst waiting at a bus stop on her way to work at a local factory. She died instantly.

Life in the Mews was unorthodox when compared to most other Glaswegian households in the nineteen-seventies. The door was almost always open and a seemingly endless stream of artists, musicians, artisans and activists would pass through on a daily basis. At times, the Mews resembled a social club, rather than a home. Moira and Kelvin were truly at the heart of this bohemian society and were liked and respected. Virtually all of the visitors to their home doted on young Kirsty. As far as possible, Moira would involve her niece in whatever was happening at any given time, whether it be painting, music, handicrafts or cooking and consequently, she had an extremely open and very stimulating childhood. As she grew up, her friends loved coming to play with her at the Mews and although, at first, some of their parents were wary of letting their children visit a house 'full of hippies', as one mother put it, once they got to know Moira and Kelvin better, their fears were allayed. Whilst Moira and Kelvin enjoyed the occasional drink with their artistic friends at home, they operated a strict no drugs policy. It led to lengthy debates amongst their friends at times, drugs such as cannabis and even hallucinogenic drugs and opiates were seen in a very different light in the nineteen-sixties and seventies than they are today. One view was that they were liberating and they were certainly fashionable, judging by the number of young pop stars and actors who indulged. However, Moira and Kelvin had seen the damage that drugs could do and they wouldn't tolerate them in the Mews and that was that.

Unsurprisingly, when Kirsty reached her teens and most of her friends of a similar age were going through a rebellious period, she found very little to rebel against. In fact, rather than complaining that she didn't enjoy enough freedom, for a year or two she became more reserved and at times would chastise her aunty for her seemingly reckless behaviour.

By this time, Moira and Kelvin had turned fifty and Kirsty began to feel quite protective towards them. She also became very proud of her Aunty Moira whose paintings, mostly portraits in oils, had been gaining attention throughout Glasgow and beyond, culminating in an exhibition of her work being shown at a commercial gallery in Finnieston, a nearby district of Glasgow. The portraits, mainly of local artists and musicians started to fetch a good price and following the exhibition, Moira received a number of commissions. Happily, Moira's and Kelvin's financial situation, which had always been precarious to put it mildly, improved beyond recognition.

Like many other girls in their early teens, Kirsty was unhappy with her appearance, she was tall and was often described as gangly and she wore braces to straighten her teeth, which she thought only added to her awkwardness. However, by the time she had reached the age of seventeen everything seemed to have changed, she had beautiful bone structure, long blonde hair, blue eyes and thanks to the braces, near perfect teeth. Her height, she was five foot ten, was no longer an issue and merely accentuated her slim figure and presence. She had grown into a beautiful young woman, who regularly turned heads in the street and her friends were always telling her that her future lay in modelling but Kirsty, in that charming easy-going manner she had, just laughed it off. Whilst she wasn't particularly academic, she had left school with acceptable, but average qualifications, the young Glaswegian did have excellent social skills possibly, she thought, due to her unorthodox upbringing at the Mews.

Just after her eighteenth birthday, Kirsty found a job in a fashionable bar in the West End, not far from her home. She enjoyed the work and if it hadn't been for a chance encounter one evening, she would have been content to remain working at the bar for the foreseeable future. It was a Thursday evening and a lively group of six or seven customers had come into the bar for pre-dinner drinks. Kirsty had got talking with two of the men in the party and they told her that they had travelled up from London that morning and the group were working on a fashion shoot, using the impressive Kelvingrove Art Gallery and Museum as a backdrop. She had noticed earlier that two of the party were young women and although they were not particularly beautiful, they were tall and slim and fashionable, she now understood that they were fashion models working on the shoot.

The following evening, the party returned to the bar for drinks and just before they left to go to the restaurant they had booked for dinner one of the men in the group, who Kirsty assumed was in charge, came across to thank her for looking after them over the past two evenings and explained that they were returning to London in the morning. He told her that he was a creative director, but also owned a fashion model agency in London with his partner, who ran the business on a day-to-day basis. Kirsty was surprised when he told her that the whole party, including the two fashion models on the shoot, had noticed her during the past two evenings and had all agreed that she could become a fashion model herself if she was interested. Kirsty blushed and thanked the man for being so kind and as she did she looked across the bar to the others in the party, who were preparing to leave. They were smiling and waving at her, obviously aware that their boss was talking with her about a possible career as a model. He gave Kirsty his partner's business card and told her that he had already spoken with his partner and if she was seriously interested in a career in modelling, she should call her.

# CHAPTER SEVEN

# BLACKMAIL

"Well, it looks as though my brother has a fan club up here." Mathew said.

The two old friends had made their way down to breakfast and apart from the two Italian men, they were the only ones in the dining room. Morag had brought them coffee and taken their order, a full Scottish breakfast for Mathew and porridge for Peter.

"He certainly has Matt and I have a feeling Caroline has completely fallen for him, she was definitely jealous of Kirsty, lucky old John that's what I say." Peter said.

"Crafty old devil, he never said a word to me about Caroline, he knew that we'd worked for years for her husband." Mathew said, shaking his head.

"Well, Caroline told us that it was only recently that she had realised that John is your brother." Peter reminded Mathew.

"Yes she did and I found that hard to believe, didn't you?" Mathew asked.

"I did a bit, perhaps they wanted to keep their friendship to themselves." Peter replied.

Morag soon arrived with their breakfast and asked Mathew to send her love to John, if he gets to see him when he visits the hospital later that morning.

"Thank you Morag, I will, by the way, has Caroline Hemsworth been down to breakfast yet?" Mathew asked.

"Och, you're kidding, Lady Caroline nearly always has her breakfast in bed when she stays here, she's a late riser.

41

Mind you, if John's been working in the gardens early, she might come down and join him for a cup of coffee and some toast about ten, like most of us here at The Sound, she has a soft spot for your brother." Morag replied and as she returned to the kitchen, Kirsty arrived in the dining room and spoke briefly with her two Italian guests, before coming over to see Peter and Mathew.

"Good morning gentlemen, I hope you slept well, I heard you had a late night, chatting with Lady Caroline, she's quite a character that's for sure." Kirsty said.

"Oh yes, we go back a long way Kirsty, longer than I care to remember to be honest." Peter joked, "We've been sat here admiring the Tower, now that it's light and we can get a better view of it, it's so unusual on that island in the middle of the loch, you must tell us how it came to be there."

"Isn't it wonderful!" Kirsty exclaimed, as the three of them looked out over the loch, where the morning mist was rising and had partially hidden the Tower making it look even more mysterious than it normally did.

Kirsty pulled up a chair and joined Peter and Mathew. "Our hotel was built in the mid nineteenth century by a wealthy diplomat and it was his home whenever he returned from foreign postings all over the world. The Tower is actually called Stuart's Folly after the diplomat Sir Edward Stuart. Nobody is certain why he built the Tower, but we think it may have been to house his collection of flags which he brought back from countries all over the world during his travels. There were only three rooms, one on each floor, when we arrived but we renovated the first two floors, so that on the ground floor we now have a kitchen/diner and on the first floor a bedroom with ensuite bathroom. The second floor is just as Sir Edward left it, with cupboards containing dozens of foreign flags as well as access to the rooftop, where you can see the flagpole.

We've added to the collection of flags over the past ten years, Angus and I travelled throughout South America last year, it was the one continent Sir Edward seemed to have missed during his travels all those years ago, so we took the opportunity whilst we were there to bring back with us the national flags of Brazil, Colombia, Chile and Argentina. Angus raised the St. George's flag yesterday to welcome you two Sassenachs to Scotland." Kirsty laughed.

"What a magical story Kirsty and you row across to the Tower from time to time?" Mathew asked.

"We do indeed Mathew, there's a small stone jetty we can reach from the gardens and we keep three rowing boats moored down there, sometimes friends join us and if the weather is good in the summer, I will swim across, keeps me fit. We have quite a bit of fun with the flags you know, I might row across to the Tower and raise a particular country's flag if I want to send a message or, make a point to Angus and he might do the same for me sometimes, we've developed a sort of code, semaphore I suppose you could call it, one flag means this and another flag means that, I won't go into any more details." Kirsty said, with a twinkle in her eye.

"When did the country house first become a hotel Kirsty." Peter asked.

"The Stuart family sold the house in the late nineteen-fifties and shortly afterwards it became a hotel. Morag's parents both worked here during the nineteen-sixties, her father was the head gardener and her mother worked in the kitchen. The house has a fascinating history, it was requisitioned during the second world war and rumour has it that it was used by the Special Operations Executive. Although we've never found out anything official, it makes some sense because the Stuart family had strong connections with the diplomatic service and with the military." Kirsty explained.

"Well, we are honoured to have the St. George's flag flying Kirsty and thank you so much for your hospitality, I'm going to drop Peter off at the Lodge and then I'm driving to the hospital, are you sure we can't settle the bill before we leave?" Mathew asked.

"Absolutely not, as we said last night, this is the least we can do after what's happened to poor John and please send him our love when you get to see him. Come and see us whilst you are staying at the Lodge, I'm sure Lady Caroline will also be delighted to see you both again." Kirsty smiled and left the dining room.

Peter and Mathew enjoyed a final cup of coffee and they both agreed that, as well as being a stunningly attractive woman, Kirsty had a charming manner and was a wonderful hostess.

*******************

Peter let himself into the Lodge with the key that Mathew had collected from his parents' house in Surrey. As he approached the front door he had noticed that the Lodge had been built with the beautiful pale yellow and pink Devonian sandstone often found in the Highlands of Scotland.

It was now more than forty-eight hours since John had left the Lodge to walk down to the loch and Peter checked all the rooms, lounge, kitchen and dining room downstairs, as well as the two bedrooms and bathroom upstairs. When he had established that nothing was amiss and there had been no break in, he checked the fridge and the old-fashioned larder and as agreed earlier with Mathew, sent a text message to him with a short list of shopping for him to pick up on his return from the hospital.

Peter unpacked his small case in the second bedroom, leaving John's bedroom free for his brother. The Lodge was quite tidy, bearing in mind it was occupied by a single man and furnished conservatively, but tastefully. Peter noticed it was warm, thanks to the storage heating, but he had spotted the beautiful open fireplace when he had first gone into the lounge and decided to prepare a log fire, should they want to light it later on. He had spotted some logs and kindling wood in a log store at the front of the Lodge when he arrived.

When he had finished, he made himself a mug of coffee and settled down at the large wooden table in the kitchen, which looked as if it was where John spent a lot of his time when he was at home. It contained a pile of national and local newspapers, as well as a number of utility bills and bank statements, but what really caught Peter's attention was half a dozen or so computer print outs of old newspaper cuttings, held together by a bulldog clip. Interestingly, they were sat next to some nineteen-nineties issues of *Elle* and *Harper's and Queen* magazines.

Firstly, he looked through the magazines, puzzled why John would have these in his kitchen, until he recognised the beautiful young model on the front page of all three copies. Even though twenty-five years had passed since the magazines had been published, Peter was in no doubt that one of the fashion models featured in all of them was Kirsty Mackenzie. On the first two covers that he looked at, Kirsty was wearing, what looked like, very expensive grunge fashion, loose oversized clothing. He was no expert on women's fashion, but he remembered his wife Gloria wearing a similar style of clothes around this time. They had both been fond of the band *Nirvana*, who had been instrumental in popularising grunge music. He smiled when he spotted that Kirsty was wearing a pair of *Dr. Martens* boots on another one of the covers. Inside one of the magazines, which was dated May 1991, Kirsty was wearing what was described on the cover as a slip dress and it was clearly a more glamourous look than the other two photographs.

Kirsty must have given the magazines to John, Peter thought to himself. He then thumbed through the newspaper cuttings, which had been printed. Two of them were from the *London Evening Standard* and *The Times*, both dated 2003 and concerned the trial of a drug smuggler at Woolwich Crown Court in south-east London. Daniel Tyler, aged 39 from Shepherd's Bush, West London, had been jailed for twenty-two years for smuggling cocaine and heroin into the UK over a six-year period.

Tucked behind the press cuttings was a photocopy of a typed letter, dated just over a month ago.

*24 October 2015*

*Dear Gus*

*Since I regained my freedom I've been considering how best to progress matters so that it results in a satisfactory conclusion for all parties.*

*For a number of years, we had a business arrangement whereby colleagues of yours sourced the product, you provided logistics and shipping and I took delivery of it in the UK, prior to its subsequent distribution, netting substantial profits for the organisation. After losing my freedom for twelve years, I am now in need of financial assistance to help rebuild my life and enable me to plan for the future.*

*Until now, thanks to me, the details of the sourcing, logistics and shipping behind the operation, as well as the names of those involved, have remained a secret and have not been disclosed to law enforcement agencies. To continue with the status-quo, a one-off payment of £100,000 is required.*

*I have kept my part of the bargain over the past twelve years, it's now time for you to keep yours. You can write to me at my old address, I look forward to hearing from you.*

*Danny*

\*\*\*\*\*\*\*\*\*\*\*\*\*\*\*\*\*\*\*

Mathew had returned from the hospital and Peter had prepared an omelette for the two of them. The news about John was not good, he was still confused and too unwell at present to travel to Inverness for an operation. Mathew had been able to see him for a short time, but because of the sedatives he had been given John was extremely drowsy and uncommunicative. Mathew had phoned his sister Judith in New Zealand immediately following the visit and given her the latest news, she would be travelling back home from Auckland in a few days' time.

The two friends sat at the kitchen table to eat and after Mathew had updated him on his brother's health, Peter showed Mathew the magazines, newspaper cuttings and the copy of the letter he had come across earlier. Peter felt slightly guilty that he had been reading through John's personal possessions but when he mentioned his unease to Mathew, who naturally seemed preoccupied because of his brother's health, his old friend just said that he was sure he'd done it with the best intentions. After they had eaten, Mathew read through the various news cuttings and the letter.

"The magazines must have come from Kirsty," Peter suggested, "what I don't quite understand is how John got hold of the letter from Danny Tyler."

Mathew was quiet for a few minutes whilst he re-read the news cuttings and the letter.

"I remember the Danny Tyler trial, I didn't cover it for the newspaper personally, I was investigating another drugs cartel at the time but naturally, I took an interest in Tyler's case. He offered little defence and wouldn't speak to the police, it was clear that he carried the can for the others who had worked together smuggling drugs into the country for years. There were huge profits to be made you know and by

47

the look of things, Danny Tyler didn't get much of a share. The sentence was so harsh because he refused to talk to the police. The cocaine was smuggled in from Colombia and Ecuador I seem to remember and the heroin from Afghanistan, via the Balkans." Mathew explained.

"The letter is clearly an attempt at blackmail, it's written to 'Gus', perhaps that's Angus Mackenzie?" Peter surmised.

"Possibly, he mentioned last night that he had worked in the shipping industry, perhaps he had played a part in the drug smuggling operation. But why would John have a copy of the letter? That's what's puzzling me Peter. Maybe John was working for the Met on the Danny Tyler case back then, that's possible, but unlikely, I don't remember him ever mentioning this case to me. I still can't work out why he's got a copy of the letter." Mathew said.

"Yes, someone has clearly photocopied this letter and given it to John by the look of things, which makes me think that it may have come from Angus Mackenzie himself or, perhaps even Kirsty. Caroline said that she thinks John would occasionally bump into Kirsty near the loch, insinuating there might be something going on between the two of them. Whatever the answer is, I think I'd like to find out a bit more about Danny Tyler, his letter implies that he's no longer in prison, he was sentenced to twenty-two years in 2003, so it's quite possible that with good behaviour he's recently been released. If John had arranged to meet someone at the loch on the night he had his heart attack and that was Tyler, it may explain why he was carrying his truncheon." Peter suggested.

"Possibly, but on the other hand, from what Caroline told us he could have been meeting Scotty Perry." Mathew said, thumbing through the fashion magazines. "Kirsty was a successful model by the look of things."

"Definitely, hardly surprising though having seen her yesterday. Do you fancy a pint at the Roebuck Inn in Mallaig this evening Matt?" Peter asked.

"I do old boy and in the meantime, I'm going to make a few calls to some old contacts in London to see whether they know the whereabouts of a Mr. Danny Tyler." Mathew replied.

Peter smiled, he well remembered from their days working for the newspaper that Mathew had built up a broad spectrum of contacts from different walks of life, some of whom he preferred not to know about.

# CHAPTER EIGHT

# THE ROEBUCK INN

"So, what do you think of John's brother Kirsty?" Morag asked. The two of them were sat in the deserted dining room, overlooking the loch, having lunch. A few snow-flakes had fallen and a light covering of snow had been forecast for later in the day.

"To be honest, he's just what I expected Morag, educated, sophisticated and very English. What about you, what do you think?" Kirsty asked.

"I agree, all those tweeds and brogues, he'd fit in very well up here." Morag said and the two of them laughed.

Morag had worked for the Mackenzies since they bought the hotel ten years ago. She was about the same age as Kirsty, in her mid-forties and lived in Mallaig with her husband Craig, a fisherman and their two teenage sons.

"Peter's interesting," Morag continued, "very different to Mathew, handsome man, more *Paul Smith* and *Armani* than tweeds by the look of him and there's something steely about him, don't you think so Kirsty? I saw you sharing a joke with him at breakfast time."

"Och, away with you, I'm a happily married woman, as you well know Morag McClair." Kirsty replied, but it was said with a twinge of sadness, rather than the humour intended.

"You're a city girl at heart Kirsty, Glasgow, London and we're a long way away up here, the back of beyond you could say, it can be very claustrophobic you know. It's different for me, I grew up here, me and Craig are used to living on top of each other, but for you and Angus it's not so easy, even after ten years at The Sound. He left early this morning didn't he? I passed him on the drive when I was coming in to prepare the breakfasts." Morag asked.

"He's gone to Inverness, he still has legal issues to sort out on his father's estate even after all these years, or so he says. I asked him about it recently, I know the family owned a lot of land in the Highlands and after his father went bankrupt because of the *Lloyd's* insurance crash he had to sell nearly all of it, but that's as much as he'll tell me. Whenever his family is mentioned he just clams up, it's very odd. Perhaps it's my fault because I haven't loved him as much….." Kirsty stopped talking abruptly and looked down at the table.

"Loved him as much as what hen?" Morag asked sympathetically. Kirsty looked up, regaining her composure.

"As much as I should have. Anyway, I do hope John is going to recover Morag, other than you, sometimes I feel he's the only one I can depend on." Kirsty said changing the subject and Morag noticed she had tears in her eyes.

"I'd miss John too, mind you, you've still got your mad Aunty Moira, she's a character." Morag said, attempting to cheer Kirsty up.

"She'll be eighty-three next year, I keep asking her or even pleading with her to come and live here with us, even Angus has asked her to come, he can be quite kind and considerate when he wants to be, but she won't leave Glasgow, they broke the mould when they made Aunty Moira that's for sure." Kirsty smiled, thinking about her Aunty. "You would have thought when Kelvin passed away last year she would have jumped at the chance to come and live up here in relative luxury, I told her we would build a studio for her so she could still paint if she wanted to, but oh no, she said she's still needed in the community in the West End of Glasgow, it beggars belief."

51

"I hope I'm still needed in the community when I'm nearly eighty-three Kirsty." Morag said, shaking her head as Kirsty poured them more coffee.

********************

It was a bitterly cold evening and had started to snow when Peter and Mathew set off for Mallaig. The drive would only take about half an hour and Mathew, who was driving, put *Katy Lied* by *Steely Dan*, a favourite of theirs, in the car's CD player.

"Pleased to see you're appropriately dressed Matt, tweeds are just what you need in this climate." Peter said smiling and Mathew laughed. It was a running joke between the two of them that Mathew was nearly always dressed in very traditional British clothing, tweeds, pin-stripe suits, blazers and so on, whereas Peter favoured a much more casual look, mainly *Paul Smith* and one or two other designers.

"So, I made a few calls before we left the Lodge and I've managed to find out some information about Danny Tyler. He was released from prison in September this year. Apparently, he served just over twelve years and has been released on license for the remainder of his sentence. A model prisoner, spent the past few years in open prisons. As we thought, he would never have been given such a long sentence in the first place if he'd cooperated with the authorities when he was arrested, but he didn't and he took the rap himself. The scale of the drug smuggling and distribution operations were obviously far too big for one person to have acted alone, but he flatly refused to talk. I'm told he played quite a small part, driving and so on and I suspect he was frightened to talk and had probably been threatened with violence, or worse, by the criminals masterminding the operation if he did, it's quite common in their world." Mathew explained.

"Do we have any idea where he is Matt?" Peter asked.

"Yes, Shepherd's Bush, same house that he shared with his sister before he went down twelve years ago. I've been told it's the house he grew up in as a child and when his parents died he inherited it along with his sister. To be honest old boy, he doesn't really fit the bill for an international drug smuggler." Mathew said.

"We need to tread carefully here Matt, it looks as though Tyler is attempting to blackmail Angus Mackenzie and if he doesn't come up with a hundred thousand pounds, he'll be telling the police that Angus was somehow involved in the drug smuggling operation. I agree with you that Tyler doesn't seem to fit the bill and I'm not convinced he wrote the letter we found either, it's written like a business letter might be, it just doesn't feel right." Peter suggested.

"So why is my brother interested in all of this?" Mathew asked, looking worried.

"As I said before, he's probably trying to help Angus or Kirsty or even both of them. John would be quite aware of the risks in getting involved, he was a Chief Inspector, major crime, blackmail and threats were all part of his daily life." Peter replied.

"I'm nervous about speaking to the Mackenzies about any of this until we've spoken with my brother about it, we could open up a whole can of worms and John might not thank us for that." Mathew said.

"I agree Matt, we don't know enough about the characters involved in all of this. Perhaps we should find Danny Tyler first and have a chat with him, although I expect all he'll be interested in is the money he thinks he's owed." Peter suggested.

"Yes, we should do that and we should also speak with Caroline, discretely, to find out a bit more about Angus and Kirsty Mackenzie and any other staff at the hotel who might be involved. She's a dreadful old gossip and would love the attention, particularly from you Peter." Mathew smiled.

"Mmm....let's not go there." Peter replied, shaking his head.

"First of all, let's see what Scotty Perry has got to say for himself." Mathew said, as he drove into the pub's car park.

********************

The Roebuck Inn is just a short walk to the ferry port in Mallaig, from where you can sail to the Isle of Skye, as well as the "Small Isles", Canna, Muck, Rum and Eigg. For this reason, as well as the railway station being the terminus for the West Highland railway line, Mallaig is a busy port during the Spring and Summer, priding itself on its fresh seafood.

On a freezing cold night in late November, the bar of the Roebuck Inn wasn't too busy and Mathew and Peter had no problem finding a free table.

"I'm not sure Caroline's losers' bar description is fair," Peter commented, hanging his jacket on the back of his chair, "I've been in a lot worse, I think it's quite a cosy bar, I like it."

"Your idea of a decent boozer compared to the Countess's idea is probably a million miles apart old boy." Mathew said, with a wry smile.

Peter went to the bar and ordered two pints of the locally brewed pale ale and a platter of seafood for the two of them, including hot smoked salmon and pickled herring. Whilst waiting for their food to arrive, they looked around the bar trying to work out which one of the customers was Scotty Perry. Their problem was solved when the young barmaid arrived with their food.

"Thank you, that looks delicious," Mathew said and then in a quieter voice, "can you tell us whether Scotty Perry is in tonight please?"

"Aye, he's sat at the end of the bar with his back to us, do you want me to give him a message?" The barmaid asked with a smile.

"No, that's fine thank you." Mathew replied, feeling slightly foolish.

After the two of them had finished their meals, Peter went up to the bar to order another pint for himself and a tonic water for Mathew, who would be driving them home. He positioned himself next to Scotty Perry at the bar to get a better look at him. He looked to be in his forties, tall with fair hair and a ruddy face, probably due to the quantity of beer he drank if Caroline was to be believed.

"Scotty Perry?" asked Peter, whilst waiting to be served.

"That's me, who's asking?" Perry replied looking Peter up and down. Peter was slightly surprised that he didn't have a Scottish accent, in fact, coming from Birmingham himself Peter thought he could detect a Black Country accent, perhaps Walsall or Wolverhampton. Wherever he was from he cut a sad figure, he had a dishevelled appearance and even at this relatively early hour in the evening sounded as though he had been drinking for some time.

"I'm Peter Wilson and my friend sat over there is Mathew Phillips-Lehman." Peter replied, nodding in Mathew's direction.

Perry turned around on his stool to get a better look at Mathew.

"That'll be John's brother then I expect, I can see the likeness, what do you want with me?" Perry asked nervously.

"Just a chat about John, let me get you a drink and you can come and join us." Peter replied and Perry nodded. His hunch that the offer of a free drink was enough to tempt Perry over to their table was correct.

"I'll be over in just a minute, I don't want any trouble though." Perry said turning back to face the bar.

"There'll be no trouble from us, just a friendly chat that's all." Peter told him.

Peter rejoined Mathew with their drinks and was followed by Perry a few minutes later.

"I'm sorry to hear about your brother, I hear he's in hospital." Perry said looking at Mathew.

"How do you know he's in hospital?" Mathew asked suspiciously.

"This isn't London, we're a small community up here and in this part of the world news travels quickly. I didn't see eye-to-eye with your brother on everything, but I don't wish him any harm." Perry replied. The pub was beginning to fill up and the barmaid must have turned on some music, Peter recognised *Gerry Rafferty's* voice.

"It was my brother who caught you stealing from the Mackenzies and you lost your job, isn't that reason enough?" Mathew asked, feeling angry.

"John could have told the police and that would have been worse for me, so I might even have something to thank him for." Perry replied, taking a swig of his lager. Peter thought it was time he joined in the conversation, before it became acrimonious.

"Scotty, we're just trying to find out why John would be walking down to the loch on a freezing cold November evening carrying a truncheon in his jacket pocket." Peter said in a more conciliatory tone. Perry looked genuinely puzzled.

"A truncheon? I've no idea. Look, I'm not a gossip and I don't tell tales, I just want a quiet life but when I hear that John was going down to the loch to meet someone in the dark it probably wouldn't be a bloke he'd be meeting and he certainly wouldn't be needing a truncheon. Perhaps you should be asking Kirsty Mackenzie about evening meetings with John down by the loch when she's supposed to be taking the dogs out for a walk. He's a single man and Kirsty's a good-looking woman who's having marriage problems, if what I've heard is true. As I said, we're a small community up here and it's difficult to keep secrets. That's all I've got to say and you can keep me out of this, it has got nothing to do with me. Thanks for the drink and I genuinely hope your brother makes a speedy recovery." Scotty Perry picked up his half-finished pint of lager and made his way, slightly unsteadily, back to his seat at the bar.

# CHAPTER NINE

## FASHION MODEL – LONDON 1988

Aunty Moira offered to travel with Kirsty to London, but she decided to go alone. She was eighteen and although she appreciated her aunt's offer, she thought it was about time she stood on her own two feet. Kirsty had never been to London before and was looking forward to it, an adventure was how she viewed the trip. She had phoned Barbara Tripp on the Monday morning, following the chance encounter with her partner in the bar.

Barbara had sounded friendly over the phone and suggested that Kirsty should come to London for an interview with her and one of her colleagues in a fortnight's time. In the meantime, Barbara said she would post her some information about the Barbara Tripp Model Agency for her to look through before the interview. She asked Kirsty to send some photographs of herself, stressing that there was no need for her to go spending a lot of money with a professional photographer, a few simple pictures, taken by family or friends would be better. Barbara also told Kirsty to keep her travel and any accommodation receipts which, regardless of the outcome of the interview, the agency would reimburse.

Moira had ordered a taxi to take Kirsty to Glasgow Central Station and both her aunty and Kelvin were at home to see her off and wish her luck when the taxi arrived. It was a long train journey, the best part of six hours and on arrival at Euston Station she took a short taxi journey to Camden Town, where Moira had arranged for her to stay with Kelvin's sister who lived with her husband in a smart terraced house in Delancey Street. She was made to feel welcome and the three of them went out for a pizza, followed by a drink in a pub on the bustling Camden High Street.

From the moment Kirsty arrived in London, she knew she wanted to live there. Camden seemed to be alive with young fashionable people enjoying themselves, even on a Tuesday evening. By 1988, the City of London was starting to benefit financially from the deregulation of the financial markets, better known as the 'Big Bang'. The effects of this major change were not only being seen in The City, but also throughout many parts of the capital, particularly the West End and other fashionable districts, such as Camden. There was a feeling of optimism in the air and there seemed to be more money around. Unemployment was falling, property prices rising and many Londoners were benefiting through share ownership from the privatisation of some previously state-owned businesses, such as *BT*, *British Gas* and *British Airways*.

However, not all was well, Margaret Thatcher, who had been re-elected the previous year and was serving her third term as Prime Minister was facing growing opposition to the planned Poll Tax, which would replace the Rates, a property tax system to fund local government. There were also reports circulating of a homes for votes scandal or, gerrymandering, involving the Conservative led Westminster City Council in London. In marginal wards, the homeless were being moved to other, less prosperous, parts of the capital and council properties were being sold off to people who were more likely to vote Conservative.

Amongst the young, dance music and designer fashion were popular at the time and Acid House and Techno nights were held at trendy clubs such as *The Trip at the Astoria* and *Heaven*. Rave parties grew out of the Acid House movement and started being held in empty warehouses and huge events were held near the M25 motorway. DJs had experienced these events in Ibiza the previous summer and exported the subculture back to the UK.

This was partly the backdrop to the London that Kirsty had arrived in when, on the following morning, armed with a copy of the *London A-Z*, she took the Northern Line underground train from Camden Town to Leicester Square. The Barbara Tripp Model Agency's small offices were situated above a delicatessen on St. Martin's Lane, close to Covent Garden and Soho. It was a warm, sunny, late Spring day and Kirsty had dressed casually and simply in a pair of denim jeans, a white t-shirt and a pair of brown flat heeled shoes. Standing at five-foot-ten inches tall, she had no need to accentuate her height by wearing high heels.

The moment Barbara Tripp set eyes on Kirsty she understood why her partner had taken the unusual step of suggesting that she contacts the agency and travels down to London for an interview. Barbara recognised immediately that she not only had beautiful cheekbones and facial features, but her height, slim figure and posture could result in her working on high-fashion runway shows. Barbara, an attractive woman in her mid-forties, welcomed Kirsty and introduced Melanie, her Model Manager. Barbara explained that Melanie provided guidance and development for the models working for the agency. Kirsty had already read that it was one of the smaller agencies in London but had an extremely good reputation amongst their clients, which included some of the top advertising agencies and fashion designers from all over the world.

Barbara and Melanie were keen to hear about Kirsty's life in Glasgow and were intrigued by her slightly unconventional upbringing. Kirsty had begun to feel relaxed by now and was pleased that they seemed to be genuinely interested as she told them about her Aunty Moira and Kelvin and their life together in the Mews. After about an hour of conversation, it didn't feel like a formal interview, she was delighted and excited when Barbara

60

asked her if she would like to spend the afternoon and probably the following morning with Melanie to discuss accommodation and a training programme. Melanie would also take her through the planning for some test shots and explain how they would prepare a modeling portfolio and composite or, 'comp' card, the business card used by models showing their best professional photographs.

It was only much later that Kirsty realised that she was being given preferential treatment by the agency and that many aspiring models would be expected to provide and pay from their own pocket for some of the services the agency was arranging for her free of charge. Before the interview ended Barbara asked Kirsty whether she would like her to speak with her aunty to explain that the agency would like to represent her niece as a fashion model. She smiled and thanked Barbara and Melanie, but told them that she didn't think that would be necessary and that she would speak with Moira on the phone and explain everything herself.

The young Glaswegian was impressed with the care and consideration that the two women had shown her and she spent the afternoon with Melanie discussing training and being introduced to the rest of the staff working at the agency. Everyone seemed so bright and fashionable and instinctively she knew that she had arrived at the right place and landed on her feet, all because of a chance meeting in the bar in Glasgow where she worked. On leaving the agency, after an exhausting but exhilarating day, Kirsty sat on an open top bus touring the sites of London, thinking to herself that this was going to be her new home.

\*\*\*\*\*\*\*\*\*\*\*\*\*\*\*\*\*\*\*\*

Kirsty ended up spending a further two days at the agency before returning to Glasgow for a week, visiting her friends to say goodbye as well as handing in her notice at the bar where she had been working.

The most difficult part for her was saying goodbye to Aunty Moira and Kelvin. They were both so pleased for her and gave her a leaving present of £500, which Kirsty knew was a lot of money for the two of them, but she accepted it with grace and vowed that one day, once she had got on her feet in London, she would pay them back. Melanie had called her on the phone before she left Glasgow to tell her that her portfolio book and comp card, showing her best shots, were ready for her to collect when she next came into the agency. Melanie had also told Kirsty that she had arranged a casting call for a magazine shoot and she would tell her more of the details when she saw her. Finally, she was told that accommodation had been arranged for her at a three-bedroom flat in Maida Vale in West London, which she would be sharing with two other fashion models who were also on the agency's books.

Back in London, the taxi journey from Euston Station to Maida Vale took less than twenty minutes and Kirsty was soon lugging her heavy suitcase up the steps leading to the large terraced house on Sutherland Avenue. She rang the bell for the third floor flat, as instructed by Melanie, and when the front door opened she struggled up three flights of stairs with her luggage. The door to flat three was open and as she entered the untidy sitting room, she was welcomed by a tall young blonde with an American accent.

"Hi, I'm Grace, you must be Kirsty." The American girl was as tall as Kirsty and perhaps a year or two older, she looked as if she had just got out of the shower and was wearing a dressing gown and by the look of things was about to dry her hair, which was soaking wet. A large square glass coffee table dominated the centre of the living room and Kirsty noted a cigarette burning in the ashtray, next to a tall stack of *Marlboro Red* packets. A large glass of, what looked suspiciously like, whisky on the rocks was also on the coffee table, it was two-thirty on a Monday afternoon.

"Nice to meet you Grace, can I put this suitcase away somewhere?" Kirsty asked, tired of lugging it around all day.

"Sure honey, your room is through the door over there and first on the right, I'm afraid it's the smallest bedroom but Hanna and me were here first, so we had first choice. Hanna's Hungarian, she's out on a shoot." Grace explained, taking a long drag on her cigarette. "Melanie was right, you look as though you've got what it takes Kirsty, you're a real beauty! Is that a Scottish accent?"

"Yes, Glaswegian." Kirsty replied laughing.

"Wow, Glaswegian! I'm from Kansas City in the USA. Help yourself to a drink, there's a cabinet full over there and there's shit loads of cigarettes, I did a shoot for the tobacco company a few months ago, freebies honey." Grace said.

"I don't smoke, but I'll have a wee dram a bit later." Kirsty replied cheerfully.

"A 'wee dram', shit, this is a whole new language I'm gonna have to learn, just wait 'til Hanna hears this, she has enough trouble with English." Grace said and the two young women laughed.

Kirsty went to unpack and have a shower, still smiling and thinking to herself that life should be interesting in Sutherland Avenue, if Grace was anything to go by.

\*\*\*\*\*\*\*\*\*\*\*\*\*\*\*\*\*\*\*\*

Following a successful casting call, Kirsty's first fashion magazine shoot took place in an industrial warehouse in Limehouse. It was soon to be converted into apartments, which, according to the newspapers, were increasingly being snapped up by 'yuppies', a popular term at the time often used in a derogatory manner to describe young upwardly-mobile professionals in employment. The warehouse was currently being used as work space for budding artists. A number of creative directors liked to use the space for fashion shoots, partly because it still retained many of its original industrial features and offered views over the River Thames.

Melanie picked Kirsty up from the flat in Sutherland Avenue in her estate car at eight o'clock in the morning and they set off for Limehouse. Although the distance was only eight or nine miles the journey seemed to take an eternity, crawling through the London rush-hour traffic. On the way, Kirsty told Melanie how she was settling into her new home in Maida Vale. Hanna, the flat-mate from Hungary was dating a guitarist in a rock band, which had recently won its first recording contract and consequently, she was rarely in the flat. Kirsty said that she got on well with Grace, who was quite a character, and the two of them had plans to go out clubbing at the weekend. She smiled when Melanie, who she thought could only have been in her early thirties, proceeded to give her a lecture on some of the dangers for young women living in London.

Melanie also gave Kirsty a taste of what to expect when they arrived at the shoot in Limehouse and without saying so she was impressed at how calm the aspiring model appeared. She had taken many young models to their first fashion shoot during her career at the agency and it wasn't unusual for them to be a bag of nerves and on more than one occasion, physically sick. Kirsty's demeanor boded well for the future Melanie thought to herself.

On arrival at the warehouse, Kirsty was introduced to the team working on the shoot, which included two other more experienced models, two male assistants who were busily setting up lighting, Alison and Bev, the hair and make-up artists who were readying one of the models for the shoot and two male stylists who were arguing about a dress which seemed to have gone missing. She was quickly introduced to the creative director, a middle-aged man, who was anxiously waiting for the arrival of the client from the fashion magazine. Finally, Melanie pointed out a tall young man with long fair hair who was sat alone quietly fiddling with a camera on his lap.

"His name's Sandy and he's a brilliant photographer, he's a freelancer and he's often hired for these type of shoots." Melanie explained.

"But he looks so young." Kirsty said, staring across the large room at the photographer.

"Yes, he's only twenty-three or something like that, but he's already built up quite a reputation in the industry. He doesn't have a lot to say I'm afraid, but come and say hello to him anyway." Melanie said, leading the way.

Kirsty studied him as they crossed the room to where he was sat. He was extremely good looking, with noticeably refined features. Oddly, she thought to herself, he was wearing what looked like second-hand clothes that were all slightly too small, but for some strange reason suited him and looked fashionable. Melanie introduced him to Kirsty and it was clear to her that he was painfully shy, he barely looked at her. When he spoke, she recognised a slight Scottish accent but it was nothing like hers, his was much softer and gentle, but she couldn't really place it because he said so little. Kirsty couldn't take her eyes off the young man and suddenly realised that she'd been staring and momentarily, felt embarrassed.

"When he takes photographs he comes alive, you'll see what I mean later." Melanie said as she left Kirsty with Alison and Bev to sort out her makeup and hair. Kirsty took to the two hair and makeup artists immediately. They looked a good few years older than her and were both from East London, true Cockneys in fact, having been born in Bethnal Green and by the way they laughed and joked with Kirsty it was clear that they liked the young Glaswegian as well. The three of them swapped stories about growing up in a big city and it was only later that Kirsty realised that perhaps their joviality had been part of a ploy to relax her before the shoot. If that had been their aim, then it worked and she thoroughly enjoyed her first experience as a fashion model, learning all the time as she took part from the more experienced models and Sandy, the brilliant young photographer.

********************

"It was as though he became a different person, it was incredible, as soon as this introverted young guy started photographing us he became a confident professional in total command of every shot." Kirsty was telling Grace about Sandy whilst they were getting ready for a Saturday night out 'Up West'.

"I've heard he's special." Grace replied, pouring them both a glass of champagne. "So, tonight honey, I thought we'd start with a cocktail or two at *Rumours* in Covent Garden, it's a favourite with the agency crowd early in the evening and then maybe *Stringfellows*, trashy but fun!"

"I'm in your capable hands Grace." Kirsty replied, taking a sip of champagne as Grace lit another *Marlboro* cigarette. Kirsty couldn't help noticing how fashionable the young American looked, wearing an oversize navy-blue blazer and a beautifully cut pair of white trousers. She felt a lot better when Grace complimented her on the simple black dress she had chosen to wear on their night out.

"You're a lucky gal honey, you could wear anything and still look a million dollars!" Grace told her.

They arrived at *Rumours* at about eight o'clock and Kirsty noticed that Grace had been right about the agency crowd frequenting the bar, she recognised a tall East European model, who had been on the shoot in Limehouse with her earlier in the week, the two stylists, Terry and Chris as well as the two make-up artists, Alison and Bev.

They were all sat on a long table near the bar and Kirsty and Grace joined them. They were a fun group to be with and Kirsty enjoyed the atmosphere in the cocktail bar, which had gained a good reputation as one of London's trendiest places to hang out. Grace was enjoying her second Harvey Wallbanger cocktail and Kirsty had opted for a Buck's Fizz, seeing she had already drunk a glass of champagne before they left the flat and didn't want to mix her drinks. After a few minutes she noticed Alison waving at a young couple who had just come into the bar, she was beckoning them to come and join the group. Kirsty couldn't quite see who they were until they emerged from the crowd and then she recognised Sandy, the young photographer, with a very pretty young woman by his side.

The two new arrivals squeezed into two chairs on opposite sides of the table and Kirsty suddenly found herself sat next to the handsome young photographer. Introductions were made around the table and she was secretly relieved to hear that Linda, the young woman who had arrived with Sandy, was Alison's younger sister and the two of them had just happened to turn up at the bar at the same time. She also noticed that Sandy was dressed more smartly than he had been for the shoot, wearing a pale blue suit, white shirt and a pair of brown loafers.

"They probably told you it was my first shoot the other day, but anyway you helped me a lot and I just wanted to say thank you." Kirsty thought she would try and break the ice.

She wasn't sure whether the music had been turned up since they had arrived at the bar but she had to lean over and speak into Sandy's ear to make herself heard. The laughter and conversation had certainly risen by a few decibels since they had arrived, probably due to the cocktails being consumed. Sandy leant over to reply and their closeness gave their conversation a sense of intimacy, which Kirsty was enjoying.

"If I hadn't been told, I wouldn't have known you were new, you were quite easy to photograph, your blonde hair helps, it catches the light." Sandy replied softly. Out of the corner of her eye, Kirsty could see Grace watching them from the other side of the table and smiled when she saw her American flat-mate wink.

"Thank you so much, but I'm sure you're just being kind to me and say that to all the models on their first shoot." Kirsty replied and leaned back in her chair so that she could see his reaction. Sandy smiled and seemed to study her for a moment.

"It's the truth, you're a natural and kind of different to the others, anyway, one piece of advice, don't be so modest, it won't get you anywhere in this business." Sandy said. Kirsty could feel herself blushing slightly and lent over again so she was closer to him, hoping he hadn't noticed.

"You're from Scotland Sandy, but not from Glasgow where I come from, your accent is so much nicer." She said trying to find out a bit more about him.

"The Highlands, but I don't really like to talk about it too much, I've been in London for about five years and like to think of myself as a Londoner now. Anyway, I like the Glasgow accent, especially hearing you. I've heard that you're sharing a flat with Grace and Hanna." Sandy said, clearly wanting to change the subject and just as Kirsty was about to reply, two of his friends appeared at their table and he was already getting up out of his chair to join them.

"Look, I have to leave, my friends have booked a table for dinner. Can I call you and perhaps we can have dinner one night?" Sandy asked.

"I'd like that, have a good evening." Kirsty replied feeling excited, but also a little disappointed that their conversation had ended so abruptly.

Like many others, she had read and heard people describing love at first sight and until now she had always been sceptical, probably because she had hardly any experience of relationships with the opposite sex. When she had first seen Sandy at the shoot, she had known that he was the one for her and their conversation in the bar only reinforced her feelings towards him, she also had a feeling that he liked her which made the experience even more exciting.

The remainder of the evening went by in a bit of a blur. Grace got outrageously drunk, but was so much fun to be with that it didn't really matter. Two beautiful young models together in *Stringfellows* weren't short of attention. Thankfully, Grace was an expert at freeing them both from the attention of any guys who had outstayed their welcome, either on the dance floor or even at the bar, where they didn't have to buy a drink all night.

The night out ended at two a.m. with a taxi ride back to the flat in Maida Vale, where Kirsty thanked Grace for a wonderful night out.

"It wasn't just me that made it wonderful was it honey," Grace said and continued, but more seriously, "be careful Kirsty, he might be difficult to handle."

# CHAPTER TEN

## MAUREEN TYLER

"I rather feel as if I've been summoned to attend this lunch, I'm sure you two are up to no good, anyway, here I am what is it you want to know?" Lady Caroline Hemsworth had a twinkle in her eye as she joined Peter and Mathew in the popular seafood restaurant in Fort William, overlooking Loch Linnhe.

Mathew had received a telephone call from the hospital earlier that morning telling him that his brother John was now well enough to be taken by ambulance to Inverness, where he would undergo heart surgery. Mathew had decided to drive to Inverness and would stay in a hotel in the city, whilst John was in hospital. On the way, he would drop Peter off at Inverness airport, from where he would take a flight back to London.

Peter was looking forward to returning to London where he would be having dinner with Taraneh Saderzadeh, his old friend dating back to his days as a newspaper reporter in Oxford. Taraneh would be flying to London from Tehran in the next day or two. Whilst back in London he would take the opportunity to visit Danny Tyler in Shepherd's Bush. Peter had rung Caroline earlier that morning and when she told him that she would be in Fort William for the day doing some shopping, he thought it would be a good idea to invite her for lunch.

"When you told us you were going to be doing some shopping here whilst we were passing through on our way to Inverness, the opportunity was too good to miss Caroline, think of it as a special treat from two old friends." Peter smiled.

"Well, I'm still suspicious that I've been ambushed, there's no such thing as a free lunch." Caroline replied and the three of them laughed.

After they had ordered and Mathew had updated Caroline on his brother John's condition, Peter told her about their meeting the previous evening with Scotty Perry.

"We're not sure Perry's had anything to do with John since he stopped working at the hotel, what we would really like to find out is a bit more about Angus and Kirsty Mackenzie. On the face of it they seem a very nice couple, they've certainly been kind to us since we've been in Scotland and by all accounts they think a lot of John, but as you well know, appearances can be deceptive. You see Caroline, we have a feeling that Angus might be the victim of a very serious blackmail attempt and it looks as though someone has asked John for help, so any background information you have on the Mackenzies would be very helpful and strictly confidential of course." Peter said.

"Of course, it hasn't taken you two long to find something to get your teeth into has it, my ex-husband would be delighted if he knew. Blackmail, that's very serious, can I ask you how you found out about it, you've only been up here five minutes, it can't be anything John has told you he's in hospital." Caroline replied, raising her eyebrows.

"No, John hasn't said anything to us Caroline," Mathew said, being slightly economical with the truth, "and to be honest, even if we told you how we've found out I don't think it would mean anything to you. It's the Mackenzies we want to know a bit more about and you're the only person we know, other than John, who can help us. You know the kind of thing we're looking for, have either of them been acting oddly over the past few months?"

71

"Well, you're obviously not going to tell me what's really going on but I trust you both, God only knows why. Look, I don't live permanently at the hotel as you both know, but I do spend a fair amount of time there throughout the year and I've got to know them both quite well I suppose. Their relationship certainly appears to be under some strain at the moment which is a shame and somewhat surprising, they've always been so close, the perfect couple some would say. Anyway, something odd did happen recently and I'll tell you about it, but it must not go any further than these four walls, is that clear?" Caroline gave the two of them one of her icy stares.

"Of course, mum's the word Caroline." Mathew replied.

"It was last month, end of October, twenty-seventh in fact, can't ever forget that date, wedding anniversary." Caroline rolled her eyes and her two old friends smiled. "I remember it was unusually mild for the time of year and after dinner at the hotel I went for a stroll by the loch. To be honest, I was feeling a bit sorry for myself what with the anniversary on my mind. Anyway, that was soon forgotten when I spotted Angus sat under one of the beautiful Scots Pine trees. I don't suppose you city boys know but the Scots Pine can live for up to seven hundred years and can grow up to thirty-five metres tall. Your brother told me, he's an authority on trees you know Mathew. Where was I? Oh, yes, I walked over to Angus to say hello and the first thing I noticed was that he had a half empty bottle of Scotch in his hand, which was unusual in itself because he's not much of a drinker. It's a running joke at the hotel that he's the only Scotsman in the Highlands who doesn't enjoy a wee dram of an evening. The sad thing was that he looked so unhappy. I sat down next to him and asked him whether he wanted to talk. He was quiet for a few moments and then he told me that he'd made a terrible mistake years ago and now he was in trouble."

"Was Kirsty at home?" Peter asked.

"No, she'd gone out with some girlfriends and was staying the night in Fort William. I asked him what had happened in the past, another woman perhaps, but he just rambled on in a drunken stupor about this terrible mistake he'd made without actually being clear what the mistake was, it didn't help that he was half cut. At one point, I remember him mentioning his younger brother, saying that he'd messed that up as well, whatever that meant I've no idea. It was all so out of character, this handsome, dignified man who's normally totally in control, was in a right state."

"I don't suppose he mentioned someone called Danny Tyler, by any chance?" Peter interrupted.

"Who?" Caroline asked, looking puzzled.

"Danny Tyler." Peter repeated.

"Not that I remember, well, we sat there for about half an hour I suppose and then it became very embarrassing. I asked him whether he had spoken with Kirsty about the mistake he had made and he just shook his head and looked so sad. I don't know whether it was the maternal instinct coming out in me, but I held his hand to comfort him and the moment I did, I realised, with horror, that he'd taken it the wrong way. It was the way he looked at me." Caroline explained, looking slightly sheepish.

"You mean he came on to you?" a wide-eyed Mathew asked.

"Don't sound so bloody surprised. I still get plenty of admiring glances, I can tell you." Caroline replied glaring at Mathew.

"I'm sure you do Caroline." Peter butted in, smiling.

"Anyhow, he's not my type, I more interested in a mature man, such as your handsome brother Mathew." Caroline said, putting John's younger brother in his place. "Angus has not mentioned that evening again whenever I've seen him, it's as though it never happened."

"Perhaps he was so drunk, he doesn't remember." Peter suggested.

"Possibly, but I don't think so, he was so desperately unhappy, it's not the kind of thing you forget, I should know I've been there myself a few times." Caroline said, wistfully.

The three of them were just finishing their deserts, an assortment of ice cream and sorbet, when Caroline mentioned Kirsty's modelling career.

"She's very modest about it you know, it's hardly ever mentioned, she was extremely successful for a while, late eighties, early nineties I seem to remember, a familiar face on the cover of lots of fashion magazines around that time and then she suddenly disappeared from the fashion world. I'm pretty sure her picture even appeared in our newspaper once or twice, Anthony couldn't resist a pretty girl on the front page and neither could half the readership if the letters we received from them were anything to go by." Caroline told them.

"Do you know the reason why she suddenly stopped modelling?" Peter asked.

"No, not really, she very rarely discusses it and if the subject crops up in conversation, she's extremely adept at changing the subject. She'd make a good politician. I've always put her reluctance to talk about her days as a model down to modesty, but who knows? If you think it's important why don't you have a chat with Maggie Riley, she'll know more about her than me. Kirsty Blair, that was her maiden name when she was modelling. Do you two remember Maggie? She was the fashion editor for the paper all those years ago, eccentric woman, used to wear these outrageous outfits. I certainly remember Anthony had his eye on her for a while, the cheating so and so." Caroline told them, wearily.

"He'd have had to form a queue Caroline, Mathew was dating Maggie for a year or two." Peter reminded them and they laughed.

"I'll text you Maggie's phone number, perhaps you can become re-acquainted with her Mathew." Caroline said sarcastically, whilst finishing her coffee.

"Thank you, I'll bear it in mind." Mathew said, raising his eyebrows.

********************

The *British Airways* flight from Inverness to Heathrow airport landed exactly twenty-four hours after Taraneh Saderzadeh's flight from Tehran touched down at the same airport. Peter had first met Taraneh when he was a young reporter working for the Oxford Mail in the early nineteen-seventies. It was due to his success at the local paper that he was offered a job with one of the national newspapers, then based in Fleet Street. Investigative journalism had been a passion throughout Peter's working life and along with his old friend Mathew, they had won a number of prestigious press awards over the years. Although they were both officially retired, Peter still dabbled with some media work concerning defence matters, on which he was a recognised expert, but it was uncovering crime and solving mysteries which really interested them both.

Taraneh Saderzadeh had returned to Tehran after the 1979 revolution in her country following her divorce from a young doctor, whom she had met whilst nursing in Oxford. She would be spending a month or two in England, mainly staying at her father's apartment in Kensington. Her old Liverpudlian friend Rita, who she had first met when they were student nurses, would be coming to stay for a week over Christmas and Taraneh was planning to travel to Liverpool to stay with her friend in the new year. On the face of it, the two of them were very different, Rita being self-assertive, loud and extremely funny, some less kind people would describe her as brash, whereas Taraneh was a quiet, slightly introverted character. Even so, the two of them had remained great friends over the years. Taraneh had stayed with her friend in Liverpool on occasions and Rita had even visited Iran, staying with Taraneh and her elderly father in Tehran.

Taraneh was looking forward to her dinner date with Peter. Apart from a brief chance meeting the previous year in a pub in Kensington, she hadn't seen Peter for more than forty years and she was curious when she considered whether or not two people could possibly catch up and enjoy each other's company without having seen one another for so long. In fact, it was the first question she asked Peter after they had greeted each other with a warm embrace at *Il Portico*, the excellent Italian restaurant on Kensington High Street.

"You're a mind reader Taraneh Saderzadeh, I was asking myself exactly the same question on the tube on the way over here." Peter said, admiring the attractive Persian woman sat opposite him. They were both in their sixties now, but Taraneh could easily have passed for someone ten years younger. She was wearing a navy-blue cashmere polo neck sweater under a beautifully cut, cream trouser suit.

"Really, and what was the answer you came up with?" Taraneh asked.

"I came to the conclusion that we shouldn't dwell on the past and just let the interesting things that we have done in our lives since we were friends in Oxford emerge naturally, as our relationship blossoms." Peter suggested, struggling to keep a straight face.

"You're incorrigible Peter Wilson, I could still be sat with the cheeky twenty-three-year-old reporter in the Radcliffe Infirmary if I didn't know better, 'relationship blossoms' indeed!" and they both laughed.

"I'm only joking Taraneh, although it's a lovely thought." Peter said.

"The problem with your suggestion Peter, is that there may be things we want to know about each other's past and present for that matter, immediately." Taraneh said, putting on a smart pair of designer glasses to read the menu.

"That is very true, so why don't we order and then enjoy our meal whilst we both consider the most immediate question we want to ask each other." Peter replied, playing along. He found it interesting and pleasant that the two of them seemed relaxed in each other's company and their mildly flirtatious relationship hadn't changed much in over forty years.

Peter ordered sardines to start and Taraneh chose the asparagus with parmigiana. They both selected the dover sole for their main course and when the food arrived Peter told Taraneh about the Coleville affair and reminded her of the key role she had played in the celebrated case.

"I knew there was something not quite right about the Colevilles when I nannied for them. I was so young and not completely sure though. I'm just surprised that you were listening to me when I told you about my suspicions, you'd not long had the operation on your eye and were badly bruised from the car accident, quite impressive you remembering my story all those years later." Taraneh said.

"Journalistic training Taraneh, listening is the key, I can remember our first editor Sidney Newman telling us that. Mind you, when it's a beautiful young Persian nurse telling you a story, it makes listening very easy." Peter said, only half joking and Taraneh just shook her head and smiled.

She considered Peter as they enjoyed their food, he was wearing a smart navy-blue suit, *Paul Smith* by the look of the cut she thought to herself, with a crisp white open neck shirt. His hair was still fashionably long, but now predominantly grey and he had pretty much the same physique, tall and slim, that he had as the young man she had known all those years ago.

Peter had chosen a bottle of *Gavi di Gavi*, a delicious white wine from the Piedmont region of Italy, to compliment the fish and whilst they ate, Taraneh told Peter about her life in Tehran, where she lived with her father in their home near Gheytarieh Park in the north of the city.

She told him about her busy social life and her large network of friends, with whom she enjoys dinner parties at each other's homes, as well as night's out at some of the best restaurants in Tehran. She also told him that she occasionally still worked as a private nurse in the city, helping families cope with housebound patients. Her father was still in reasonably good health for someone of his advanced age and he had a good support system around him, should he need it, whenever Taraneh was abroad.

"I remember our last meeting in Oxford you know Peter, I was about to be married and you were about to embark upon a career in Fleet Street. I'm pleased to see that your career fared better than my marriage." Taraneh said, as they finished off the last of the wine.

"How do you know that?" Peter asked.

"It wasn't difficult, a quick search on the internet told me that you've had a glittering career." Taraneh replied.

"Your husband was a doctor wasn't he?" Peter asked, deliberately changing the subject.

"Yes and we were divorced within a few years, it was a mistake, we were both too young, fortunately we had no children." Taraneh explained.

"I'm sorry to hear that, I was lucky, I was very happily married but sadly, Gloria died suddenly a few years ago, I struggled with her death for some time afterwards but I've come through the worst now. Unfortunately, we didn't have any children." Peter told her.

"I'm very sorry to hear that Peter." Taraneh said, quietly.

"So, those immediate questions we'd both been thinking about for the past two hours that couldn't wait, ladies first Taraneh." Peter smiled.

"Age before beauty Peter, you can go first." Taraneh jokingly replied.

"If I must, well my question is very personal I'm afraid, I just wondered whether you are in a relationship with anyone at the moment?" Peter asked, feeling slightly embarrassed and avoiding eye contact.

"Peter Wilson! That is very personal. However, the answer is no and it's a coincidence, because that is exactly the same question that I wanted to ask you." Taraneh answered with a smile.

"That's very good news then, because I can provide exactly the same answer that you just gave." Peter said and the two of them laughed. They enjoyed coffee and a glass of limoncello as the evening drew to a close, before Peter ordered a taxi.

After dropping Taraneh off at her apartment, nearby in Kensington, Peter asked the driver to take him home to Marylebone. The evening had been a success, he thought to himself in the taxi and he was pretty sure that Taraneh felt the same. He found it fascinating that even after a gap of more than forty years their relationship was very much the same as it had been when they first met, light hearted and relaxed, which was just what he needed at present. Perhaps people don't change that much as they grow older, other than their appearance of course he thought and as far as Taraneh's appearance was concerned, he felt that she had matured into a very beautiful woman.

She had told him that she would be in London for a couple of months and they had agreed that another night out in the near future would be nice. Her Liverpudlian friend Rita would be coming to stay over Christmas and they decided that it would be fun to go out one evening as a foursome, if Mathew was back in London before Christmas and could join them.

\*\*\*\*\*\*\*\*\*\*\*\*\*\*\*\*\*\*\*

Maureen Tyler got off the Central Line train at Shepherd's Bush station and decided to spend an hour in the *Westfield Shopping Centre*, before walking home. It was a Friday evening and she'd finished for the week at the law firm near St. Paul's, where she worked as a PA for one of the partners. It was pretty much the same journey she had been taking every working day since she turned eighteen, thirty-four years ago, although she had only been with Martindale, Buckle and Shaw (MBS) for the past ten years. Her experience gained working in the shipping industry, prior to her current position, had been instrumental in her being offered the job, MBS specialised in maritime law.

Maureen bought herself a beige-coloured jacket from *Zara*, she still had a slim figure and rarely had any difficulty finding clothes off the peg that would fit her, whenever she went shopping. She still had a youthful appearance and on more than one occasion, the younger lawyers at work had asked her out. Sadly, as she had often told her oldest friend Janice whenever they went out for a meal together, she'd lost faith in men a long time ago. Even though her friend was forever telling her that she shouldn't let one bad experience ruin her life, she paid no attention to her, after all, what did Janice know? Yet another fifty-something woman without a partner.

Anyway, she thought to herself as she walked down the Goldhawk Road, Daniel as she always called him, not Danny, was back home now and she had enough on her plate worrying about him, never mind about any other bloke. As she let herself into their terraced house on Stowe Road it crossed her mind that, even though Daniel was technically back home, he was more often than not to be found in his second home, his favourite boozer near Shepherd's Bush Green.

Maureen had spent the past twelve years living alone in the house she had grown up in with her brother and her parents, whilst Daniel had spent this period in various prisons dotted around London and the South of England. She had regularly visited her brother throughout this sad period in their lives, becoming an expert on public transport throughout the region during her travels. The latter part of his sentence was spent in two open prisons, which made life a bit more bearable for him. Maureen had even struck up relationships with two of Daniel's fellow inmates' wives, long-suffering women with serial offenders for husbands. She readily understood that technically, she was in a different situation than they were, she wasn't married to Daniel they were brother and sister, but she was all that he'd got since they had lost their parents. Their mother and father had tragically died in a car accident when Maureen and Daniel were in their early twenties and the Victorian terraced house on Stowe Road where they had been brought up had remained their home ever since.

In the nineteen-sixties and seventies, when they were growing up, this part of West London had been a traditional working-class district. Now, many of the houses in Stowe Road, including their own, were fetching more than a million pounds. Maureen often thought to herself that it was a pity that Daniel had turned to crime all those years ago, because if he had only known that one day he'd be sitting on a goldmine his life may have taken a different course. Even before his long spell in prison, Stowe Road and the surrounding district was becoming a popular location for young professionals to live and many aspects of the area had changed beyond recognition. Excellent transport links to the West End and the City had resulted in Shepherd's Bush becoming what estate agents described as 'a desirable location'. The opening in 2008 of the Westfield Shopping Centre, the largest covered shopping development in London, had further enhanced Shepherd's Bush's reputation as an up-and-coming district.

Maureen went into the kitchen and poured herself a large glass of red wine, noting that the sink was full of unwashed dishes. She took the wine with her out into the back garden, where she had recently had some decking installed and lit a cigarette. It was her guilty secret, enjoying one cigarette each day after work to help her unwind.

The neighbours on both sides were new, a married couple, both accountants, on one side and a young female advertising executive on the other side. One of the only people still living in the street from her childhood was old Mrs. Brent who lived opposite. She was well into her eighties now and still a nosy cow, as far as Maureen was concerned. Daniel had only been back home a few days when she stopped Maureen one morning in the street, as she was setting off to work, to say that it was nice to see Daniel again, telling her not to worry she wouldn't be letting any of the neighbours know about his past. Maureen was tempted to tell her to mind her own business, but didn't have the time or patience to get into a long conversation about her brother, so she just smiled and continued walking towards the Goldhawk Road and Shepherd's Bush Underground Station.

Maureen looked forward to going to work, she was good at her job and was valued by the law firm. The experience she had gained from working in the shipping industry was proving to be invaluable at MBS and although she was only employed as a PA, the partners often consulted her about some of the more detailed aspects of the business. She had remained in contact with a few old colleagues from the shipping industry, most of whom were now retired, who she would occasionally meet up with and every now and then she would take the opportunity to quiz them on some detailed point about the shipping business that one of the partners needed answering.

Daniel arrived home from the pub just after eight o'clock and the two of them settled down in the kitchen to share a *Marks & Spencer* beef lasagne, with a green salad, that Maureen had prepared earlier. Maureen drank two more

82

glasses of wine with her dinner, whilst Daniel said he would stick with lager because he didn't want to mix his drinks, which made them both laugh. Over the past few weeks since he had been home Daniel had been telling his sister, for the first time, the truth about the crimes he had committed, which had resulted in his twelve year stay in prison. Maureen had asked him on a number of occasions why he had not told the police the names of his accomplices because it would have almost certainly dramatically reduced his sentence. All that Daniel would say was that it would have been dangerous to do that, some of the gang were ruthless criminals who would go to any length to retain their freedom and anyway, he had now served his time, he was a free man and there would be no repercussions.

On one evening though, when he had drunk a bit too much lager, he told Maureen the names of three of the people involved with the crimes. Two of the names meant nothing to her, but the name of the third one stunned her. For a few moments she could no longer hear what her brother was telling her and later on, thinking back to that moment she believes she had gone into some kind of shock, her heartbeat had raced and she'd felt anxious and cold. Daniel had recognised that something was wrong with his sister and comforted her until she recovered. He apologised, saying it was wrong to dwell on the past and promised not to mention the subject again.

It was too late though, Maureen now knew that one of the men responsible for putting her brother behind bars was the same man she blamed for ruining her life ten years ago, when he dumped her for another woman.

# CHAPTER ELEVEN

## KIRSTY AND SANDY 1990 - 1994

By 1990, Kirsty Blair was an established fashion model. Her bookings were mainly concentrated in London, but she had already travelled to New York, Tokyo, Paris and Milan for work. She was becoming recognisable to the public from the many fashion magazine shoots she had undertaken and she had most recently worked on two high-fashion runway shows in Milan and Paris. Kirsty's least favourite bookings were the commercial modelling assignments for advertisements in magazines or on television and cinema. Brand work for fashion chains was lucrative, but again, not particularly enjoyable.

At times, she had to pinch herself to remember just how lucky she was, her social life in London was exciting and sometimes glamourous, every young woman's dream she was often told. Over the past eighteen months, she had gained a reputation for being professional and reliable, traits not always synonymous in the fashion world. She looked after herself, exercised regularly at the gym near the flat in Maida Vale, didn't drink excessively and kept what Melanie liked to call, reasonable hours during the working week. She had also fallen in love.

The dinner date she had with Sandy eighteen months ago at a small Japanese restaurant in Soho was the start of her first ever serious relationship. Looking back, Kirsty remembered it as an awkward occasion. Even though he was a few years older than her, Sandy had about as much experience of relationships with the opposite sex as she had and on top of this, he was painfully shy. She knew from the beginning of their relationship that if it was going to work out she would have to make a lot of the running and at times, it was hard work. Thankfully, whilst Sandy was clearly a sensitive soul, he was caring and affectionate. When they first met, Kirsty had still been a virgin, her flatmate, Grace, couldn't believe it when she told her one evening over pizza and a bottle of wine.

"Holy shit! You're having me on honey." were her exact words, Kirsty remembered fondly. Grace was not only her flatmate, but by now also her best friend and sometimes behaved like the older sister she'd never had. They still shared the same flat in Sutherland Avenue, although Hanna had left and moved in with the rock star and consequently, the third bedroom was still vacant.

Kirsty looked back happily on the years she spent sharing a flat with Grace. She had that American way of being positive about almost everything, which Kirsty admired. She was also tremendous fun to live with, regularly arranging parties for their friends at the flat. Luckily, the neighbours were young and Grace would get around any issues about the noise by inviting them all to the parties as well. After a while, Kirsty had noticed that Grace had started mixing with a group of her compatriots, most of whom worked at the American Embassy in Grosvenor Square. They were a wealthy, generally formal bunch and Kirsty enjoyed watching their reaction when they met some of Grace's more outrageous friends from the fashion world. In his quiet, unassuming way, Sandy enjoyed the parties and he was very popular with the other models invited, who loved to discuss the inventive ways he often found of photographing them whenever they worked together on fashion shoots.

Sandy had asked Kirsty to move in with him on a number of occasions, he rented a one-bedroom flat in Bloomsbury, a short walk from the British Museum, but she thought it best to keep arrangements as they were for the time being. The two of them lived pretty hectic lives and even though they worked in the same industry, surprisingly, their paths rarely crossed professionally. Sometimes, if one of them was working abroad, they might not see each other for a week or more. When they were both in London, they tried to meet up two or three evenings each week for dinner, following which Kirsty usually stayed the night in Bloomsbury. At weekends, they would go to a club or, perhaps a party. Although neither of them had much experience, Kirsty found Sandy a wonderful lover and around this time she often thought to herself that she was glad that she had waited for the right man to come along before she lost her virginity. She did recognise that this only added to the intensity of the relationship and the love that she felt for Sandy. At times, this scared her. What if something happened to him she would think to herself irrationally.

Still, despite these concerns, the past eighteen months had been the happiest time of her short life. She was a successful fashion model, living in an exciting city with a lovely flatmate and she was in love with a beautiful young man. Not only that, she was also confident that her love for him was reciprocated. At times, it was like a dream, she would phone her Aunty Moira once a week and tell her about her life in London and she could tell that her aunty was delighted for her and typically very supportive.

Sometimes, Kirsty wondered how different her life may have been if her mother had lived. She was a mere two-year-old when she died and couldn't remember anything about her. Moira would sometimes speak about her sister, telling Kirsty that Annie was a good woman who loved and cared for her daughter, demonstrated by the fact that she was killed in a road accident on her way to work at a factory to support the two of them. Annie was a proud woman who wanted to provide for her daughter and give her a decent upbringing, not always easy for single mother living in a poor part of Glasgow in the nineteen-seventies. Aunty Moira once told Kirsty that her life had been very different growing up with her and Kelvin in the Mews, but she must always remember that her mother's love for her had been deep.

Kirsty had asked her aunty and Kelvin whether either of them knew anything about her father but sadly, all they could tell her was that her mother had told them she had made a mistake when she met this man and it was best forgotten. Occasionally, she wondered whether she should try and trace him and that it would be the normal thing to do for a young woman in her position, but she always came to the same conclusion that he obviously hadn't wanted her, so what was the point? Her mother had put it so succinctly when she had told her sister that, 'it was best forgotten'.

*********************

Within twelve months, Kirsty and Sandy were sharing their own flat in Camden, even though it was more by chance than design that they came to be living together. Grace had decided to move in with her American boyfriend, a young diplomat who worked at their embassy, at his flat in Victoria and Kirsty decided that she didn't want to stay in Sutherland Avenue, with the prospect of a new flatmate joining her. Fortunately, this coincided with the lease on Sandy's flat in Bloomsbury expiring. They were both earning a very good income and by pooling their savings they were able to put down a deposit and take a mortgage out on a small flat in Camden. Kirsty was delighted to be living in the very part of London where she had stayed when she had arrived from Glasgow for her interview with Barbara Tripp and Melanie a few years earlier.

For the next two years the young fashion model and the brilliant photographer enjoyed their life together in fashionable Camden, both working hard during the week and playing hard at the weekends. The only worries Kirsty had about their relationship was Sandy's use of, what their friends called, recreational drugs. She had known that from time to time he would do the occasional line of cocaine along with others that they were mixing with, it was very common in the fashion industry. He said it helped him relax and be more sociable and because, by nature, Sandy was a very quiet reserved person Kirsty accepted his explanation.

Their alcohol consumption at weekends had also increased and they would think nothing of drinking until three or four o'clock in the morning. Kirsty hated the term 'recreational drugs'. Whilst Aunty Moira and Kelvin had employed a zero-tolerance policy towards drug use at the Mews, she had seen Class A drug use wreak havoc on some of their friends' lives in London. Kirsty tried cocaine once or twice herself when she was with Sandy and whilst she was surprised at how easily it gave her confidence, she felt uncomfortable the following day and unusually sad. She wasn't certain that these feelings were directly connected to the drugs she had taken, but she decided that it wasn't for her and she never took cocaine again.

By 1993, Kirsty had become one of the leading fashion models at the agency, she had a wealth of experience built up over the previous four years and was now in a position where, to some degree, she could pick and choose which bookings suited her the best. Financially, she was also prospering. She had always been prudent and was good at saving money and she was now managing to put away a tidy sum each month, even after her part of the mortgage and bills were paid.

Unfortunately, her life was about to take a dreadful turn for the worse. Looking back on events later, she could see that the problems started when Sandy told her one autumn evening that he had to travel back to Scotland to attend a funeral. He was particularly anxious and short tempered that evening and she had to drag it out of him that it was his father's funeral that he would be attending. In all the time Kirsty had known him, Sandy had hardly ever spoken about his family and on the rare occasions that he did, it was to make it clear that he had now put his unhappy childhood behind him and that he didn't want to be reminded of his earlier life in Scotland. Sometimes, Kirsty had heard him speaking on the phone with his mother, but when she asked him about his mother he would clam up, clearly upset.

Since she had known Sandy, the two of them had enjoyed such a loving, gentle and kind relationship, that it was such a contrast to see him upset and angry. By this time, he had been living in London for the best part of ten years and other than the rare occasions when his work took him north of the border, he hadn't been back to Scotland. Kirsty offered to accompany him to the funeral, explaining that whatever had happened in the past was now over and reassuring him that family relationships could often be complicated and difficult. She could provide him with support if they went together she suggested, but he wouldn't hear of it, he was going alone. Sandy was away from home for the funeral for no more than forty-eight hours and when he returned to London, he threw himself into his work with a vengeance.

The following year, Sandy's dependency on cocaine and alcohol increased. During the week he would work, but he had started to return home later in the evening. Because of Kirsty's own work commitments, which sometimes involved long hours and nights staying away in hotels, she was not always at home herself when he returned to the flat in Camden. Much later, she would blame herself for not recognising the tell-tale signs which were beginning to appear. Sandy became morose and started suffering from depression, including panic attacks in the evenings. The weekends became one long alcohol and cocaine fueled binge. They had begun to argue on a regular basis and Kirsty would sometimes go and stay with Grace and her boyfriend in Victoria, sleeping on their couch, which was preferable to staying in the flat in Camden when Sandy was in such a terrible state. He had always been slim, but by now he had lost weight and had started to look ill and unkempt. Kirsty tried to talk to him to try and understand what was driving his self-destructive behaviour, but to no avail. On the 3rd of April 1994, Kirsty answered the door of their flat to two uniformed police officers, Sandy had been found dead at an address in South East London. She would find out later that the house where he was found was being used by drug dealers and others to buy, sell and use crack cocaine, commonly known as a 'crack den'.

# CHAPTER TWELVE

# OUT OF DANGER

The operation was successful. A blood vessel was taken from John's arm and attached to the coronary artery above and below the blockage. The procedure took five hours and forty-eight hours later, John was sat in a chair next to his hospital bed talking with Mathew and his sister Judith, who had flown to Inverness from London earlier that day, following her return from New Zealand. Judith's husband Colin was at home in Surrey with his elderly in-laws. The doctors had already spoken with John and told him that he should be able to return home in approximately a week's time and hopefully, should be able to return to most normal activities within six or seven weeks.

"I'm so happy John, we've been so worried about you." Judith leant over and gave her brother a peck on his cheek.

"Did they say anything to you about what may have caused it?" Mathew asked.

"Age, high fat diet, I'll need to make some changes I think." John replied.

"When you are discharged, I'm coming to stay with you for a while, if that's alright with you?" Mathew said.

"That's very kind Mathew, but you'll have things to take care of in London." John replied.

"That can wait John, Judith will go back to Surrey in a day or two to be with Colin and mum and dad." Mathew added.

"Of course, you shouldn't have come up here Judith, you must be exhausted after the flight back from Auckland." John said, becoming visibly more tired as he spoke.

"I'm fine thanks John, we need to leave Mathew, he needs rest." Judith said, nodding in John's direction. After a quick word with the ward Sister, the two of them drove back to the hotel in Inverness, near to the hospital. On the way back, Mathew was thinking to himself that he was glad that he didn't bring up the question of why his brother was carrying a truncheon on the night he had the heart attack and why he appeared to be investigating a drug smuggler who had recently been released from prison, his brother was too weak and it could wait.

"It was kind of Peter to travel all the way up here with you, how is he? I haven't seen him since last Christmas." Judith asked innocently, as her brother parked the car near to the hotel reception.

"He's fine, he had to get back to London for a date." Mathew replied mischievously, remembering that his sister had once had a crush on Peter and the two of them remained quite close.

There had been a time before both Peter and Judith had married that Mathew thought that the two of them might become a couple themselves. He certainly had suspicions that they'd had some kind of relationship not long after he'd started working in Fleet Street with Peter in the mid-seventies. Whenever Mathew had brought up the subject in a light hearted way, Peter had always vehemently denied it and when he teased his sister about a possible love interest with Peter, she would simply blush and change the subject. Perhaps it was because Peter was virtually part of the family, that any suggestion that the two of them had been lovers was so embarrassing for them. Anyway, Mathew thought to himself, it was all water under the bridge, his sister had a happy marriage with Colin and two terrific sons. Even so, he made a mental note to mention his suspicions to Peter again the next time he saw him, he quite enjoyed seeing his oldest friend pompously deny that anything of the sort had gone on between them.

*********************

Kirsty and Morag were having their weekly lunch together in the dining room of The Sound. They were discussing the Christmas and Hogmanay arrangements for the hotel, but Morag noticed that Kirsty appeared to be preoccupied and at times not listening, there was clearly something on her mind.

"Sometimes, a problem shared is a problem halved you know hen." Morag said, kindly.

"I'm afraid, this problem is a very serious one Morag and recently I may have even made matters worse, I really don't know what to do next." Kirsty replied sadly.

"Have you spoken with Angus about it?" Morag asked, pouring them both a glass of wine.

"No, I haven't, because it involves Angus, I think he's being blackmailed Morag." Kirsty suddenly blurted out.

"Blackmailed, what on earth for?" Morag asked, looking concerned.

"This sounds like a bad comedy sketch, but I found a letter in one of his jacket pockets when I was preparing to take a whole bundle of our clothes to the dry cleaners. I would never normally look through his pockets but it's something you do instinctively when you're doing the washing and cleaning isn't it?" Kirsty asked, looking for reassurance.

"Yes, of course it is Kirsty, you didn't do anything wrong." Morag replied supportively.

"Anyway," Kirsty continued anxiously, "the letter I found is from someone who seems to have been in prison for a long time, twelve years I think, and he claims that Angus owes him a lot of money. He says in the letter that they were involved in some kind of business agreement, but reading between the lines it sounds more like a criminal

93

enterprise. The bottom line is that if Angus doesn't pay up, this man will go to the police."

"That sounds very serious Kirsty, you said that you've made matters worse, how on earth have you managed to do that?" Morag asked, looking increasingly concerned.

"I didn't know what to do Morag and I panicked, I confided in John, well you know he's a former policemen, I just thought he would know what to do so I gave him a copy of the letter." Kirsty explained.

"And did he know? Surely he should have told you to speak to Angus and then report it to the police." Morag asked.

"You're right, he did, but I told John I wanted to know more about it before I spoke to Angus and he agreed to make some discrete enquiries and let me know as soon as possible what he'd found out. That was two days before his heart attack, so I've no idea what's going to happen now, everything's such a mess. I'm sure he just felt sorry for me, him being so kind and now I've gone and involved him in all of this, it's the last thing the poor man needs at the moment." Kirsty said, close to tears.

"Have you heard how John is, he was having surgery yesterday wasn't he?" Morag asked.

"Yes, sorry, I meant to tell you, I spoke with his brother earlier and the operation went well and hopefully, he'll return home in about a week's time, Mathew is going to stay at the Lodge with him whilst he convalesces." Kirsty replied.

"You know the answer to this Kirsty love, you are going to have to speak with Angus about it all at some point." Morag said, giving her old friend a knowing look.

"Yes, I know and that's what's worrying me." Kirsty replied.

\*\*\*\*\*\*\*\*\*\*\*\*\*\*\*\*\*\*\*

"The last time I spoke with you at length I made a complete fool of myself." Angus said, passing Lady Caroline Hemsworth a small glass of gin and tonic.

The two of them were meeting at Angus's request in a sea front bar near to the Kyle of Lochalsh. Caroline would be driving across the bridge to her home on the Isle of Skye following their meeting, hence the small G&T, rather than the customary large one.

"It was a bit embarrassing for both of us as I seem to recall. Still, water under the bridge as they say, cheers." Caroline said, clinking their glasses, Angus was holding a glass of beer.

"Your good health Caroline and thank you for coming, I was drunk that evening and was talking nonsense." Angus said, avoiding eye contact with her.

"Well darling, I hope that isn't some excuse for why you made a pass at me." Caroline replied.

"Of course not, I was..........."Angus stammered, before he was interrupted.

"I'm only teasing you Angus, there is no need to try and explain, if I had a pound for every time I've made a fool of myself after too many drinks I'd be an even richer woman that I am today. Now, why have you asked to see me?" Caroline smiled.

"Mathew Phillips-Lehman and Peter Wilson, I heard through the grapevine that you've known the two of them for a long time and I just wanted to find out a bit more about them and thought that you might be able to help me out, that's all." Angus asked, sitting back in his chair.

"Well, I spoke with Mathew this morning, he told me they've operated on John and it went well." Caroline said, buying a bit of time, whilst she tried to work out where their conversation was heading.

"That's splendid news, it'll be great to have John back, he's an important part of the team." Angus replied.

"Anthony owned the newspaper that the two of them worked for in the eighties and nineties, Peter was officially the defence correspondent, but as a pair, their strong point was investigative journalism, they were the best around. You can probably look up the awards they won on the internet, I should think it's all there. Peter got most of the attention because he took risks, Mathew was the details man, contacts everywhere, a brilliant combination. Anthony rated them very highly, which was praise indeed, miserable bastard that he is." Caroline laughed, but noticed that Angus had a more serious look on his face.

"They're retired now, aren't they?" Angus asked.

"From full time work, yes they are, but it was their private investigation last year that uncovered Sir Robert and Margaret Coleville's crimes, so they're still at it, so to speak. I suppose you could say it's become a hobby for the two of them now that they both have more time on their hands. I know one thing, I wouldn't want them investigating me if I'd been up to no good." Caroline said deliberately, just to see Angus's reaction.

"Oh, I read about the Coleville affair, I didn't know that those two were behind the story." Angus replied calmly.

"Look Angus, our conversation is private and as far as I'm concerned it won't go any further than these four walls. I've absolutely no idea what's going on, but can I ask you the reason you want to know more about them." Caroline asked, taking a sip of her gin and tonic.

"Nothing underhand Caroline, I always like to know a bit about the guests who stay at our hotel and you never know I might want them to help me one day," Angus replied, unconvincingly, "are you sure I can't tempt you with another gin and tonic?"

"Very kind Angus, but no, I wouldn't want to get squiffy, I might make a pass at you." Caroline replied and the two of them laughed.

96

Caroline left the bar and drove across the bridge to Skye, puzzled and slightly unsettled by the conversation she'd just had with Angus Mackenzie.

# CHAPTER THIRTEEN

# FLOWERS IN THE RAIN – LONDON
# 1994 -2002

Later, when Kirsty had time to reflect on events, she was
not sure how she would have got through Sandy's funeral
without Barbara Tripp's and Melanie's help. Sandy had
been a freelance photographer and had not been an
employee of the agency, but from the moment Kirsty had
rung the agency to tell them the terrible news the two of
them couldn't have been kinder. They helped Kirsty with
the funeral arrangements, even managing to track down
Sandy's mother in Scotland, although by this time she was
suffering from the early stages of dementia, living in a care
home and was too sick to attend. Other than Finlay
Robertson, a cousin of Sandy's mother, they were unable to
trace any other relatives. Kirsty stayed with Grace and her
boyfriend in Victoria whilst the funeral arrangements were
made.

Sandy was cremated and his ashes were placed in an urn
in the Garden of Remembrance in Hampstead Cemetery,
not too far from the home he had shared with Kirsty in
Camden. A plaque commemorating him was inscribed,
*Sandy Mackenzie, born 2nd February 1966 - died 3rd April
1994. RIP.* He was just twenty-eight years old.

The funeral was attended by friends and colleagues from
throughout the fashion industry. Someone joked at the
reception, held afterwards at the model agency's offices in
St. Martin's Lane, that they'd never seen so many beautiful
people in one place at the same time. It raised a few smiles,
but it was a desperately sad occasion. Moira and Kelvin had

travelled down from Glasgow and were made a fuss of by Kirsty's young friends. She spent some time speaking with Finlay and the cousin of Sandy's mother told her how he had introduced Sandy to photography and how quickly he had picked up the basic skills, even though he was only young. Although Finlay was not a very close relative of Sandy, it was clear to Kirsty that he thought of him affectionately. He told her the story of how he gave the young budding photographer his first camera as a gift.

Kirsty didn't feel in the mood to discuss Sandy's past but she did, half-heartedly, ask Finlay about his childhood in the Highlands. She wasn't surprised when he told her that Sandy wasn't a very happy child at home, but said that as he got older he eventually learnt to stand up for himself. Finlay was clearly upset and Kirsty could sense that this was not the time, or place, to discuss such a sad period in Sandy's short life. Finlay left the reception soon afterwards to head back to Scotland.

Kirsty travelled back to Glasgow with her Aunty Moira and Kelvin the following day and she stayed at the Mews with them for the next fortnight whilst she decided what to do next. She had told Barbara and Melanie immediately after the funeral that she wanted to take a break from modelling for a while and they were very supportive. In fact, it was Barbara who rang her one morning, whilst she was helping Moira prepare breakfast in The Mews, to tell her about an unexpected opportunity that had arisen. She told Kirsty that a fashion editor friend of hers was planning to write a book about British fashion during the 1940s and 1950s and needed someone to help her research the project. Since becoming a model, Kirsty had been interested in fashion from this period and had become quite knowledgeable, often discussing the subject with Barbara whenever they met at the agency. Kirsty told her that she would be returning to London in a few days' time and would be delighted if her name was put forward for the position.

\*\*\*\*\*\*\*\*\*\*\*\*\*\*\*\*\*\*\*

The funeral had brought home to Kirsty just how little she really knew about Sandy. She was travelling back to London on the train from Glasgow and thinking about their life together. She knew next to nothing of his past, it was almost as though his life had started when he arrived in London in 1984, just four years before she had arrived there herself from Glasgow. He very rarely spoke about anything that happened during his early life in the Highlands of Scotland and not for the first time, she thought it was strange, unusual. Since his death, it had become more and more obvious to her that this was not normal behaviour whereas, when he was alive she was so much in love with him and too preoccupied with her work to fully realise or understand the damage that was being caused. As the saying goes she thought to herself, she had been blinded by love, failing to grasp that Sandy's secretive behaviour was damaging.

This was the first time she had given herself time and space to reflect on her life with Sandy and the dreadful events that led to his death. His return to Scotland for his father's funeral had seemed to send him into a spiral of self-destruction. Should she have done more to help him? But how could she, when he would never engage in discussion regarding his early life and anyway, in every other respect he was so caring, kind and gentle. Why would she have dwelt on the negative side of his character when there was so much to enjoy about its positive aspects.

During her stay back home in Glasgow, Aunty Moira had reminded her that she was very young when she met Sandy and it was hardly surprising that they didn't spend hours on end reflecting on life when they were together,

100

they were a happy young couple having the time of their lives. It was Moira's way of telling her, sensitively, not to dwell on the past and not to blame herself.

When discussing these thoughts with her Aunty she could tell that Moira was acutely aware that she had already lost her mother in a shocking accident and now her partner had died, in equally dreadful circumstances. Moira's words were, as usual, wise. You will never forget what happened to Sandy, her Aunty told her one sunny afternoon as the two of them strolled through Victoria Park in Glasgow, you will think about it most days for years to come, perhaps forever, but the pain you will feel will lessen as the years pass. Kirsty recognised that she was speaking from experience, after all, Moira had also lost a sister all those years ago when her mother Annie died.

\*\*\*\*\*\*\*\*\*\*\*\*\*\*\*\*\*\*\*

Kirsty's first task when she had returned to Camden was to decide what to do with Sandy's very expensive cameras and photographic equipment, which virtually filled the small spare room in the flat. She remembered Sandy telling her one day about an organisation that helped young aspiring photographers who came from disadvantaged backgrounds and instinctively she decided to donate to them all of the equipment, lock, stock and barrel. She found their phone number amongst some letters in Sandy's files and within days a young couple arrived in a van and collected everything. They were delighted, but respectful and clearly grateful. Kirsty was not surprised when the young woman told her that Sandy had occasionally given photography lessons at the organisation's studio in Hackney, free of charge.

The next decision Kirsty made was to ring the fashion-editor regarding the job that Barbara had told her about. Kirsty had no real experience of research, but she was interested in the history of British fashion and needed to do something positive. Two days later, she met Maggie Riley in her cramped office in a national newspaper's headquarters in Wapping, East London. The two of them hit it off immediately. Maggie was clearly a slightly eccentric artistic type and her dress sense accentuated this image, she wore layers of chiffon and lace, along with a shawl and an elaborate head scarf, all in vivid colours. She was also totally disorganized. Kirsty thought her office looked as though a bomb had just gone off in it and Maggie struggled to find anything she was looking for without an extensive search, which must have added hours to her working day. However, when she spoke about fashion, she was full of knowledge, articulate and enthusiastic.

Maggie asked Kirsty to start researching the period during the Second World War, when British fashion was forced to be inventive to overcome the shortages and rationing that were in place across the country. Kirsty was soon to learn that it wasn't just food that was rationed during this period, buying clothes was rationed as well. Maggie gave Kirsty a list of relevant museums in London and beyond to visit, including the Imperial War Museum, the V&A and the Fashion Museum in Bath, as well as a few books which covered fashion in the nineteen-forties.

Maggie offered Kirsty £100 per week, which Kirsty accepted with thanks, she hadn't really considered what the remuneration, if anything, would be for the research she would undertake, her primary objective was to keep herself busy doing something that interested her. Maggie took her out for lunch after the meeting and the two of them shared a bottle of wine with their meal. It was the first time she had drunk alcohol since Sandy's death and she felt quite happily tipsy when she left the restaurant to make her way home from Wapping Station.

Kirsty enjoyed research. Surprisingly, it was the detail she found satisfying. She spent hours in the various museums she visited, preparing notes and then cross-referencing them against the information she had gleaned from the books that Maggie had given her to read. After two months she had prepared a document, divided into sections, covering aspects such as the utility clothing regulations, uniforms worn by women in the services, dressmaking and tailoring, wartime weddings and so on. Maggie was delighted with the results and treated Kirsty to lunch at *Quo Vadis* in Soho. The staff there looked after Maggie, she was obviously a good customer and popular, it all reminded Kirsty of happier times when lunch or dinner in Soho was the norm. Maggie asked her to undertake some similar research, this time on British fashion during the 1950s and offered her an additional £20 a week for her troubles, which Kirsty happily accepted.

It was at this time that she decided that her modelling career was over and she would find herself a normal job, preferably working nine-to-five in an office. She had come to the conclusion, reinforced by the enjoyment and peace of mind she had gained from the mundane nature of research, that what she needed, even wanted, was a secure job providing stability. At one point, she even considered becoming a librarian, but thought that might be a step too far in a different direction! She was convinced that the ordinary nature and security that office work would provide was perfect for her.

Kirsty completed the research on 1950s British fashion in no time at all. After the austerity of the war years, the fifties were exciting and fresh and Kirsty reflected this in the document she prepared for Maggie. The drab regulations during the war years and the immediate aftermath had now been replaced with bright sections on cocktail dresses, ballgowns and wonderful designers, such as *Hardy Amies, Mary Quant and Norman Hartnell*. Strangely, the fashion changes she had documented mirrored the change in her own mood, for the first time since Sandy's death she felt more positive and optimistic about the future.

Kirsty told Maggie, over a farewell lunch at *Kettner's* in Soho, that she had enrolled for a secretarial course at night school and following this, she would be applying for office jobs in London. Maggie told her in typically frank fashion that it was a terrible waste that someone so beautiful would not be photographed anymore, but she totally understood why her life was changing course and said that she would provide very good references, if she ever needed them. Kirsty thanked the fashion editor and they parted on very good terms. It felt as though a chapter in her life was drawing to a close and her life in the fashion world was finally over.

Kirsty took Barbara Tripp and Melanie out for lunch and told them about her decision. Surprisingly, it was Melanie who tried to talk her out of it, Barbara was quiet for long periods during the lunch which was uncharacteristic. When they had finished their lunch, Melanie excused herself, she had a meeting arranged and had to get back to the office in St. Martin's Lane.

"You've been quiet Barbara." Kirsty said, once Melanie had left.

"Yes, I thought you'd noticed. Look, I totally understand your decision and if it doesn't work out you will always be welcome back. This whole terrible episode has got me thinking about whether we, I mean me I suppose, do enough to look after our models outside of their working life." Barbara explained.

"Sandy didn't work directly for you Barbara and you did more than enough to help me when he died." Kirsty said, kindly.

"Yes thank you Kirsty, it was the least we could do but I just want to think a bit harder about the care and welfare of our models. Anyway, enough about that, I wish you every success and happiness Kirsty." Barbara said smiling and the two of them embraced.

Kirsty knew deep down that it was Sandy's tragic death that had initiated the radical change of direction in her life. What she didn't know at the time, was that it would eventually lead to the most extraordinary and dramatic times of her life.

*********************

Throughout the remainder of the decade, Kirsty happily worked as a secretary for a number of businesses in London. The secretarial studies she had undertaken at night school had stood her in good stead and she enjoyed her work. Whenever she tired of working for a particular company, she would simply find a position elsewhere. Maggie Riley had been true to her word and always provided a good reference when required, as did Barbara Tripp. She rarely had any difficulty finding a new job, particularly once she had been interviewed and the employer had met her in person. She had taken up cycling following Sandy's death and one of her main criteria before accepting a new job, was that their offices were within cycling distance from her home in Camden.

By the start of the new millennium her life was stable and comfortable. She had a circle of friends, which she had met mainly through her office work over the past five years, with whom she would meet, usually at weekends, for dinner or drinks. Her old flatmate, Grace, had recently moved to Argentina and lived in Buenos Aires, where her diplomat partner had been posted by the American government. They had seen each other less and less since Sandy passed away, which was more to do with Kirsty not really wishing to mix in the fashion world anymore, rather than any reluctance to meet Grace, for whom Kirsty still felt affection.

105

Unsurprisingly, Kirsty was never short of male attention, but she was careful not to let any relationship become too serious. Relationships with men were one aspect of her life which reminded her of Sandy and consequently, she was mindful not to become too involved with any one partner. She found this difficult at times, she was naturally gregarious and tactile and whenever she ended a relationship, it was normally her that would end them, she felt guilty about her selfishness. She knew that it would have to be someone extremely special for her to contemplate a serious relationship and even after more than six years since his death, she knew that she could never really replace Sandy.

At times, she had a strong feeling that her female friends thought that she was a bit strange. Whenever, after a few drinks, they discussed men Kirsty could sense that they knew that she was deliberately taking a back seat during the conversation and because of this, if she did occasionally pass an opinion she was often listened to in silence as if she had something important to say, it was just embarrassing.

Aunty Moira and Kelvin came to stay with her two or three times a year and Kirsty always returned to Glasgow for Christmas and Hogmanay. When Moira and Kelvin stayed with her in London, she would always arrange days out for the three of them at either the Royal Academy of Art, the National Portrait Gallery or the V&A, Moira's favourite galleries in the capital, followed by dinner in the West End or in Mayfair.

More recently, when she was alone with her aunty, Moira would discretely ask her whether there was anyone special in her life. Kirsty smiled to herself whenever this happened, somehow, Moira knew her so well and must have recognised that this was part of her life which was not being fulfilled. Unbeknown to Kirsty and her aunty, the situation was about to change in a way in which neither of them would have ever imagined.

\*\*\*\*\*\*\*\*\*\*\*\*\*\*\*\*\*\*\*\*

Kirsty had started the new millennium working for a firm of accountants in Belsize Park in the London Borough of Camden. It was an ideal location for her, she could cycle to work from home in less than twenty minutes and she could also cycle the short distance along the Finchley Road to the cemetery where Sandy's ashes were kept whenever the mood took her, which was always at least once a month. On two occasions, during the first eighteen months that she had been working for the accountancy firm, she had been surprised to see a large bouquet of flowers left on the ground next to the plaque commemorating Sandy. On both occasions she had looked more closely and found a small card attached to the bouquet, which merely contained the handwritten words, 'To Alex'. Other than Finlay Robertson, whom she had met briefly at Sandy's funeral, she knew of no one who had known him as Alex and it was very unlikely that Finlay would have travelled all the way from Edinburgh to leave flowers. Of course, she was aware that Scots often called someone christened Alexander, by the name Sandy. It puzzled Kirsty, the flowers were being left by someone who knew him before he became known as Sandy and therefore, presumably, before he moved to London, she thought to herself.

The mystery was solved on the eighth anniversary of his death, the 3$^{rd}$ of April 2002. Kirsty had cycled to Hampstead Cemetery from her office at lunch time, she had a doctor's appointment later for a recurring problem she had been experiencing with headaches and she had taken the afternoon off as a holiday. She locked her bicycle to the railings outside the cemetery and ventured inside. As she made her ways towards Sandy's resting place, as she liked to think of the spot where his ashes were kept, clutching some fresh flowers it started to pour with rain, a typical

April shower she thought to herself as she looked up at the darkening sky.

At first, she didn't see the large figure on his haunches looking at the plaque commemorating Sandy, nor the beautiful bouquet of flowers which had been placed on the ground next to the plaque. Kirsty stopped her approach and moved off the pathway onto the grass to get a better look, hoping that she wouldn't be seen. For some strange reason, unknown to her at the time, she was sure that it was best that she wasn't noticed. After a minute or two, the person stood up and turned around and Kirsty noticed that it was a man and he had a puzzled look on his face, it was as though he had suddenly become aware that it was raining and he was wet. Looking slightly annoyed, he raised a large black umbrella above his head. Kirsty found herself shaking as the man walked back along the path towards the cemetery gates. It was uncanny, it wasn't just that he looked like Sandy, it was his mannerisms that she had noticed, particularly the look of irritation on his face when he suddenly realised that it was raining and he was wet. She had seen that same expression of annoyance or irritation on Sandy's face so many times, usually when he'd been concentrating on something connected with photography and had been disturbed.

Kirsty knew that this was her opportunity to find out who this man was and she may never get a better chance as she followed him at a discrete distance out of the cemetery gates and onto the Finchley Road. She had a hunch that he was heading for Hampstead Underground Station and she was correct. Thank goodness he hadn't driven to the cemetery, she was not sure what she would have done, written down the number plate of his car presumably. Panic struck her for a moment when she followed him into the station, only to realise that she didn't have a ticket. Whilst he was heading towards the lift, she quickly bought a ticket from the machine, thankfully there was no queue and she rushed after him through the ticket barrier. The lift door was just about to close as she managed to squeeze herself in behind a woman with a pushchair. It was only when she had got into the lift that she realised that she was still clutching the fresh flowers she had intended to leave for Sandy. Irrationally, she just hoped he didn't turn around and see her standing there, drenched to the bone, holding a bunch of soggy flowers.

When the doors to the lift finally opened, she followed him onto the Northern Line platform and watched as he boarded the first train heading to Morden and sat down. Kirsty entered the same carriage, it wasn't busy at this time of day, but she remained standing, ensuring she would have a good view of him when he decided to get off. As the train pulled into Old Street station there was a commotion when a short elderly man, possibly from Eastern Europe, boarded the train and started playing a small accordion. By the time they had left Moorgate station he had stopped playing, it had been the theme music from the movie, *The Third Man* and for some reason, Kirsty remembered she had watched the film on television with Sandy one wet Sunday afternoon.

By now, the accordionist was passing through the carriage offering his battered trilby hat for passengers to drop coins into. For a few moments he had become the focus of attention with everyone watching him partly to see, out of curiosity Kirsty suspected, which of their fellow passengers would give him some money. She just hoped he didn't reach her and she would also become the focus of attention, the mad woman, standing by the door soaking wet gripping a sad bunch of ruined flowers. She needn't have worried because the train noisily pulled into Bank station and the man she was following had already stood up and was ready to get off the train.

Thankfully, the remainder of her journey was relatively straightforward. She followed him at a discrete distance up the escalators and out onto the street outside Bank station.

Within three or four minutes he had entered a smart office block on Bishopsgate. Kirsty watched him through the glass doors as he strode past the reception desk towards the lifts and she could tell by the smiles and nods that greeted him, that he was well known at the grand offices of Mackenzie, Blount.

# CHAPTER FOURTEEN

## PETER WILSON INVESTIGATES

"She had a boyfriend who died you know, tragic, an up-and-coming fashion photographer, can't remember his name for the life of me, memory like a sieve Peter, how's that old devil Mathew Phillips-Lehman?" Maggie Riley asked, stirring her tea and Peter noted that every so often she still spoke in that staccato style, short, choppy broken speech.

The two of them were sat in the beautiful café at the V&A in Kensington, enjoying afternoon tea and cakes. Since retiring, after more than forty years mostly spent as a fashion editor, Maggie had become a volunteer at the V&A. She found that it provided her with an interest and enabled her to pass on her vast experience of the fashion world to others, when called upon. Her flamboyant fashion sense hadn't waned much since the days when they worked together, along with Mathew, at the newspaper owned by Caroline's then husband, Anthony Hemsworth. Today, Peter was pleased to see she was sporting a leopard-print midi dress and a faux fur pom-pom hat, well it was a freezing cold winter's day he thought to himself.

"Mathew's fine Maggie and he sends his love, it's his brother who's been in the wars I'm afraid, Matt is staying with him in Scotland whilst he recovers from heart surgery." Peter explained.

"John, the policeman, sorry to hear that, you see my memory's not totally shot." Maggie replied with a smile.

"Ex-policemen now and you wouldn't believe it, but when we were up in the Highlands visiting him last week we bumped into the Countess, Caroline Hemsworth, it was her that gave me your phone number." Peter said.

"Christ! What are you two on, some kind of friends re-united trip?" Maggie said making Peter laugh. "Caroline was convinced her husband was having a fling with me you know. Every time she came into the office, we were still in Fleet Street back in those days, she'd seek me out and interrogate me, mad as a March hare. It wasn't even true, Anthony was cheating on her with that blonde girl who wrote the cookery page at the time, can't remember her name either. Mind you, he did try it on with me once or twice. I told him I didn't go out with married men. Funnily enough, I think he was a bit scared of me, can't think why."

"Caroline hasn't changed much Maggie, she's divorced now, spends a lot of her time on the Isle of Skye."

"Yes, so I heard, bloody cold place to spend your retirement, still I suppose she was given the place as part of the divorce settlement." Maggie said, pouring them both another cup of tea.

"So, Kirsty Blair, that's why you're here Peter, such a beautiful girl, early nineteen-nineties, she was everywhere. For a time, every magazine you picked up she'd be modelling something or other, she did some runway work as well, I remember seeing her once or twice, she was good at that too, a natural. Sandy, that was his name!" Maggie seemed relieved that she'd suddenly remembered the name of Kirsty's boyfriend, Peter noticed. "Good looking boy, genius with a camera apparently, I think it might have been drugs. There was so much of it about then, that and AIDS, it really hit the fashion industry hard, terrible time really." Maggie said, sadly.

"Did you ever meet them when they were together?" Peter asked.

"No, in fact, the first time I actually met Kirsty was shortly after Sandy's death, I was looking for someone to help me with a series of books I was writing at the time on

British fashion, research and so on, she was recommended to me by Babs Tripp, who ran the model agency that Kirsty had worked for. She was brilliant, hardworking, attention to detail, all that stuff, did a great job, worked for me for about six months. The thing I remember that made me smile at the time, was that she was such a beautiful girl, tall, slim, blonde hair, fabulous bone structure and when she opened her mouth she had this broad Glaswegian accent, so unexpected. Lovely girl, but sad what happened to the boyfriend. It definitely had a dramatic effect on her, hardly surprising though." Maggie said.

"Do you know what she did after she had completed the research work she did for you?" Peter asked.

"She told me she was giving up modelling to become a secretary. To be honest, I felt a bit sorry for her, I think she just wanted a fresh start in life after Sandy's death. For a number of years, I used to receive requests for a reference from her prospective employers, accountancy firms, lawyers and so on. I always wrote her a good one, I liked her. The last request I received was from some shipping company in the City, which was unusual I thought, must be fifteen years ago at least. I remember it because the company's address was in Bishopsgate and I was born nearby in Spitalfields. Never heard anything from her since then, you're not going to tell me something terrible has happened to her are you Peter?" Maggie looked worried, it had suddenly dawned on her that something might be wrong.

"No, not at all Maggie, as a matter of fact I saw her last week and she was in good health by the look of her." Peter replied, reassuringly.

"I read about the Robert Coleville business in the papers last year, it was you and Mathew that were behind the story wasn't it, I remember now. All these questions about Kirsty Blair, you're on to something else, you two will go on forever won't you?" Maggie asked, but it was a rhetorical question.

"You've been a great help Maggie, she might be in a spot of trouble and we are just trying to help her and I promise that everything you've told me today is in the strictest confidence." Peter said.

"Oh, I trust you Peter, I just hope that whatever trouble she's in sorts itself out. Kirsty had a close friend, another model, American girl, they may even have lived together, not sure, too long ago, but ring Barbara Tripp, Babs will know, tell her I gave you her number and she'll be fine." Maggie reached inside her large shoulder bag and after much rummaging around, pulled out an address book and a pen and paper and scribbled down a number and handed it to Peter.

"Lovely to see you again Maggie, you look great." Peter said and he meant it. Maggie had got to her feet and was putting on a bright orange double-breasted wool coat, which she'd hung on the back of her chair.

"Mmm......I would have married Mathew if he'd asked me you know, I'm sure we must have made quite an odd couple back in the day, all those tweeds and blazers he used to wear and me dressed up like a Christmas tree most of the time, but we had a good thing going for a while, that's men for you, mind how you go Peter."

*******************

Maureen Tyler saw him cross the road, open her front gate, walk along the path, climb up the steps to her front door and then ring the door-bell. She thought he looked as though he was in his late fifties or early sixties, he was handsome with long greying hair and was casually, but expensively dressed, in a navy-blue overcoat, probably *Burberry* she thought, maroon polo neck sweater, dark blue jeans and Chelsea boots. He also had hanging from his shoulder what looked like an expensive brown leather bag. Maureen was watching from her bedroom window, but positioned so that he couldn't see her from outside, she had no intention of answering the door and her brother Daniel was out, probably down the pub on Shepherd's Bush Green. She had been furious with Daniel for the past few months, since he had told her that one of the crooks that he had been mixed up with was none other than her old boyfriend.

She was normally at work on a weekday lunchtime, but had taken the day off to attend a dental appointment later that afternoon. She hadn't been up long either, a late night out up West with her old friend Janice, who had news for her about a new man she had met via the dating app that she used. Although Janice had encouraged her to download the app on a number of occasions, Maureen wouldn't be doing that, she'd had enough of men. The bell rang once more and then, after a minute or two, she heard the letter box open and something drop onto the floor in the hallway. She stepped back from the window and watched the man walk back onto Stowe Road and head towards the Goldhawk Road.

Danny Tyler was handwritten on the front of the plain white envelope and when Maureen opened it, there was a short message saying that the sender was a journalist and if Danny wanted to talk about his twelve-year prison sentence and give his side of the story he could call him on the mobile phone number provided. It was signed, Peter Wilson. Maureen was relieved and intrigued as she put the letter back in its envelope and into her handbag. Relieved that Daniel hadn't opened the letter or, worse, answered the door, God only knows how he would have reacted. She was intrigued by the wording, short and deliberately vague. Had the man at the door seen the letter she had sent to Angus Mackenzie? Perhaps that rat Mackenzie had asked the handsome journalist to act on his behalf and hand over the money that Daniel was owed. There was only one way to find out Maureen reasoned, she would contact the mysterious Peter Wilson after her visit to the dentist.

********************

Peter sat in the corner of the Copper Kettle café, a short walk from St Paul's Cathedral, where he had a good view of the door. The text message had arrived on his mobile phone the previous evening, providing the details for their meeting. He was pleasantly surprised that the location was a decent café in the City, over the years he had met many ex-criminals and their choice of venue tended to be down-market pubs, more often than not in some grim suburb of London. Peter had ordered a cappuccino, even though he remembered an Italian friend telling him years ago that cappuccinos should never be consumed after eleven o'clock in the morning, something to do with the digestive system.

As he scanned the café, he noticed that the only other customers in there were a young couple enjoying bacon sandwiches and mugs of tea and an attractive looking middle-aged woman ordering something at the counter. Peter was surprised when she turned and headed towards his table holding a cup and saucer in her left hand.

"Maureen Tyler." She said, holding out her right hand and Peter instinctively got to his feet.

"Peter Wilson," he replied shaking hands, "I was expecting a man, but I can tell by the smile on your face that you already know that, do you want to explain?"

"I will explain in good time, but first of all I think you should tell me why you want to speak with my brother Daniel about his prison sentence." Maureen demanded, getting straight down to business. It was the first time he had heard her brother referred to as Daniel and for some reason it made him focus on the woman, who was now sat opposite him. She spoke with a London accent, was direct

116

and had a steely look in her eyes, which he found strangely attractive. Peter suddenly remembered the advice his first newspaper editor Sidney Newman had given him, that when you're in a tight spot the best policy is to stick to the truth, as far as possible. Sidney had been a bit of a hero to both Peter and Mathew and when faced with difficult problems later on in their careers they would often consider the good advice he had given them when they were young reporters.

"Fair enough, I've seen a copy of a letter sent by your brother to Angus Mackenzie asking him for one hundred thousand pounds and I'm interested to know more about it all." Peter replied calmly.

"Are you working for Angus Mackenzie? Because if you are, we can end this conversation now and save ourselves a lot of time." Maureen said and the way in which she emphasised the name 'Mackenzie', made it clear that this was extremely personal for her. Peter quickly recognised that he was dealing with a very determined woman in Maureen Tyler and instinctively knew that if he was going to get any information out of her about the blackmail attempt, straight talking was probably the best way forward.

"No, I'm a retired journalist and I'm not working for Angus Mackenzie or anyone else for that matter, I'm not going to tell you how I came to see the letter your brother sent, but if it helps, I'm pretty sure Angus Mackenzie doesn't know I've seen it. A good friend of mine has inadvertently become mixed up in this business and I am going to make sure that he comes to no harm." Peter said, deliberately making eye contact with Maureen, who visibly relaxed on hearing that Peter wasn't working for Angus Mackenzie.

"Angus Mackenzie is a crook, a liar and a cheating bastard. He's responsible for my brother spending some of the best years of his life locked up and as well as that, he's done his level best to ruin my life too. Daniel didn't write that letter, I did, my brother knows nothing about it." Maureen said.

"And why should Angus Mackenzie hand over one hundred thousand pounds?" Peter asked, encouraging Maureen whilst she was clearly in full flow.

"Let me tell you a story Peter, you might find it will help you with your enquiries. Twenty-five years ago, Angus Mackenzie started work at what was then his family's shipping firm, Mackenzie, Blount. As the son of one of the part owners he was fast-tracked to the top. I was already working there as a secretary and a few years later we started a relationship, which would last ten years. His fortunes changed dramatically after he'd been at the company for about four years when his father, Cameron Mackenzie, a miserable nasty old man went bust, he lost millions as a *Lloyd's Name* and ended up having to sell his share in Mackenzie, Blount, as well as the family estate in Scotland. Angus suddenly had to work for a living." Maureen paused and drank some tea.

"Must have been quite a shock for him, but he stayed at Mackenzie, Blount?"

"Yes he did, the directors had already invested a lot of time and money into his career and saw no reason to lose him. The company kept the Mackenzie name, the brand was important I suppose and they felt it would be useful to still have someone from the Mackenzie family involved, so I was told. It hurts me to say it, but he was good at his job and was learning quickly by all accounts. His problem was money, if his extravagant lifestyle was to continue he would have to find some way of funding it now that daddy's money had all gone, his MB salary wouldn't have covered it, that's for sure." Maureen said checking her watch.

"How are you for time?" Peter asked, suspecting that she was due back at work soon. He had warmed to Maureen by this time and importantly, he believed that the story that was unfolding was true. He had thought she was an attractive woman when he had first spotted her at the counter and now that they were sat opposite each other he guessed she was probably aged about fifty, slim, with delicate features and he couldn't help noticing she had elegant hands and wore no wedding ring.

"I'm alright for a while thanks." Maureen replied and Peter noticed that she had relaxed now and seemed to feel more comfortable in his company. "I made a big mistake around this time by introducing him to my brother. It was at our cousin's wedding I think, I went along with Angus and surprisingly he got on really well with my brother who was three sheets to the wind, which was usual in those days. Angus liked a drink, he's Scottish for goodness sake and I can remember them at the reception stood together at the makeshift bar in the marquee telling each other jokes and laughing. At the time, I was pleased, it was a nice family occasion and my fella was having a good time with my brother, who I'd been worrying about for years.

Daniel had been in trouble from quite a young age, our mum and dad died when we were both in our early twenties and he turned to petty crime, nothing nasty, no weapons or drugs, but by the time he met Angus he'd started to become involved with a gang of professional criminals. He was out of his depth to be honest, they'd get him to do odd jobs at first and then used him as a driver from time to time. He'd always been good with cars, he did an apprenticeship at a local garage when he left school. Anyway, one day, Daniel let slip to these crooks that he knew a guy who was high up working for a London shipping company, which had offices in South America. Introductions were made and 'business opportunities' discussed, as they say. Well, to cut a long story short, before long Angus was using Mackenzie, Blount's offices to help the gang smuggle cocaine in from Colombia. Cartagena/Felixstowe was one of MB's major shipping routes. Looking back, I can remember Angus spending six months at the company's offices in Cartagena around this time as part of his career progression programme and it must have been during his stay there that he recruited someone to manage the illegal shipments from their end. Daniel would pick up the drugs at Felixstowe in a lorry after they'd been through customs hidden amongst legitimate cargo and then he brought them back to London. Just two or three shipments each year, for five or six years, brought enormous profits for the criminals, including Angus Mackenzie. Daniel saw next to nothing of the profits for his part in the crimes and eventually, he was caught red handed one night driving a lorry on the A12 containing a consignment of cocaine." Maureen looked close to tears.

"I've read the newspaper reports of the trial and I understand he refused to talk to the police, hence the long sentence he received." Peter said.

"He was terrified that they'd kill him or hurt his family if he grassed. I only found all of this out when he was released from prison earlier this year. I've been so angry since he told me, these crooks got away with literally millions of pounds scot-free and Angus Mackenzie played a major part in it all. Well, he's not getting away with it now, not anymore, enough is enough."

The Copper Kettle was beginning to fill up with office workers buying their sandwiches, some of them presumably taking them back to their desks, others finding a table to eat them on the premises.

"Was it Daniel that told you all of this Maureen?" Peter asked.

"Yes, but as I said, only recently since Daniel's been back home. I've spent the past twelve years using my holidays from work to visit him in prison whenever I could, travelling all over the south of England, grim at times, but I'm all he's got." Maureen replied, sadly.

"He's very lucky to have you Maureen, by the sound of things. When did you split up with Angus?" Peter asked,

120

wanting to move the conversation on, he was aware that she probably had to get back to work soon.

"Kirsty Blair joined the company as a secretary, must have been at the end of 2002 I think, not long before Daniel went down. I recognised her face from the fashion magazines about ten years earlier, *Cosmo*, *Elle*, she was always in them for a couple of years and I'd always taken an interest in fashion. Oddly enough, at first, I really liked her. She was totally down to earth and had a kind nature. She was one of those beautiful women who was popular with other women, she never flaunted her good looks and she rarely spoke about her days in the fashion industry. I was really interested in her background and on the few occasions our paths crossed in the office, I would ask her all sorts of questions about the fashion world, but very soon I could tell that it was a part of her life that she didn't really want to talk about, she was very good at changing the subject when fashion was raised. It seemed odd to me that she was now working as a secretary, I never understood that, still don't, I did it because it was the one way I could earn a living and I had little other choice. To cut a long story short, eventually, someone in the office tipped me off that there was something going on between her and Angus."

"That must have been awful for you, what did you do?" Peter asked, genuinely caught up in Maureen's sad story.

"What was really strange, was that it was her chasing after him, you'd have thought it might have been the other way around, but it wasn't. The person who tipped me off about them, told me that she'd been after him from the day she joined the company, it was very odd. I mean, he's a reasonably handsome bloke and I know that it's not always about looks, but she could have had any fella, she was beautiful. Well, as soon as I found out, I didn't give him the pleasure of telling me it was all over between us, I just left Mackenzie, Blount one Friday afternoon after work and never returned. It still puzzles me to this day what she saw

121

in him, anyhow, now that I've discovered what he was up to and the part he played in Daniel's downfall, Kirsty is very welcome to him." Maureen said, regaining some of her spirit.

"Blackmail is a very serious crime Maureen, why not just go to the police and tell them what you've just told me?" Peter asked.

"Because Angus Mackenzie owes Daniel, it's not for me that I'm doing it and reporting it all to the police is not going to help my brother. Mind you, if he doesn't cough up I will go to them just to spite the bastard. So, if you do see him, you can give him that message from me." Maureen said.

"Thank you Maureen, you've been very honest, particularly with someone you've never met before, it's really appreciated." Peter said.

"I *Googled* you before I arranged the meeting, it was quite easy, you're quite well known by the look of all the stuff about you on the internet, so I trusted you. Perhaps we'll meet again sometime." Maureen stood up, smiled and shook hands again with Peter and left the café.

Peter watched her leave and cross the busy road, heading back to her office he supposed. He ordered a mug of tea and a bacon sandwich and thought about the story he'd just heard. He'd met many 'Maureens' in his life, particularly during his early years growing up in Birmingham and later when he worked for the local newspaper in Oxford, loyal, hard-working women who, invariably, had been treated badly by some man along the way.

He also thought Maureen was very attractive, not just for her good looks, but for her attitude towards life. He found the story of her trudging around the various prisons throughout the South of England where her brother was being held, *'because I'm all he's got'* quite moving. He had a feeling that Maureen Tyler was not the sort of woman you would necessarily want to cross and that Angus Mackenzie would need to watch his step.

\*\*\*\*\*\*\*\*\*\*\*\*\*\*\*\*\*\*\*\*

When Peter told Barbara Tripp that it was Maggie Riley who had given him her phone number, she had no qualms about passing on Grace Garcia's number to him. She told Peter that Grace and her husband had not long been back in London following several postings for her husband overseas. Joseph Garcia Jr. had accepted a senior post at the US Embassy and the couple and their two children were now living in Belgravia.

When Peter arrived at the beautiful mews house just off Eaton Square the nanny, a young Latvian woman, was just getting Grace's two young daughters ready before taking them to their nursery school, which was in walking distance. Grace invited Peter inside and led him through the open plan reception area and dining room and into the large kitchen.

"Do you mind if we talk in the kitchen Mr. Wilson, I can make us some coffee, we spend a lot of our time in here." Grace said and Peter noticed she still had a strong American accent.

"Of course, and please, it's Peter." He replied with a smile. Grace Garcia was in her late forties, tall, with blonde hair tied back in a pony tail. She was dressed casually, in a pair of pale green tracksuit bottoms and a navy-blue V-neck jumper. It came as no surprise to Peter that she had been a successful fashion model when she was younger.

"Joe, my husband looked you up on the web when I told him you were coming to see me, he thought he'd heard your name in connection with defence matters, he's a diplomat at our Embassy in London." Grace said.

"Well, I'm retired now, but still keep my hand in from time to time, it's very kind of you to invite me and I'll try not to take up too much of your time." Peter replied.

"So, you said on the phone you wanted to ask me some questions about Kirsty, can I ask you why?" Grace said, preparing the coffee. Peter had anticipated Grace's question and decided that the truth, or something very close to it, was usually the best response in these circumstances.

"Of course, and if you feel at all uncomfortable about anything please say at any time and I'll leave." Peter said.

"Thank you Peter." Grace replied.

"As well as a defence correspondent, I worked as an investigative journalist for many years and whilst visiting Scotland recently I met Kirsty and her husband Angus Mackenzie. Without going into too much detail, it's possible that they may be in some trouble and it may be connected to their past lives. I want to try and help Kirsty and I'm just trying to get a better understanding of her life when she was a model. It may have a bearing on the predicament the Mackenzies now find themselves in and I heard from Maggie Riley, who I used to work with, that you and Kirsty were close friends. Just so it's clear Grace, neither Angus nor Kirsty Mackenzie know that I'm here today." Peter explained.

Grace considered Peter for a moment and then her face lit up with a broad smile.

"Maggie Riley. Wow! that's a name from the past, quite a character, working with her must have been a blast." Grace said and they both laughed. "Sure, I was good friends with Kirsty, we shared a flat in Maida Vale when she arrived from Glasgow, she was just eighteen, I'd arrived from Kansas City not long before her and we both worked for the same model agency, Barbara Tripp's, a lovely lady."

"I believe Kirsty stopped modelling very suddenly following the death of her partner." Peter said, tasting the excellent coffee Grace had made.

"I'll tell you what I remember Peter because I certainly want to help Kirsty if she's in any trouble. First of all, I'll be forthright with you, I'm American after all, as well as looking on the web, Joe made one or two calls to check you out before you came and he told me you have a good reputation as a journalist, so I'm trusting you. Kirsty was a good girl, she didn't sleep around, didn't do drugs, didn't smoke and hardly drank and believe me, that was pretty rare in the world that we inhabited. When she first met Sandy, it was literally love at first sight, he was such a good-looking guy, they made a beautiful couple and they clearly loved one another. They even shared a Scottish heritage. He was a brilliant young photographer you know, outstanding and in great demand." Grace said and Peter made a mental note to look through the old fashion magazines he'd discovered in John's kitchen when he returned to Scotland. Sandy may well be credited with some of the photographs in them, he thought to himself.

"But the trouble was," Grace continued, "there's always a 'but' isn't there, Sandy had a problem that Kirsty just couldn't see or, didn't want to acknowledge. When they met, a lot of people in the fashion world knew he had a cocaine habit, but then so did many others. I tried to warn her, but she was too young and deeply in love and in every other respect, he was a lovely guy. Lots of us did the odd line of Charlie for fun, the trouble with Sandy was that he was a really shy, sensitive kind of guy and he used cocaine to boost his confidence. Ultimately, it gotta hold of him. There was something else too, he seemed to be running away from his past. Kirsty mentioned it to me occasionally, I don't think she ever found out hardly anything about his family, but you know, they were young and carefree and had busy lives and at the time maybe it wasn't that important to her." Grace shook her head, sadly.

"Did you keep in touch with Kirsty after Sandy died?" Peter asked.

"Well, of course, there was the funeral to get through first. Kirsty came and stayed with me and Joe whilst the arrangements were made, it was before we were married and we were living in Victoria at the time. I seem to remember Barbara Tripp and her assistant did a great job organising everything, Kirsty helped out a bit, but she was so upset, in shock probably." Grace explained.

"Do you remember any of Sandy's family attending the funeral?" Peter asked.

"Just one, I seem to remember his father hadn't long died and his mother was too ill to attend, dementia I think. But the man who did attend was a distant relative and the reason I remember him was that he was also a photographer, he specialised in wedding photography. Joe and I were thinking about getting married around this time, so I was interested in talking to him about weddings and photos and all that stuff. He was a nice guy. I have his business card somewhere, I'm a terrible hoarder you know, Joe reckons I need to get help! If I can find it, I'll send you a text message with his details. Mind you, I guess he'll be in his eighties now, that's if he's still with us." Grace said.

"That would be very helpful Grace, thank you." Peter replied.

"Not long after the funeral, Joe got posted abroad and I kept in touch with Kirsty for a while, but I guess around the time of the millennium, or soon afterwards, she no longer replied to my emails, was it emails then or letters? I forget, whatever, we lost touch with one another. When you said you were coming, I looked out a photo of a whole gang of us taken in a bar in Covent Garden to show you, must have been taken in about 1990 I guess." Grace reached inside her handbag and passed the colour photograph to Peter. The bar was crowded and a group of five young people were raising their glasses as the picture was taken. Peter recognised Grace and Kirsty immediately, even after twenty-five years.

"Sandy is on the end there, with his arm around Kirsty's shoulder, such a handsome young guy." Grace was smiling at the memory.

Peter looked closely at the photograph and the first thing that struck him was how much Sandy reminded him of Angus Mackenzie. His features were not as rugged as Angus's, but other than that the similarities were remarkable.

"If you see Kirsty again please give her this and tell her I'd love to hear from her now that I'm back in London. I heard a rumour she's running a luxury hotel in Scotland." Grace said, handing Peter her card and taking back the photograph.

"Yes, it's in a beautiful spot on the banks of Loch Morar in the Highlands. I'll pass on your message to her should the opportunity arise and thank you Grace, you've been a great help." Peter said, still thinking about the photograph she had shown him.

# CHAPTER FIFTEEN

# KIRSTY AND ANGUS 2003 - 2004

It was exactly six months after she had followed the man from Hampstead Cemetery to his office in Bishopsgate, that Kirsty saw the job vacancy. In the meantime, she had provided a recruitment agency which specialised in jobs in the shipping industry with her CV, hoping that a position would become available at Mackenzie, Blount. She had also sent her CV to their Personnel Department, who told her they would keep it on file and should a suitable vacancy arise they would be in touch and as well as this, she regularly searched through the Sunday papers in the hope that she would find a job advertised at MB, but all to no avail.

In the event, it was by complete chance that she found out about a vacancy. She was travelling on the underground after work one evening between Belsize Park and Leicester Square, where she was meeting some friends for dinner, when she noticed that someone had left a copy of the *Evening Standard* on the shelf behind her seat. She picked it up and thumbed through the paper to pass the time, the news in the paper was still dominated by reports of the war in Iraq following the American led coalition's invasion earlier in the year, when she came across an advert in the paper's small job vacancy page.

*A leading International Shipping Company is looking for an experienced secretary to report to the Finance Director. For a job application form, please apply to the Personnel Department at Mackenzie, Blount.*

The advertisement also provided the company's address in Bishopsgate. She was so surprised to see the advert in the paper that she read it several times, missing her stop and eventually getting off the train at Charing Cross.

Kirsty had decided six months earlier that she was going to get to know the man who had been leaving flowers at the cemetery. She had returned there to collect her bicycle after following him to his office and checked the flowers he had left for Sandy, they had the same basic inscription on the card that she had seen on previous occasions, *"To Alex."* It was only when she got home later in the afternoon that she realised that she had completely forgotten all about her doctor's appointment.

Kirsty hadn't been idle during the six months since she had first seen him, she had travelled to Bishopsgate on a number of occasions after work and twice even during her lunch break, in the hope that she might see him near his office. She wasn't quite sure what she would do if she did come face to face with him, but she was determined to keep him in her sights whilst she waited for a job vacancy to arise.

At times, it did occur to her that her behaviour was becoming slightly obsessional, but she would put these thoughts to the back of her mind, after all, she wasn't doing any harm and every other aspect of her life was what would be described as normal.

There was a café on the other side of the road to Mackenzie, Blount's offices in Bishopsgate from where, if she sat on one of the high stools by the window, she could clearly see the entrance. She would look across to their imposing offices hoping to see him leave for the evening or, perhaps pop out for a sandwich if it was lunchtime. She did actually catch a glimpse of him one evening when he came out of the offices onto Bishopsgate with a good-looking woman and immediately hailed a passing cab, in which they disappeared in the heavy traffic heading towards Liverpool Street Station.

By this time, she was fairly confident that he was Sandy's brother. Even though Sandy had never mentioned that he had a sibling, Kirsty could think of no other reason why a man of roughly the same age and with similar looks and mannerisms as Sandy would be leaving flowers in the cemetery next to his ashes. It also occurred to her, that the shipping company where he worked shared Sandy's surname and she wondered whether the man she had followed was one of the owners.

In an attempt to confirm that there was a brother, she had even contacted the nursing home where Sandy's mother was living at the time of his death. She knew that his mother had been suffering from dementia and consequently, she was not surprised to hear that Mary Mackenzie had died. When she asked the Sister of the nursing home, over the phone, for the contact details of any living relatives she was told, rather abruptly, that the nursing home would never divulge such details to a stranger, it was against their policy and probably illegal. This incident upset Kirsty, she had clearly overstepped the mark and realised that she had behaved irrationally. Although, within a few days she had forgotten the incident and continued with her pursuit of this mysterious man.

Sometimes, often late at night when she awoke feeling restless, she had thoughts that she was destined to be with him, purely because he was the closest person to Sandy that she would ever find. Her imagination would sometimes run wild, picturing herself and the mystery man living out some idyllic life with children in a beautiful house in the countryside. At other times, she would lie awake wondering who the woman was that she had seen him leaving Mackenzie, Blount's offices with, his wife, long term lover or, perhaps just a work colleague accompanying him to a business function? She would consider the endless possibilities, before drifting back to sleep.

By now, Kirsty was thirty-three years old and as she prepared herself for the interview she decided that, for the first time in her life, she would use her femininity and if necessary her sexuality to ensure she got offered the job. The wait, to see whether she had been granted an interview had seemed like an eternity, even though she had received a phone call from the personnel department, confirming the date and time, less than a week after she had posted them her application form. She had never even considered employing such tactics when preparing for previous interviews, even though it would not have been difficult, she'd spent several years as a fashion model in front of a camera and had learnt the tricks of the trade. This interview was very different though, she was desperate to get the job and was acutely aware that she may not get another chance to work at Mackenzie, Blount for some time, if she wasn't successful.

She had phoned her aunty Moira the night before, as she usually did when she had an interview the following day. Moira was an excellent listener and Kirsty told her about the job and the preparation she had undertaken, deliberately leaving out her plans to use her sexuality, she knew Moira would have disapproved. Not that her aunty was prudish, far from it, but she would definitely have concerns over a woman using these tactics to get a job.

It was a mild, sunny day when Kirsty arrived at Mackenzie, Blount's offices, wearing a smart lilac linen suit, crisp white shirt and heels. She was collected from reception by a secretary and taken in the lift up to the third floor and then through an open plan office space, where she noticed that she had turned a lot of heads. Finally, she was shown into a large private office where, disappointingly, she was met by two women, the Director of Personnel and a senior accountant.

Following introductions, Kirsty was told that this was a first interview, they had a number of other candidates to see, and if she was successful, a second interview with the Finance Director would be arranged. The interview went smoothly, she had done her homework on Mackenzie, Blount and their successful shipping business. She had even researched the company's history and could tell that the two women were impressed by her knowledge of its origins. The senior accountant, a rather earnest young woman, asked her about her secretarial role at the firm of accountants she worked for in Belsize Park and seemed comfortable with her knowledge of various accountancy terms.

The Personnel Director, an older woman, was more friendly and relaxed and seemed to be more interested in Kirsty's previous life as a fashion model and asked her why she had given it up. She had been waiting for this question, it cropped up in nearly all of her previous interviews since she had stopped modeling and she gave her well-rehearsed answer, explaining that it had been a wonderful time in her life and she wouldn't have missed it for anything but eventually she knew that it was time to move on and join the grown-ups in the real world. She delivered her response with a smile, tongue in cheek you could say, which deflected from the fact that she deliberately hadn't answered the question. However, she received nods of approval from the two interviewers.

Kirsty received a telephone call the next day whilst she was at work, she had provided her office number on the application form, asking her whether she would be able to meet the Finance Director for a second interview the following week.

The wait for the second interview seemed to last forever, when in reality it would take place only five days since Kirsty had attended the first one with the Director of Personnel and the senior accountant. Normally, before an interview she would hardly have given it a second thought, she certainly wouldn't be nervous, but this was different and in her mind the stakes were high. She had convinced herself that to get so close, be granted a second interview, but fail to be offered the job would be a disaster and consequently, Kirsty had spent several sleepless nights before the big day arrived.

*********************

Kirsty noticed that Malcolm Carswell's office was even bigger than the Personnel Director's office, all to do with his status she supposed. She had been collected from reception and shown into his office by his outgoing secretary, Gillian, who complimented Kirsty on her stylish grey trouser suit. As she was waiting for the Finance Director to arrive, apparently he had been delayed in a board meeting that was overrunning, she busied herself reading through some notes she had made earlier about the company. After about five minutes, two men suddenly appeared in the corridor outside the office and to Kirsty's consternation, one of them was the mystery man from Hampstead Cemetery. She wasn't entirely sure why she was surprised and slightly flustered at seeing him, after all, he worked in the building and he was the reason she was sat in the Finance Director's office in the first place. Perhaps it was seeing him so close up that unsettled her, she could see him much clearer now than when she followed him from the cemetery and on the London underground. His resemblance to Sandy was remarkable and for some reason, disconcerting.

The two men were quite animated during their discussion, probably something that had occurred at the board meeting she thought to herself, gradually regaining her composure.

"I'm so sorry to keep you waiting Miss Blair." Malcolm Carswell said, as he joined Kirsty in his office. He was a balding, late middle-aged man with a nice smile and a friendly manner.

"It's fine, thank you for seeing me and please, call me Kirsty." She replied, as Gillian wheeled in a trolley containing tea, coffee and bottled water. After tea and coffee had been poured and Gillian had left, Malcolm took off his jacket, hung it on the back of his chair and opened the folder on his desk in front of him.

"Penny, sorry I mean the Personnel Director, prepared a report for me following your interview last week and it's very complimentary. I tend to rely on her judgement in these matters, but I thought it best for us to meet and give you the chance to ask any questions you may have about the job or, the company." Malcolm said.

Kirsty relaxed and asked one of her pre-prepared questions regarding the company's recently published plans to expand, which she hoped would impress and Malcolm gave her a brief summary of Mackenzie, Blount's ambitions. After about twenty minutes, during which she told the Finance Director a little bit about her current role with the accountancy firm in Belsize Park, he closed the folder in front of him.

"So, Penny will put this in writing, but the position is yours if you still want it Kirsty. No need to answer now, have a think about it until the offer arrives in the post and let us know. Obviously, we hope you will accept." Malcolm said with a smile.

Kirsty could tell he was very busy and merely thanked him and said she would be in touch when she receives the offer letter.

"Penny mentioned your previous job as a fashion model Kirsty, whatever made you change career?" Malcolm asked as Kirsty was preparing to leave. Feeling confident, now that she had been offered the job, she thought she would try

134

something different from her usual, well-rehearsed, reply to the question.

"Oh, it may sound glamorous Mr. Carswell, but it's a very shallow world, believe me." Kirsty replied enigmatically.

"Well, I can't pretend to understand that world, but I'm sure my wife and teenage daughters will be fascinated to hear about it all one day." Malcolm replied cheerfully, before Gillian took Kirsty back down to reception.

********************

Kirsty soon settled in working at Mackenzie, Blount. Gillian spent her final week and Kirsty's first week, handing over her duties. Just like many young women Kirsty had met since she had given up modelling, Gillian was more interested in talking about the fashion world that her successor had once inhabited rather than office duties.

Malcolm Carswell's office was on the third floor of the building and Kirsty had soon established that the mystery man she had followed from the cemetery was Angus Mackenzie, the Chief Operating Officer (COO) and his office was on the floor above, next door to the Chief Executive Officer (CEO). She was already pretty sure that he was a close relative of Sandy's, probably his brother and finding out that they shared the same surname, merely confirmed her suspicions. She was excited  and pleased with the progress she had made, it had taken her more than six months to get to this stage of her plan and everything seemed to be falling into place.

Interestingly, she had also discovered that the good-looking woman she had seen getting into the taxi with Angus a few months ago was Maureen Tyler, the Personal Assistant to the CEO. Gillian told her over a drink after work one evening, during the handover period, that Angus and Maureen had been in a relationship for years and years

135

and she'd heard that he wouldn't commit to marriage or even moving in together. Gillian was quite tipsy by the end of the evening and Kirsty had been careful to ask her about all of the directors, to disguise the fact that it was Angus's life that she was really interested in exploring. She discovered that he had a luxury apartment within walking distance of the office and whilst, as far as Gillian knew, he had never been caught out for cheating on Maureen, there had been plenty of rumours circulating around the office for years regarding his philandering. Kirsty learnt that his family had once part owned the company, hence the name Mackenzie, Blount, but his father had gone bust in the nineteen-nineties leaving huge debts and was forced to sell his share in the business.

It had been an interesting evening finding out all the office gossip Kirsty thought to herself on the way home, because of the distance between the office and her flat in Camden she had taken to travelling to and from work on the London underground. Some good news she found out was that according to Gillian, who was moving to Bristol to live with her partner, Malcolm Carswell was a lovely man and a great boss.

*******************

It was three weeks before Kirsty managed to speak with Angus Mackenzie and it wasn't a particularly auspicious start. She had caught fleeting glimpses of him a few times when he passed through the third floor and also on one occasion in reception when he was leaving the office with the CEO, but nothing more than that. It was late one afternoon when Malcolm came out of his office, handed her a buff folder and asked her to urgently take it upstairs to Angus Mackenzie's secretary Janet. Kirsty took the stairs and when she arrived at Janet's desk she found that she wasn't there. She could see Angus through his office

136

window sat at his desk reading and as she was deciding whether to interrupt him, Maureen Tyler passed by heading back to her desk outside the CEO's office. They had been formally introduced when Kirsty had first started, but had not had the chance to speak at any length since then. She took the opportunity to tell Maureen that she had a folder for Mr. Mackenzie and it was urgent. Maureen was friendly and after asking her how she was settling in at MB, told her that Janet had phoned in sick today and she should just knock-on Angus's door and pop her head inside.

Kirsty had been thinking about an opportunity such as this arising for more than six months, ever since she had seen him in the cemetery, but now that it had arrived she wasn't quite sure what to expect. She knocked, opened the door wide and Angus Mackenzie briefly looked up from his desk. For a few seconds Kirsty froze and just stared at him, he was a handsome man with more rugged features than Sandy, but the expression on his face, one of annoyance at being disturbed, could easily have been her deceased partner, the furrowed brow, raised eyebrows and piercing stare.

"Can I help you?" he asked in quite a loud, commanding voice with no hint of a Scottish accent, Kirsty noticed.

"Oh…yes, yes," she stuttered nervously, "I have a folder for you from Mr. Carswell, it's urgent, but your secretary…….."

"Just put it over there." Angus said brusquely, pointing to a side table in his office and he continued reading making it patently clear that their brief discussion had ended.

Kirsty left his office feeling slightly light-headed. Whilst she hadn't been sure what to expect, it certainly wasn't this, he had barely even acknowledged her. Virtually all of her adult life she had been used to receiving admiring glances from both men and women. She had been told, on more than one occasion by her old friend Grace, that she was one of those women whose beauty attracted men but didn't seem to threaten other women, which Grace said had a lot to do with her personality, she didn't 'flaunt it'. She obviously didn't enjoy men leering at her, but this man had completed ignored her and was rude, it was almost as though she didn't exist and by the time she had returned to her desk she felt angry. 'Who the hell does he think he is?' she asked herself and decided there and then that a change of tactics was in order. Finding a way to attract Angus Mackenzie was going to be more difficult than she had first thought.

*******************

Back home in Camden, Kirsty, who normally slept soundly, had a restless night waking at three o'clock in the morning following a strange dream in which Aunty Moira and Kelvin were having dinner in a restaurant with Angus Mackenzie and Maureen Tyler. Moira was explaining to Angus and Maureen how, after years and years of chasing after Kelvin, she finally got her man and he asked her to marry him. Moira was in the middle of telling them that jealousy was the key when Malcolm Carswell's wife and their two daughters arrived at the restaurant, which had been transformed into a fashion show runway. There was an even more bizarre moment when Maggie Riley suddenly appeared on the runway wearing a Wren officer's uniform form the second world war and it was at this point that Kirsty woke up sweating.

Kirsty often tried to decipher odd, jumbled up dreams when she awoke from them. On this occasion, it was Moira explaining to the other diners that it was Kelvin's jealousy which had led him to propose to her that stuck in her mind and she drifted back off to sleep, contentedly.

*******************

Mackenzie, Blount had a rather quaint tradition that, according to the company's archived records, stretched back to the early twentieth century. On the first day of each month the CEO hosted a lunch for all employees whose birthdays fell in that month. Nowadays, the event was a buffet lunch held in the board room and if the CEO was not able to attend, one of the other senior executives would stand in as the host.

Until the late nineteen-seventies, the lunch had been a formal affair held in the directors' dining room and the Chairman of the Board would host the lunch and then give a speech. The lunch was a much more informal affair nowadays and consequently, was generally looked forward to by the staff. It provided a chance for all employees, regardless of their position in the company, to get to know each other better.

Formal invitations for the lunch were sent out in the internal post a few weeks before each event to remind employees to attend. Kirsty's invitation arrived in mid-May and she was invited to the birthday lunch on the first of June. She had been working at Mackenzie, Blount for several months by now and she had become quite friendly with the company's senior lawyer, Harry Steele. Whenever he had meetings in Malcolm Carswell's office, Harry would always stop at her desk beforehand and share a joke with Kirsty, he could be quite flirtatious but in a humorous way and she found herself enjoying his attention. He was about forty years old, good looking and like Kirsty, single. He had clearly picked up on the office gossip that she had once been a fashion model when she was younger and he would gently tease her about her past and she would join in the fun. Kirsty had come to like Harry, perhaps not in a romantic sense but he made her laugh and feel good about herself. When he discovered that they were both born in June and would be attending the birthday lunch on the first of June, he told her that he was delighted and at last they could share a glass of champagne together, joking that she could think of it as their first date, if she liked.

\*\*\*\*\*\*\*\*\*\*\*\*\*\*\*\*\*\*\*\*

The CEO was abroad on business visiting Mackenzie, Blount's offices in Cartagena, Colombia so Angus Mackenzie had agreed to stand in and host the birthday lunch on the first day of June. There were a dozen invitees, all born in June, assembled in the board room including Kirsty and Harry Steele who were drinking champagne when Angus made a short, humorous, well received welcome speech. Kirsty was unaware that Angus and Harry had never really seen eye-to-eye over a number of business matters, Angus being of the view that he was a typical over cautious lawyer whose sole aim was to slow down or completely halt new business initiatives. He had even once described Harry, during a particularly heated meeting discussing a potentially lucrative contract, as the 'head of the business prevention department'.

A tradition of the birthday lunches was that the host would make a point of speaking individually with everyone present. The current CEO, Godfrey Green, who was nearing retirement age, even went as far as topping up everyone's glass with either champagne or fruit juice whilst circulating around the board room. Kirsty and Harry were already enjoying their second glass of champagne and having a good time when Angus approached them.

"Cheers you two." Angus said cheerfully and the three of them clinked their champagne flutes.

"Cheers Angus, have you met Kirsty Blair, Malcolm's secretary?" Harry asked, but before Angus had the opportunity to answer, Kirsty interjected.

"Yes, we have met, quite soon after I started I had to deliver a folder to Mr. Mackenzie's office and he was so kind, welcoming me to the company, but you probably don't remember." Kirsty said mischievously, giving Angus her best smile and looking him in the eyes.

"Of course, I remember it," Angus replied, looking slightly embarrassed, "how are you enjoying life at MB Kirsty?"

"Oh, I love it, everyone is so friendly." Kirsty said, deliberately touching Harry's arm, ensuring that Angus noticed.

"You must know that Kirsty is a former fashion model Angus, brains and beauty. Now you two must excuse me for a moment, I've just spotted Penny and must catch her before she leaves. I've been trying to get five minutes in her diary for ages." Harry crossed the board room to speak with the Head of Personnel and for once, Kirsty was pleased that someone had mentioned her former life as a model.

"Harry can be so embarrassing at times, but he's so charming." Kirsty sipped her champagne and smiled at Angus and just for a brief moment their eyes met and neither of them said anything.

"Yes, I've heard you were once a model," Angus said, breaking the silence, "I can't say I'm surprised and that's a Glaswegian accent if I'm not mistaken. I'm a Scot myself you know, I'd love to hear about your fascinating story Kirsty, that's if you want to share it with me sometime?" Angus was flirting now and Kirsty thought to herself that he could be quite charming when he wanted to be.

"I would be delighted to share it with you and yes, you're right, I'm a proud Glaswegian, but whatever happened to your Scottish accent Mr. Mackenzie?" Kirsty asked.

"Oh please, call me Angus, we try not to be too formal here at MB. I'm afraid I was sent to boarding school in England at a very young age and never developed the Scottish accent. So, Kirsty, I'll be in touch in the next day or two, how does that sound?" Angus asked.

"I'd like that." Kirsty replied, just as Harry returned with an opened bottle of champagne and Angus excused himself to circulate and meet the other invitees attending the party.

Kirsty enjoyed what was left of the birthday lunch, laughing and joking with Harry Steele. Once or twice, she glanced across the board room to see Angus Mackenzie playing the genial host, talking with the other employees who shared a June birthday. In the short time she had known him, she was sure that he was a man who was used to getting what he wanted and unless she was badly mistaken, she was now firmly in his sights. Perfect, she thought to herself.

********************

It didn't take long for Kirsty to hear from Angus Mackenzie. A letter was waiting for her when she arrived at her desk on the Friday morning following the birthday lunch. In the handwritten letter, Angus had said that he had enjoyed their discussion and would love to find out more about her. Consequently, he asked whether she would be free for lunch on Saturday and suggested a restaurant called *The Bleeding Heart* not far from Farringdon underground station. Oddly, he said that there was no need for her to reply to his invitation, he would be at the restaurant at one o'clock and he hoped that she would be able to join him.

Kirsty was both excited and intrigued by the letter. Why didn't he want her to let him know whether she was able to meet him? Perhaps he was afraid of being turned down or, he was so used to people doing whatever he wanted that he simply assumed that she would turn up or, maybe he always had lunch there on a Saturday. Kirsty chuckled to herself at the thought of him being shown to his usual table at exactly one o'clock each week. She knew that he would be out of the office all day at a meeting because Malcolm would be joining him at a client's office in the afternoon and anyway, he hadn't left his personal phone number in the letter so there was no way that she could contact him even if she wanted to.

Of course, Kirsty knew that she would going for lunch with Angus on Saturday, she had been planning for an opportunity such as this for months and she wasn't going to let his ego, if that was what was behind his strange behaviour, get in the way. As a matter of pride though, she decided that she would arrive late for their lunch date.

As it turned out, she needn't have planned to be late, the Circle Line train got stuck in a tunnel outside King's Cross station and she ended up being twenty minutes late by the time she had found the beautiful restaurant, which was tucked away in Farringdon. Angus looked genuinely pleased to see her and waived away her apologies for being late.

"Well, you look fantastic Kirsty, I get the impression that you don't have to try very hard to look special though." Angus said, warmly. She had dressed casually in a pair of brown leather trousers and a cream-coloured cashmere jumper.

"I'll take that as a compliment and you don't look too bad yourself Angus Mackenzie." Kirsty replied and they both laughed.

It was a wonderful lunch date. Kirsty recognised that Angus was very different to Sandy in a number of ways, he was gregarious, confident, could be extremely funny and was very masculine. From time-to-time, Kirsty couldn't help noticing those tell-tale mannerisms, the furrowed brow when he concentrated on the menu and the wine list, the puzzled look when he was confused by something she had said, that reminded her that he was Sandy's brother. It was perfect, she had found a handsome, intelligent, wealthy man and all the time that she was with him, she would remain close to Sandy.

143

# CHAPTER SIXTEEN

## CARTAGENA, COLOMBIA - 2015

Andres Alvarez stepped outside the television studios just after midday and noticed that the car to take him to the airport was waiting on the opposite side of the road, the driver waived to him from inside the car. A small group of teenage girls were waiting outside the studios and as soon as they recognised the young actor, they asked him politely whether they could take a 'selfie' with him. Andres found that this was happening more often lately as the television serial or, telenovela, as they are known in Colombia was becoming more popular. Andres had just spent four days in the capital, Bogota, filming a number of scenes for the next two episodes of *El Amante*, in which he had been cast as a young heart-throb. Throughout his late teens he had built up a huge *YouTube* following with more than eleven million subscribers.

He was now twenty years old and this was his first major acting role on mainstream television in Colombia, the telenovela was also broadcast in several other Latin American countries. Andres had got into a routine over the past six months whereby he would spend the weekdays in Bogota filming and then fly back to Cartagena, where he lived with his mother, on a Friday afternoon before returning to the capital on the following Monday. Depending upon the traffic, the journey to the airport would take about forty-five minutes and the flight to Cartagena about one hour twenty minutes. His mother had encouraged him to stay in Bogota some weekends, she was worried about him constantly flying, but Andres preferred to return home, where he enjoyed the beautiful coastline, his friend's company and his mother's cooking.

Valeria Alvarez was a good cook and although she still worked part time at the international shipping company she had been with for twenty-five years, she still found time to rustle up a delicious Cazuela de Moriscos, a seafood stew or, perhaps Soncocho, a filling soup with meat and root vegetables.

Andres happily posed for the selfies with the girls outside the studios, this kind of situation was still a novelty for him and if he was honest with himself, he quite enjoyed the attention. Less enjoyable, was some of the attention that he was beginning to attract from certain sections of the media. He had begun to experience photographers suddenly appearing from nowhere when he was out socialising with his friends and taking pictures without asking for permission and on one occasion, even his mother had been photographed when she was out shopping in Cartagena. It certainly wasn't too intrusive at present and he accepted that this kind of attention from the media was all part of the job, but he also acknowledged that it was part of his life that would probably need managing at some point and he may well need to employ someone to provide professional help and advice in the future. He had already spoken with his agent, who looked after a number of young actors and musicians, about his concerns and had a meeting arranged with him for the following week in Bogota to discuss the matter.

Valeria was at home in their beautiful apartment in Manga, Cartagena, preparing a meal for Andres ahead of his return from Bogota. The two of them had lived in Manga, a mainly residential district of the city, for more than ten years. The apartment, on the fashionable Avenue Miramar overlooking the Bay of Cartagena was conveniently situated for Valeria to travel to work at the shipping company's offices. Manga is connected to the

145

more bohemian district of Getsemani and to the historical centre of Cartagena by the Puente Roman bridge. It certainly raised a few eyebrows amongst her work colleagues and friends, when she bought such an expensive apartment.

Both Valeria and Andres were born in the beautiful port of Cartagena De Indies, to give it its full name and felt proud of their city with its delightful colonial architecture and distinct Colombian character. Valeria's great-grandparents had travelled to Cartagena from their home in Spain in the late nineteenth century to work in the shipping industry and her elderly parents still lived nearby in the old San Diego quarter of the city. Valeria grew up there and despite being the Alvarez's only child, had a very happy upbringing. She excelled at school and went on to study English and Economics at the Universidad di Cartagena.

In 1990, she joined the international shipping company, Mackenzie, Blount, working at the port in her home town. Five years later, she gave birth to Andres, following a failed relationship with a work colleague. Valeria returned to the office quite soon after Andres was born and her parents happily took on a lot of the child care, whilst her career progressed.

Only recently, after twenty-five years at the company, had she significantly reduced her hours to enjoy more time with her family and her Argentinian partner, Mateo de Caro. Mateo, who was of Italian extract, owned a popular Italian trattoria in Getsemani and it was at an office party held at the restaurant ten years ago that they had first met. They enjoyed what could best be described as a very easy-going relationship and even though they had tried living together for a short period soon after they met, they both accepted that it didn't work and they were more than content to continue their relationship whilst living separately. Mateo never pretended to be a replacement father to Andres, but he was kind and provided support whenever Valeria needed it, which was what she preferred.

She had spoken to her son when he reached his teens about her relationship with his father and been open about the matter and the mistake she had made, telling him that if he ever wanted to discuss the subject further, he must say. Since then, they had very rarely spoken about it and Andres had shown little interest in wanting to meet his father, who his mother had told him lived abroad. What neither of them knew, whilst Valeria prepared dinner for her son, was that events about to unfold would turn their lives upside down, resulting in Andres showing a lot more interest in his father.

*********************

The weekend passed far too quickly for Valeria, no sooner than Andres had arrived back in Cartagena that he seemed to be flying back to Bogota to film further episodes of *El Amante*. He had spent Saturday and Sunday with his friends at Marbella Beach, a favourite spot with the locals and generally quieter than Bocogrande, where the beaches were often crowded.

On Sunday evening, Valeria and Andres went to the trattoria in Getsemani and had dinner with Mateo. Annoyingly, at one point, the dinner was rudely interrupted by a young photographer who just happened to be in the district and had spotted Andres arriving at the small Italian restaurant. Without asking, he started taking photographs of the young actor having dinner with his family and an argument broke out. Andres lost his temper and if it hadn't been for Mateo intervening and calming the two young men down, it could easily have become violent.

It was a disappointing end to what had been a lovely weekend. He had enjoyed swimming and sunbathing at the beach with his friends and always loved the food that his mother had cooked for him and the Italian dishes served at

Mateo's trattoria. Until recently, he had always looked forward to returning home at weekends and he was determined not to let some selfish photographer spoil the arrangement.

Andres flew back to Bogota on the Monday morning, giving a lot of thought about the forthcoming meeting with his agent. The incident the previous evening had upset him and he knew that it was time to start protecting his privacy. When they did meet, over breakfast on the Wednesday morning at Andres's hotel, he was pleasantly surprised that his agent, Enrique, had also been giving some thought to his young client's rising celebrity. Enrique recommended that the best strategy to counter the media pestering him and trying to unearth details about his private life, was to be proactive and make sure he got the story he wanted to tell in the news.

His agent suggested a number of ways to achieve this goal, one of which was an appearance on *El Dia Hoy Dia*, one of Colombia's daily prime-time television chat shows. It was an extremely popular show and because the questioning from the glamorous presenter, Sofia Valentina, was friendly and generally lighthearted, it was popular with celebrities wishing to enhance their reputations and be shown in a good light.

*******************

Valeria returned home from work earlier than usual, turned on the television in the lounge and poured herself a glass of aguardiente, an aniseed flavoured alcoholic drink, popular throughout Colombia. Andres had rung her from Bogota earlier in the day to tell her that he would be appearing live on *El Dia Hoy Dia* at seven o'clock that evening. Sofia Valentina presented the show, which was broadcast on three consecutive evenings every week. The format of the show was tried and tested. Two guests were invited to each thirty-minute episode and invariably, the guest interviewed first remained on the famous 'red sofa' after the commercial break and was then joined by the second guest.

On this particular evening the first guest, Antonella Lopez, was a well-known columnist who wrote for one of Colombia's leading tabloid newspapers. Lopez had courted notoriety throughout her career and had gained a reputation for uncovering cheating husbands, corrupt politicians, as well as highlighting hypocrisy, often amongst the rich and famous. Her forthright approach had made her popular with ordinary Colombians and she received a warm welcome from the studio audience when she was introduced.

She expertly used up most of her twelve minutes on the show to promote her debut historical novel. Tonight's live audience for the show was noticeably younger than usual, as well as being predominantly female and when, after the commercial break, Andres Alvarez joined Lopez on the 'red sofa', he was given a raucous reception, including one or two wolf whistles.

Back in Cartagena, Valeria turned up the sound on her TV and switched her mobile phone to mute mode, she was excited to see her son on the popular show and didn't want any unnecessary interruptions.

The interview started with Valentina asking the handsome young actor about his early career as a successful '*YouTuber*' and to the delight of the mainly young studio audience, Andres explained how he used to rehearse his one-man comedy routines with his friends on Marbella beach in Cartagena. He even recited one of his more famous routines for the audience, who clapped and cheered him on. Andres had a slightly shy, modest demeanor, which endeared him to the studio audience as well as the viewers watching on TV.

Sofia Valentina jokingly flirted with the young actor as the interview progressed, at one point asking him where he got his rugged good looks and blonde hair from. Lopez joined in the fun, suggesting that he must have a very handsome father. The audience were enjoying themselves by this time, but Andres had suddenly become subdued and even looked slightly tearful. Lopez sensed the tension in the studio and never one to miss an opportunity, seized the moment and asked Andres about his parents, suggesting that they must be so proud of him, mentioning that she had read somewhere that he still lived at home with his mother at the weekends, when he wasn't filming in Bogota.

It was a combination of a lack of experience and poor preparation that prevented Andres from just laughing off the teasing from the two women. Instead, he responded, straight faced, that yes he lived at home with his mother, but had never met his British father. There was an awkward silence and Lopez reached out and squeezed the young actor's hand, seemingly to comfort him. The show was drawing to a close and sensing the young actor's discomfort, Valentina wound it up a minute or two early and asked the audience for a round of applause for her two guests.

As the credits rolled, in Cartagena, Valeria poured herself another drink. She was horrified that the interview had ended with her son looking so uncomfortable and tearful, she reached for her mobile phone to try and call him.

Backstage at the television studios in Bogota, Antonella Lopez was already on her mobile phone to the editor of the tabloid newspaper for which she wrote a weekly column, telling him to hold the front page of the entertainment section, she'd got tomorrow's headline.

# CHAPTER SEVENTEEN

# A GLASGOW WEDDING - 2005

Over the next few weeks, following their lunch in Farringdon, Kirsty and Angus became lovers. They agreed it would be best for both of them if their relationship was conducted away from the office, it would remain a private matter between themselves and they wouldn't discuss it with anyone at work.

Angus never had the chance to end his long relationship with Maureen Tyler, she left Mackenzie, Blount suddenly one Friday afternoon and didn't return. Angus could only presume that she had discovered he was having a relationship with Kirsty and had decided to leave the company. He tried phoning her, but she didn't return his calls. He spoke privately with Penny and ensured that the Personnel Department would provide Maureen with an excellent reference from the company, should one ever be requested.

Kirsty and Angus spent most weekends together either in Camden or at Angus's flat in Bishopsgate. He had totally fallen in love with Kirsty. He was nearing forty and it was the first time in his life that he had been in love. It had totally shocked him and turned his life upside down. Work seemed less important to him and his feelings of guilt concerning his younger brother, which had been simmering for years, slowly began to fade.

It was now nearly ten years since Sandy had died and during this period Kirsty had severed any ties she had once had with friends and colleagues from the fashion world. She missed Grace, but her American friend had left London some time ago. Kirsty was not in love with Angus, she still loved Sandy and was acutely aware that she was reliving her life with him, through her relationship with his older brother. Occasionally, she was shocked by her own behaviour, this was deceit on a grand scale, but the shock and sometimes guilt, was always outweighed by the comfort and safety she felt when she was in Angus's company. He reminded her of Sandy so much, his voice, his smell, his mannerisms and to a certain extent, his looks. She had been anxious the first time she had made love with Angus, she hadn't slept with anyone since Sandy had died, but she needn't have worried, like his brother he was a kind and gentle lover.

Kirsty was pleased when Aunty Moira and Kelvin met Angus and liked him and made no mention of any similarity they may have noticed between her new partner and Sandy, why would they? It was such an unusual situation, who would have ever of thought that she was in a relationship with her deceased partner's brother. She had discretely asked Moira and Kelvin not to mention her relationship with Sandy whenever they spoke with Angus. She told them that it was still too painful for her to tell Angus yet, it could wait she said and she would tell him about it when the time was right. She felt uncomfortable deceiving Moira, but it had to be done, nobody must ever know that her new partner was Sandy's brother.

Kirsty did have her suspicions that perhaps her aunty already knew, she had caught her studying Angus on one occasion when he was deep in conversation with Kelvin. Moira was a wise woman and Kirsty had always thought of her as a good judge of character, so naturally she was pleased that she got on well with Angus, but at the same time, anxious that she might discover the truth about her new partner. At other times, she wondered to herself why she was even worrying about her relationship with Angus, after all, it wasn't illegal for goodness sake. In fact, when

152

she was working for Maggie Riley she discovered through her research that it wasn't that unusual for women who had been widowed during the war to end up marrying their brother-in-law. Coming across situations such as this may have reassured Kirsty from time to time, but it didn't alter the fact that she was hiding the truth from her family, her friends and of course, Angus himself.

On rare occasions, Angus would tell Kirsty about his family, it was always tinged with grief, his unloving father and long-suffering mother and of course his wayward brother Alex. The younger brother who had left the family home at eighteen years old and never returned, except to attend their father's funeral and then tragically die of a drugs overdose was how Angus described Sandy's adult life. It was clear to Kirsty, that his knowledge of Sandy's life after he had left home was virtually non-existent, the two brothers had behaved as if they were total strangers.

That was the most Angus ever revealed to Kirsty about his family, no mention of the huge debts he had inherited from his father or his mother's dementia and definitely nothing about the flowers he would leave at his brother's resting place in Hampstead. Regarding Sandy's death, she did think that it was significant when Angus told her about the six months that he had spent working for Mackenzie, Blount in Cartagena, Colombia between January and June 1994. It coincided with Sandy's death in April of that year and she thought that it may explain why he hadn't attended his brother's funeral, perhaps he was unaware of Sandy's death whilst he was abroad? Perversely, she felt a sense of relief when he skirted over his relationship with his family, particularly his brother and at times she even felt that his deliberate secrecy almost legitimised her own deceitful behaviour.

\*\*\*\*\*\*\*\*\*\*\*\*\*\*\*\*\*\*\*\*

153

By the end of 2004, Angus and Kirsty were very much a couple and extremely happy together. Kirsty was beginning to care more and more for Angus, even though she wasn't what she recognised as being in love with him. He was kind and she could see that he was clearly in love with her. One problem that they had not addressed was disclosing their relationship to their colleagues at work, although they both had a feeling that some of them had already guessed that they were an item. Kirsty decided that a change of job for herself would be healthy and at the end of the year she left Mackenzie, Blount. She started the new year temping and enjoyed working at different locations in the capital, most of which were in cycling distance either from her flat in Camden or, from Angus's home in Bishopsgate.

Two momentous changes in Kirsty's life occurred later that year. Angus told her that after fifteen years, he had decided to leave Mackenzie, Blount. A takeover of the company was in the offing and it was likely that he would become surplus to requirements. Rather than hanging on to see what the new owners had planned, he negotiated a generous leaving package with the Board of Directors. Kirsty wasn't particularly surprised, she had heard rumours about a takeover of the company even when she was still working there and she had also heard gossip that Angus would be forced out. What did surprise her though and would dramatically change her life were Angus's plans for the future.

They were spending a long weekend away in a rented cottage on the banks of Loch Lomond. They had flown to Glasgow earlier in the week and had spent two days staying with Aunty Moira and Kelvin at the Mews in the West End.

"I've got this the wrong way around Kirsty." Angus said. The two of them were sat outside the cottage overlooking the loch on the Saturday evening. It had been unusually warm for early May and they were enjoying the evening sunshine.

"The wrong way around? I don't understand Angus." Kirsty replied, slipping her arm inside his and moving closer to him.

"Perhaps we should have had this discussion before we went to stay with Moira and Kelvin." Angus said and she could tell he was slightly nervous, which was unusual for him.

"What discussion, is there something you're trying to tell me Angus Mackenzie?" Kirsty replied, playfully.

"Ask, not tell, there are two things Kirsty. First of all, I'm thinking of buying a hotel, to be more precise a luxury hotel on the banks of Loch Morar in the Highlands. That's not the important thing though." Angus had a serious look on his face.

"You are thinking of buying a luxury hotel and it's not important?" Kirsty said, slightly sarcastically.

"No, this is the important bit, I want you to run the hotel with me as my wife, will you marry me Kirsty?" Angus had turned to face her, with an anxious look on his face.

Kirsty had not been expecting this, she knew that he was looking for a new challenge since he had left Mackenzie, Blount, so the idea of buying a hotel, though foolhardy, she could just about understand, but marriage? She'd had no idea that he was going to propose and a for a few moments, she was speechless.

"I'm sorry Kirsty," Angus stammered when she didn't reply, "that really wasn't fair, surprising you like that I'm so sorry."

"I hope you're not changing your mind already Angus," Kirsty said smiling, "you've got nothing to be sorry about, I would love to run a hotel with you and I would enjoy it even more being known as Kirsty Mackenzie. I see what you mean now about getting things the wrong way around, we need to go back to Glasgow to tell my aunty and Kelvin the wonderful news!"

********************

Kirsty had never really thought about getting married when she lived with Sandy, they were both so young and incredibly busy with their working lives that she honestly couldn't remember whether they had ever spoken together of marriage, they had certainly never seriously discussed having children. For some reason, which she wasn't quite sure of, she had assumed things would be the same with Angus. Perhaps she had felt that because he was approaching forty he wouldn't be interested in marriage, she wasn't really sure. When he proposed and she had got over the initial shock, it had felt natural and almost instinctive for her to accept. She was confident that he loved her and even if she didn't feel that emotionally attached to him, she was very fond of Angus. Perhaps they would have children, she was now nearly thirty-five years old, so there was still time.

Now and then, she even wondered whether she could tell him about her relationship with his brother and tried to work out, in her own mind, what his reaction would be if she did tell him. However, deep down, she knew that she never would because if she did, she felt it would tarnish the memories she had of Sandy, as well as jeopardise her relationship with Angus and that was the last thing she wanted. Realistically, she knew that it was too late, if she had really wanted to tell him it should have been when they first met at Mackenzie, Blount and that opportunity had long gone. Being together with Angus provided a tangible link with the only man she had ever loved and she knew that the link must never be broken.

Kirsty sometimes wondered whether there was a known medical condition which was behind her unusual behaviour,

156

perhaps it had been triggered by her traumatic early childhood, losing her mother, followed by the loss of her partner. At other times, she thought to herself that she was doing nothing wrong, unusual, but not wrong. Whenever she dwelt on the tragedies that she had experienced in her life it merely confirmed her view that you must enjoy life whilst you can because you never know what awaits you around the corner. She would smile to herself when this crossed her mind, she was beginning to sound just like her Aunty Moira.

*******************

The wedding was a small, but very happy occasion. It was held at a registry office in Glasgow and Kirsty was given away by Kelvin. Angus's best man was an old friend from Cambridge University, with whom he'd studied history. Kirsty had invited a handful of friends from London, as had Angus.

There was no one at the wedding connected with the fashion industry. By this time, in her view, Kirsty had successfully managed to sever all ties she had once had with that world. Angus rarely asked her about her modelling career, it was a totally alien life to his own and not something that he was particularly interested in, although he was always pleased when Kirsty helped him choose new clothes. He recognised that she knew, better than he did, which suit or shirt and tie would look best on him. At the wedding, they had both agreed that they didn't want a church ceremony, Kirsty wore a simple vintage style full length ivory dress, with a high neckline. She looked stunning. Angus's suit, which Kirsty had helped him pick, was a blue three-piece by *Hugo Boss*.

Following the ceremony at the registry office, the wedding party celebrated at the *Ubiquitous Chip*, a beautiful restaurant located on Ashton Lane in Glasgow's

West End. After a long lunch, Moira invited everyone back to the Mews for further drinks, where Angus and Kirsty told the guests about their plans for the Sound of Sleet Country House Hotel. Angus had completed the purchase just days before the wedding. The happy couple also told their guests that the honeymoon would have to wait, they were heading straight to Loch Morar to start their new life together first thing in the morning.

# CHAPTER EIGHTEEN

# THE WEDDING PHOTOGRAPHER

"I'm on the train to Edinburgh Matt, how's John?" Peter asked.

"He was discharged yesterday afternoon from hospital and he's making a good recovery so far thanks. We're in the Lodge and Caroline has kindly agreed to come over and cook dinner for us this evening, she's staying at the hotel at the moment." Mathew replied.

"You are honoured." Peter joked.

"Mmm…she seems to have become quite maternal towards my brother." Mathew added.

"Maternal? That's what they call it these days, is it?" Peter replied.

"Anyway, I thought you were flying up to Inverness today?" Mathew asked, changing the subject.

"Change of plan Matt, I'm on my way to see an octogenarian wedding photographer who might be able to help fill in some of the gaps in this mystery, I'll probably stay in Edinburgh tonight and then hire a car and drive up to Loch Morar in the morning. Perhaps you could book me a room at the hotel for a couple of nights?" Peter asked.

"Will do old boy, I'm sorry there isn't room at the Lodge for you to stay." Mathew replied.

"That's alright thanks Matt, we need to get together when I'm back, I've got quite a lot to report back on, better go now the line's beginning to drop out." Peter said.

"Sure, safe journey Peter."

\*\*\*\*\*\*\*\*\*\*\*\*\*\*\*\*\*\*\*\*

Ramsay Garden is a block of late nineteenth century apartment buildings in the Castlehill district of Edinburgh. Peter had seen photographs of them taken from Princess Street, which he had looked up on the internet and he decided to walk from Waverley Station to Finlay Robertson's two-bedroom maisonette in the historic development. Grace Garcia had been true to her word and had rung Peter when she found Finlay's old business card. Although it had been more than twenty years ago when she had met Finlay at Sandy's funeral and the phone number printed on his business card was no longer in service, Peter had eventually been able to trace the retired wedding photographer.

When he entered the maisonette, he found it was in immaculate condition, not unlike its sprightly owner. Finlay Robertson was over six foot tall, slim and for someone who had recently turned eighty-four and lost his life-long partner only twelve months ago, he was in remarkably good spirits. He was dressed quite flamboyantly, in a pair of Douglas Green tartan trews, he told Peter they were in honour of his deceased partner Arthur, who was a Douglas and a purple twill cotton shirt, with which he sported a bottle green silk cravat. Peter liked Finlay from the moment he opened his front door and welcomed him into his home. It was early December and literally freezing outside, but you wouldn't have known it sitting in Finlay's tastefully furnished lounge, it was very warm.

"So, Peter, you want to talk about Alex Mackenzie, before we do though Arthur and I would normally have enjoyed a wee dram of single malt whisky at this time in the afternoon, will you join me, I have a very reasonable twelve-year-old Glenlivet?" Finlay asked, heading towards the beautiful art deco drinks cabinet.

"That would be marvelous, thank you Finlay." Peter replied.

Once they had settled down with their drinks, Peter reiterated what he had told Finlay over the phone, that he was a retired journalist but was investigating a crime that had been committed more than twenty years ago and wanted to find out a bit more about the Mackenzie family.

"You've been very modest Peter, a highly acclaimed journalist from what I remember, defence correspondent, uncovered Sir Stephen Ambrose's shenanigans when he was Secretary of State for Defence in the nineteen-eighties. Oh yes, Arthur and I always liked to keep abreast of the news and the Ambrose case had a special interest for us, Arthur went to the same boarding school as the rascal just after the war, swore he was gay, but hey-ho, what did we know." Finlay said and Peter noticed he had a soft, cultured, Edinburgh accent.

"Well, I hope your memory is as good on the Mackenzie family as it is on crooked English politicians." Peter prompted the elderly man, with a grin.

"Yes, of course, the Mackenzie family, I can be easily sidetracked you know Peter, put it down to my age. So, my cousin Mary married that scoundrel Cameron Mackenzie the week after the coronation in June 1953. He was an important landowner across Inverness-shire in those days and by marrying into the Mackenzie family, Mary, who'd been a school teacher, was going up in the world. It became clear to me very early on in their marriage that Cameron Mackenzie was a heartless bully and could be very cruel when the mood took him. As far as I know, he never hit Mary, if I'd have found out that he did I would have intervened. He was very adept at putting her down when the opportunity arose. I suppose times were different back then, people tended to just put up with that kind of nonsense I'm afraid. They had two sons, Angus and Alex, Angus was a year or two older than Alex and they were like chalk and

161

cheese, totally different from each other. Angus took after his father, brash, confident, self-centered, whereas Alex was quiet, shy and sensitive and he struggled at school with reading and writing. I would imagine that today, he would be given special help at school because of his learning difficulties, but in the nineteen-seventies when these boys grew up there was rarely any proper diagnosis of these types of issues, never mind about helping the wee bairns. Angus, on the other hand, was very successful at boarding school in England and then at university, he was destined to go into the family shipping business in London." Finlay stood up and poured them both another glass of whisky.

"I felt for young Alex and one day when I visited the family in Inverness, I was pleasantly surprised when he took an interest in my camera. I used to carry one with me most of the time in those days, particularly when I visited the Highlands, the scenery and sometimes the light up there were perfect for photography. By this time, I had become quite well known as a wedding photographer and had built up a profitable business, society weddings and so on. I showed him the basics and left him the camera as a gift. I couldn't believe it really, he was a natural and before long was winning local photography competitions. I was so pleased that he had found something at which he excelled.

Soon he was winning national competitions and it was around this time, when I went to visit the family, that I remember an incident which gave me an insight into the relationship between the two brothers and their father. Alex was showing me his new camera and I noticed that his hand was badly bruised and I asked him what had happened. He told me his father had hit him with a strap. I was furious, they used to use the strap on us at school in Scotland before the war, but this must have been about nineteen-eighty for goodness sake.

I confronted Cameron about it, he was with Angus in the library in their house, it must have been during school holidays because he was back from his boarding school in England. Cameron told me that if I didn't mind my own business he would let the world know that I was gay, although he used a much nastier term than that of course, he threatened me basically and I remember Angus laughing at me. What he didn't know was that I couldn't have cared less what people thought about my sexuality. I moved towards Cameron, I'm over six foot tall as you can see and I had a bit more weight on me in those days and I could tell he was worried, which was exactly what I intended. I noticed that he wouldn't look me in the eye and eventually, I told them both that if either of them ever hurts young Alex again, I would report them to social services and I let them know that I would be watching. Well, that took the wind out of Cameron's sail and he just mumbled incoherently, but I could tell from young Angus's body language that he was frightened." Finlay stood up to stretch his legs and looking at him, Peter could well imagine that he must have looked quite formidable back in those days.

"Did you attend Cameron's funeral Finlay?"

"I did, to support Mary and Alex to be honest. It would be the last time I ever saw Alex. Angus didn't speak to me all day, he'd given me a wide berth ever since the incident in the library, I think he was a bit wary of me." Finlay laughed. "I remember him arguing with Alex after the funeral, it was at the wake I think, Cameron had gone bust a year or two earlier because of the *Lloyd's* insurance crash and Angus wanted Alex to help him clear up the debt. Unbeknown to me at the time, Cameron had written Alex out of his will several years earlier, nasty old man and I remember so clearly Alex telling his brother that he was the golden boy who had inherited everything and he could sort it out himself. Of course, all that Angus had inherited was a massive pile of debt. I was quite surprised, Alex was quite aggressive and it was totally out of character for him to stand up to his brother."

163

"How did Angus take it?" Peter asked.

"He looked shocked, frightened again, just like the day I confronted his father about the injury to young Alex's hand." Finlay replied.

"Is the man in this photograph Angus Mackenzie?" Peter asked, passing Finlay a recent picture of Angus on his mobile phone that he had taken from the hotel website.

"Yes, that's Angus, I haven't seen him since Mary's funeral more than ten years ago, but that's definitely him. I heard he'd bought a hotel, is he in trouble?" Finlay asked, passing the phone back to Peter.

"He might be, it's partly connected to my investigation, I'll keep in touch and tell you what happens if you'd like me to?" Peter offered.

"Yes, I would like to know, thank you Peter. When Alex became a well-known fashion photographer in London, he kept in touch with me you know and on one occasion invited me to a fashion shoot down by the Thames on the South Bank. I went with Arthur, he loved London, particularly Soho, the old devil. It was a lovely day, the models and the crew made a real fuss of us. Unbeknown to me, Alex had told them all that I was his mentor, which was stretching it a bit, but I can't say I didn't enjoy the attention.

He was clearly at the top of his profession by this point in his career and was in complete control of the fashion shoot. You could tell by the respect that the models and the whole of the crew gave him, I was extremely proud. He was a brilliant photographer and was known to everyone as Sandy by then, but he was still wee Alex to me, what a waste." Finlay said sadly and finished his glass of whisky.

# CHAPTER NINETEEN

## HARRY STEELE'S STORY

"Kirsty's gone to London, she's meeting some interior designers about refurbishing some of the bedrooms on the second floor," Morag said, as she poured Lady Hemsworth a cup of black coffee, "we don't often see you in the dining room for breakfast Caroline, particularly at this early hour, it's not even eight o'clock yet."

"John came home from hospital yesterday, Mathew's staying at the Lodge with him and I promised I'd call in this morning to see them. I cooked them supper yesterday evening, John's still quite fragile you know, so it's all hands on deck." Caroline replied, buttering some toast.

"When you see him, send him my love Caroline, we'll be glad to have him back, we miss him."

"I will Morag, is Angus up and about?" Caroline asked.

"Driving Kirsty to the airport in Inverness, he's expected back this afternoon."

"I do hope those two patch up their differences Morag, I've been through a messy divorce myself and I wouldn't recommend it, do you have any idea what's causing the problems in their marriage." Caroline asked.

"I've no idea Caroline, let's just hope the two of them sort it out." Morag replied and quickly returned to the kitchen.

\*\*\*\*\*\*\*\*\*\*\*\*\*\*\*\*\*\*\*\*

Kirsty's appointment with Eleonora Cattaneo Interiors at their studio in Knightsbridge was at two o'clock, which would give her plenty of time to return to the hotel in Kensington after the meeting and get ready for her dinner with Harry Steele. She hadn't seen Harry for at least ten years, since she had left Mackenzie, Blount and she was intrigued at what he would now look like. If she was being honest with herself, she was quite excited at the prospect of seeing him again.

The meeting with Eleonora went well, they had known each other since Angus bought the hotel in Scotland and the interior designer was familiar with the rooms on the second floor which Kirsty wanted to refurbish. She showed her some curtain fabrics, as well as some quilts and duvets and the two of them discussed colour schemes for the bedrooms. They agreed a date in the new year when Eleonora would visit the hotel to take some measurements, prior to her providing a formal quote. After two hours, Kirsty returned on foot to her hotel in South Kensington and ran a bath.

As Kirsty soaked in the warm water she sensed that perhaps the time was fast approaching when the secret she had guarded for more than ten years was about to be discovered. She lay back in the bath and remembered the two previous occasions when Angus had come close to finding out about her previous life with his brother Sandy.

The first occasion was on a warm evening in Soho, not long after her relationship with Angus had begun. He had arranged a night out for them at *Ronnie Scott's* jazz club, a favourite haunt of theirs, with two of his old university friends. The four of them had tickets for the second house show, it was either *Dr. John* or *Marlena Shaw*, she couldn't remember who after all those years. They were enjoying a drink beforehand at the *Dog and Duck*, just a short walk from *Ronnie Scott's* and because it was such a lovely evening most of the customers, including Angus, herself and their two friends, had drifted onto the pavement outside the popular Soho pub.

At first, she didn't recognise Alison and Bev, the two make-up artists she had worked with during her modelling days, it had been years since she had last seen them. When she finally realised it was them, she thought that they appeared to be wearing fancy dress, until it suddenly dawned on her that the two of them were involved in a hen party. They certainly recognised her, that was for sure as they broke away from their friends on the hen party and headed towards her. They were both dressed as red Indian squaws and were extremely drunk. Shouting and laughing they hugged and kissed her until suddenly, Bev stood back slightly, staring at Angus, exclaiming that she had seen a ghost. Laying there in the hotel bath, Kirsty could still remember sensing danger at that moment outside the *Dog and Duck*. In her drunken state, Bev had obviously mistaken Angus for his brother Sandy.

Fortunately, Angus was deep in conversation with his two old university chums and barely seemed to notice the two drunken squaws staring open mouthed at him. Under different circumstances, Kirsty would have been pleased to see Alison and Bev again, she had always enjoyed their company and they had spent some memorable times together partying in London, but now was not the time.

Luckily, after a minute or two, Angus called over to where she was standing with her two old friends and told her it was time to leave for *Ronnie Scott's* and she quickly took the opportunity to say her goodbyes to Alison and Bev.

Angus didn't mention the incident until the following day, when he asked her who the two strange women were that she was talking with outside the pub the previous night, he said that he could sense that they were staring at him. Kirsty remembered telling him that they were just two old colleagues that she had worked with many years ago and that they were so drunk they were staring at all the men.

The second occasion was an even luckier escape, Kirsty remembered as she topped up the bath with more hot water.

167

They had been running the hotel in Scotland for nearly five years and had created a lucrative income stream by hosting wedding receptions. A Scottish bride and her American groom had booked the hotel for their reception. Kirsty remembered meeting them prior to the wedding and thinking that they were clearly a wealthy young couple. More than a hundred guests had been invited to the reception and many had travelled to Scotland from all over the world. All of the hotel bedrooms had been reserved for the immediate family and close friends and other accommodation in the area had all been fully booked for many of the other guests. The wedding ceremony had been held in Mallaig and following this, a sit-down lunch was to be held in the beautiful hotel dining room overlooking Loch Morar. The bride and groom would be spending the night in the Tower on the island before going away on their honeymoon the following day.

As the guests were arriving Kirsty thought she recognised one of them, a middle-aged man who spoke with an American accent. Although she couldn't quite place him she had a feeling that, because of the way he looked at her, they had met before. The wedding reception was a big success and she recalled the best man thanking her and Angus during his speech for their outstanding hospitality.

By early evening the guests who were not staying the night at the hotel began to drift away. Kirsty remembered that she was organising taxis for some of the guests when the American man who she thought she had recognised earlier approached her in the hotel reception area. It was as if their conversation had happened yesterday, she thought to herself whilst enjoying the warm bath.

"It's Kirsty, the model, as soon as the best man mentioned your name it all came flooding back to me, Cy Clark, great to see you again after all these years." The American man said.

At first, she wasn't in the least concerned, people she had met once or twice and sometimes, even strangers introduced themselves to her because they recognised her from her modelling days. She smiled and said she hoped he had enjoyed the wedding, not wishing to get into a long conversation when she was so busy arranging transport for some of the guests. However, it was what he said next that started the alarm bells ringing in her head.

"That was quite a career change for you and Angus moving from the fashion world to hospitality. I asked Angus earlier if he still had time for photography these days. You know Kirsty, I can't remember why but your name came up when I bumped into Grace Garcia in Kansas City a few years back, she was visiting family there and I was attending a conference and she told me you had married. Well, you and Grace definitely knew how to throw a great party all those years ago. Sutherland Avenue, Maida Vale, I can even remember the address!" Cy said, pleased with himself.

It had suddenly all come back to her, Cy was one of Grace's friends from the American Embassy in Grosvenor Square. There was a whole gang of them from the embassy who used to attend the parties she held with Grace at the flat.

She remembered being terrified when she suddenly realised that Cy had wrongly assumed that her photographer partner at the time of the parties was Angus. He must have forgotten that her partner back then was Sandy. An easy mistake to make, Angus still looked quite like Sandy and it was at least twenty years since they held the parties in Maida Vale. My God, she thought to herself at the time, what else has he said to Angus?

Cy eventually left in a taxi, she made sure he was in the next one that she called and the rest of the evening went past in a blur as she tried to decide whether or not to raise the subject with Angus. Being so busy, they had barely had a chance to speak to each other all day.

After a sleepless night, the dilemma was solved over breakfast when Angus told her about this strange American guy at the wedding who claimed to know them both when they were partners in London in the early nineteen-nineties. Kirsty sat up in the bath and smiled when she remembered her quick-thinking response and her sense of relief at Angus's response.

"Sounds as though he muddled me up with one of your ex-girlfriends darling, perhaps someone you never told me about?"

"Mmm....too long ago," she remembered Angus replying, "these days, I can barely recall what happened last week."

As she dried herself and then got ready to meet Harry, her thoughts returned to the secret she had kept for over ten years and whether or not it would remain a secret for much longer.

*******************

Harry Steele hadn't really changed that much, Kirsty thought to herself when he greeted her with a kiss on both cheeks at *San Lorenzo* on Beauchamp Place in Knightsbridge. His dark hair was now turning grey, which only seemed to enhance his good looks. He was wearing a smart dark suit with a white shirt and tie, which made her wonder whether he had come to the restaurant straight from work. Kirsty wore a simple short sleeved black dress and had tied her blonde hair back, she was pleased to see that she could still turn heads even in a smart Knightsbridge restaurant which was rarely short of good-looking people dining.

"A civil rights lawyer. I'd heard through the grapevine that you'd left Mackenzie, Blount, but that's quite a change of direction, isn't it Harry?" Kirsty asked, taking a sip of her *Campari* and soda.

"I'd split up with my partner, she'd left me after nearly five years together and I though, sod it, I need a complete change. I took a significant pay cut, but you know, the work is rewarding and very varied and most importantly, I thoroughly enjoy it. Anyway, enough about me, how is the beautiful Kirsty Mackenzie these days, come to your senses and want to make a go of it with me at long last?" Harry smiled.

Kirsty had never been sure how serious he had been about her when they worked together all those years ago and he used to joke with her about them dating. Perhaps she'd call his bluff one day she thought to herself.

"You haven't changed a bit have you," Kirsty laughed, "I'll tell you what, let's order our food and then I've got a few questions I want to ask you, test how your memory is shaping up these days." Kirsty told him.

"Sure, on one condition though Kirsty, that you let me take you to this lovely little cocktail bar I know after dinner?" Harry asked, calling over the waiter.

"It's a deal, Mr. Steele." Kirsty replied and they both laughed.

They both ordered fish, Kirsty choosing tuna and Harry opting for the Fritto Misto di Mare. Kirsty selected the wine, a bottle of white from the Puglia region of Italy.

When the food arrived, they spent an hour or so reminiscing about their days working at the shipping company before Harry told her to go ahead and ask him the questions she had in mind.

"After all," he said, "I'm curious to know why you really wanted to see me after all this time."

"That's not fair Harry, although you're right, it is what has brought us together this evening. It's something you said to me one day when I first started dating Angus or, perhaps it was when I told you over the phone that we were to be married, I can't remember exactly when it was but I distinctly remember you putting on your serious lawyer's voice telling me to be 'very careful with Angus Mackenzie'. I knew that you two had crossed swords at work a few times and at the time, stupidly probably, I thought it was just jealousy on your part." Kirsty could actually feel herself blushing, something she hadn't done for years.

"Well, I was certainly jealous, no doubt about that, but I was also concerned that you were making a big mistake. I must have been wrong, because you're still together after ten years." Harry replied.

"Yes, we are, but I want to know what your concerns were at the time. Looking back, you sounded as though you really meant it when you told me to be careful, you were very serious which to be honest, wasn't like you at all." Kirsty had leant forward, concentrating, as if she somehow knew that she was about to hear something important.

"And if I tell you what my concerns were, you'll enlighten me on why you're asking?" Harry asked.

"Yes, I will." Kirsty replied, feeling a slight tension in the air. When Harry wanted to be serious and play the lawyer, which in her experience wasn't very often, he could be very impressive and she could see why he was thought so highly of when they worked together at Mackenzie, Blount. She also found him extremely attractive when he was serious.

"There was a report prepared by the internal auditors. They were carried out on an annual basis, you probably remember from your time working for Malcolm in Finance. It must have been around 1998, I'd been working late as usual, reading the report, I sometimes wondered whether Malcolm and I were the only two board members who actually read them. Anyhow, I noticed that the auditors had spotted some shipping irregularities to do with the cargo between Cartagena and Felixstowe, nothing particularly unusual about that, mistakes were often made and rectified later. I mentioned it to Malcolm a few days later and he told me that he'd also spotted it and because it was really an operational matter, he'd asked Angus Mackenzie to look into it and report back to him. Finance 'owned' the auditor's report, so Malcolm was within his rights to ask Angus to investigate. To cut a long story short, we never saw the findings of 'Angus's investigation', he'd taken the action away and it got kicked into the long grass, as they say. I raised the matter with Malcolm a few weeks later and I remember him telling me that Angus was up to his neck with work and probably too busy to investigate any further. I just had a gut feeling that Angus was hiding something." Harry paused and drank some wine.

"And that is why you were concerned?" Kirsty asked, looking slightly disappointed.

"Not entirely, it must have been six or seven years later, you had left Mackenzie, Blount by then and I seem to remember that Angus was negotiating a leaving package with HR. I was in Nice, attending a conference and by chance I bumped into Dave Russell, the former head of internal audit, he'd left MB by then and was working for another company in the City. We got quite pissed one night, I remember we were in the Place de Garibaldi, I hadn't realised until that night that Garibaldi was born in Nice. Anyhow, out of the blue, Dave asked me whether anything ever emerged from his audit report, which had raised the shipping irregularities out of Cartagena. I told him that it had ended up in Angus's in-tray and that was the last we ever heard on the subject. Dave told me that, at the time, the auditors were suspicious that there was an illegal drug smuggling angle, but they didn't have enough evidence to say it categorically in their final report. He'd even gone as far as going to see Angus about it, off the record, but was told by him not to be so ridiculous and to go away and forget all about it." Harry explained.

"This sounds serious." Kirsty said, fearing the worst.

"Yes, but it was what Dave told me next though that made me tell you to be careful Kirsty and it was over the phone, just before you got married. He told me that Angus's long-term girlfriend at MB, Maureen Tyler, has a brother called Danny and Danny Tyler was currently spending twenty-two years in prison for smuggling drugs from South America into the UK." Harry looked across the table at Kirsty, who had turned as white as a sheet.

"Maureen," Kirsty muttered, "of course, her name is Tyler, Maureen Tyler, I'd forgotten her surname."

"Yes, Maureen Tyler, with a brother called Danny, who was banged up for drug smuggling. It just seemed too much of a coincidence that Angus had suppressed the auditor's report and his long-term girlfriend's brother had been smuggling drugs between Cartagena and the UK. That is what my concerns were Kirsty, I thought that you were about to marry a crook." Harry caught the waiter's eye and asked for the bill.

Kirsty thought about the blackmail letter, signed by Danny Tyler, what a fool she was, she hadn't made the connection between the brother and sister.

"So, why have you been asking me about my concerns Kirsty." Harry asked, calmly.

"Because, I think my husband was involved in drug smuggling and is being blackmailed by Danny Tyler." Kirsty said as she reached across the table and held Harry's hand.

# CHAPTER TWENTY

## A CREDIBLE WITNESS

Following Andres's disastrous appearance on El Dia Hoy Dia, the apartment he shared with his mother in Cartagena had been besieged by media reporters and photographers hoping to get an interview or a photograph of either Andres or Valeria. Unbeknown to the media, the two of them had taken refuge at Mateo's apartment above his trattoria in Getsemani. How long it would take them to figure out they were staying in Getsemani was anyone's guess but, for the time being, Andres and Valeria had found sanctuary where at least they could think.

In their view, the interest shown in the popular media since Andres's appearance on television had been totally out of proportion. The gossip columns and showbiz pages in the national newspapers were all asking 'who is Andres's mysterious British father?'. One story, clearly made up, even suggested a link to the British aristocracy. The interest on social media was even worse, with discussions raging about privacy laws. For some strange reason, it certainly felt strange to Andres, the story had captured the attention of a large section of the population, mainly the young and the fire was being stoked by the media.

On the one hand, there was a wave of sympathy for the young actor who it was clear to see felt terribly uncomfortable towards the end of the TV show, but on the other hand, there were those who claimed it was just a publicity stunt, along the lines that he didn't have a book to promote on the show so he deliberately put the story about his father, 'out there' for discussion.

Fortunately, Andres had completed his filming for the final episode of the current series of the telenovela and he had a two months break, before filming started for the next series. Of course, that was providing his character in El Amante was retained. Since the furore concerning his father, there were even rumours circulating on social media that his part may be axed.

Valeria was upset and angry at how stupid Andres's agent had been in booking him for El Dia Hoy Dia, bearing in mind how little experience he had of these kind of chat shows, as well as being woefully unprepared for any awkward moments, such as the one that arose. As well as that, she wondered whether his agent had been aware that the journalist Antonella Lopez was also appearing on the show, a nasty piece of work in Valeria's eyes. Apparently, Andres had been told by the producer, just before the show started, that Lopez was a last-minute replacement for a well-known tennis player who had to pull out because of a family bereavement.

Andres felt much more relaxed about the situation than his mother. To a certain extent, he was used to social media criticism during his days performing on his *YouTube* channel and had learnt to ignore the more unpleasant comments. Obviously, he was annoyed that his family's personal life was now under scrutiny and plastered across the newspapers and social media, there had even been a question raised in the Senate of Colombia concerning privacy laws in the country.

Surprisingly, the whole sordid affair became the catalyst for Andres finally deciding that he was going to find his father, something he had been thinking about, unknown to his mother, for some time. When he told her of his plans over dinner in Mateo's apartment she was very supportive. She told him she had a contact at Mackenzie, Blount's offices in London, who would probably know where his father was living. From conversations she'd had with ex-colleagues, she was pretty sure he was still in the UK and had even heard rumours that he was running a hotel. Even so, Valeria was slightly surprised when Andres told her that he would be flying to London in the next few days, it all seemed so sudden she thought. He told her that he may as well be abroad until all the nonsense surrounding his appearance on the chat show subsides and the media has found another silly story to keep them busy.

*********************

Peter checked out of the hotel in Edinburgh and picked up the hire car to drive to Mallaig. Mathew had booked him a room at the 'The Sound', although there had really been no need, the hotel was very quiet in the run up to Christmas and there were plenty of vacancies. Before checking out of the hotel in Edinburgh, Peter had rung Taraneh, whose old friend Rita was coming to stay with her in Kensington over Christmas. Peter told her that he would speak with Mathew and providing he is back in London in time, the four of them could meet up for dinner on Christmas Eve. Taraneh said she was delighted with the idea and told Peter she thought that Rita and Mathew would probably get along fine, even though on the face of it they were complete opposites.

When Peter had hung up he paused and thought about his relationship with Taraneh. She was a beautiful woman and he found her extremely attractive, they certainly got along together well when they had last met for dinner and their friendship was lighthearted and friendly. Even so, he wasn't sure whether there would be a romantic side to their relationship and at times, he found her hard to read. She had certainly made it clear when they last met that she was unattached, as he had done and it would be interesting to be out together for an evening with another couple, a different dynamic perhaps, Peter thought to himself.

The difficulty for him was that he wasn't really sure whether he was ready for or even wanted a long-term relationship with Taraneh or with anyone else for that matter. On the other hand, it was undeniable that he really enjoyed her company and it was not as if they would be living on top of each other if they did become romantically attached. Taraneh had responsibilities back in Tehran, where she looked after her ageing father and he respected this and knew that the arrangement wouldn't change whilst her father was still alive. In fact, it was one of the reasons he liked her so much, he admired her caring approach to life, which he had experienced first-hand when she had nursed him following the car accident all those years ago. Whatever the outcome, he was looking forward to the four of them meeting up on Christmas Eve.

********************

"Caroline's cooking for John again old boy, so I thought it would be helpful for me to get out of their way for an hour or two." Mathew said.

"Any excuse for a pint." Peter joked.

"She's definitely very fond of my brother, that's for sure, I've never seen this side of her before, it's quite endearing." Mathew said.

Peter had checked into 'The Sound' that afternoon, following the long drive from Edinburgh and Mathew had walked up from the Lodge to join his old friend in the hotel bar. It was extremely quiet, apparently Kirsty was still in London and Morag had told them that Angus had decided to stay in Inverness for a few days after dropping his wife off at the airport.

"Lucky old John, just what he needs at the moment, a bit of tender, loving care." Peter replied.

"So, tell me about Danny Tyler, did you get to meet him?" Mathew asked.

"No, but I met his sister Maureen, a much more interesting character than her brother I reckon, it was her that wrote the blackmail letter." Peter replied.

"Danny's sister wrote the letter?" Mathew sounded surprised.

"Maureen worked at Mackenzie, Blount, the shipping company with Angus Mackenzie and they had a long-term relationship until about twelve years ago when Kirsty Blair, as she was then known, started working there as well. Before long, Angus and Kirsty were in a relationship and Maureen had been unceremoniously dumped, she left the company as soon as she found out about the two of them getting together. During Maureen's relationship with Angus, she innocently introduced him to her brother Danny, who had been involved in petty crime for a number of years. What Maureen didn't know at the time, was that Danny had become involved with some bigger fish, who were serious criminals dealing in drugs and he had introduced them to Angus. With an intimate knowledge of the shipping industry, as well as having access to the company's offices, Angus was well placed to help an international drug smuggling gang, for a decent cut of the ill-gotten gains of course. A very successful operation it was too by the sound of it, lasting years until Danny was caught red-handed on the A12 with a lorry containing class A drugs." Peter paused to drink some beer.

"That's extraordinary, but why did Angus get involved with these crooks?" Mathew asked.

"Money, simple as that, the recent death of his father, Cameron Mackenzie, had left the family saddled with huge debts following the Lloyd's insurance crash, Cameron was a *Lloyd's Name* and this was a way for Angus to clear the family debts and provide another income stream to fund his lavish lifestyle. Maureen knew nothing of this until Danny was released from prison earlier this year and told her the whole sordid truth. You can imagine how she feels about

Angus Mackenzie, In her eyes, he not only ruined her life, but he was partly responsible for her brother spending years in prison." Peter explained.

"Which is why she and not Danny wrote the blackmail letter." Mathew suggested.

"That's right Matt, Danny has no interest in cashing in on his past whatsoever by the sound of things and seems quite happy spending his time in the boozers around Shepherd's Bush." Peter said.

"Presumably, the police didn't make a connection between Danny Tyler and the fact that his sister was in a relationship with a senior executive at a shipping company importing goods from South America." Mathew suggested.

"That's a very good point Matt and I guess the answer is no they didn't, perhaps it's one of the reasons why Danny refused to talk to the police when he was arrested, he didn't want to involve his sister. A very lucky break for Angus Mackenzie if that is what happened. Shall we have another pint Matt, I need to tell you about Angus's younger brother Alex or, Sandy, as Kirsty knew him when they lived together in London." Peter said, collecting their glasses and heading to the bar.

"Can't wait old boy." Mathew said, checking his mobile phone for any emails whilst Peter got the drinks.

"Kirsty Blair met Sandy Mackenzie when she started out as a fashion model in London in the late nineteen-eighties. According to one of her best friends at the time, an American fashion model called Grace Garcia, it was love at first sight. Sandy was a rising star in the world of fashion photography and the couple moved in together. According to Grace, who I met at her house in Belgravia, the couple adored each other. Unfortunately, Sandy had a drugs problem and died of an overdose in 1994. It seems that Sandy kept his past a secret and Kirsty knew very little about his background or his family. I traced a distant relative of Sandy's called Finlay Robertson, a grand old gentleman, hence my detour via Edinburgh yesterday. When they were growing up, the two young brothers, Angus and Sandy or Alex as he was always known by Finlay, couldn't have been more different and by the sound of things, Sandy was bullied by his father and possibly by his brother as well. He had a miserable, unhappy childhood by all accounts and as soon as he reached the age of eighteen he left home for London, where he pursued his career as a fashion photographer. He had already made quite a name for himself in Scotland as an amateur photographer, winning competitions and when he arrived in London he completely cut himself off from his family." Peter explained.

"So how did Kirsty end up marrying Angus, surely she must have known he was Sandy's brother?" Mathew asked, looking puzzled.

"Good question Matt, I agree she must know that they were brothers, but when she actually found out and how, I've no idea. The bigger question is, does Angus know that Kirsty once lived with his brother and they were lovers?" Peter wondered aloud.

"That is a big question Peter and if he doesn't know, but somehow finds out, God only knows what he might do. I wonder what an earth made Kirsty marry Angus if she did know he was Sandy's brother?" Mathew asked.

"It's certainly very unusual and we may never know the answer to that. Maureen Tyler told me something interesting on that subject though, she was adamant that it was Kirsty Blair who was doing the chasing when she came to work at Mackenzie, Blount, not Angus." Peter said.

"Could be sour grapes on Maureen's part, blaming the other woman rather than her man." Mathew suggested.

"Could be, but I don't think so, it's true that Maureen really doesn't like Angus Mackenzie and that's putting it mildly, but she made a very credible witness and I tend to believe her side of the story. There's another thing to consider too, according to Grace Garcia, when Sandy died, Kirsty was distraught and it was immediately following his death that she gave up modelling, even though she was at the top of her profession, it caused a complete change in her life. Bearing in mind that according to Grace, Sandy was the 'love of her life' and he died of a drugs overdose, what will her reaction be if she finds proof that Angus was mixed up in a drug smuggling operation? It doesn't bear thinking about." Peter said, looking concerned.

"Crikey, I hadn't thought of that, you have been busy old boy." Mathew said, smiling.

"I have been and I've kept the best bit until last. I spent a pleasant afternoon with Maggie Riley in the café at the V&A, I'd forgotten how close you two were Matt, could easily have been wedding bells, according to Maggie." Peter teased.

"Oh, don't you start." Mathew spluttered whilst taking a sip of his beer and the two old friends laughed.

*********************

"It's great to see you up and about John." Peter said, pulling up a chair to the large kitchen table in the Lodge. Mathew had made a pot of tea and was busy pouring the three of them a cup. Caroline had driven into Mallaig to do some shopping.

"Thank you Peter, it was so kind of you to come all the way up here with my brother when you heard what had happened. I understand you've been busy down in London and from what Mathew has told me you've have lost none of your talent for investigative journalism." John replied.

"Thanks for that John, but you had already completed a lot of the ground work by unearthing those newspaper reports of Danny Tyler's trial, which put us on the right track. I expect Matt has already asked you, but were you going to meet someone on the evening you had the heart attack?" Peter asked.

"Yes I was Peter, I was going to meet Kirsty Mackenzie. She had told me a week before that she'd discovered the blackmail letter and had given me the photocopy that you've seen. To be honest, she'd been confiding in me for a little while about the difficulties she was going through in her marriage. I think it was beginning to create a bit of gossip amongst the hotel staff, it's difficult to keep anything private in a small community like this, but I can assure you there was nothing going on between us, although I must say, it was very hard at times not to become involved, after all, she's a beautiful woman and I felt sorry for her. You know, I had the impression that she was building herself up to tell me something about her past and from what Mathew told me this morning about her relationship with Angus's brother, I think I was right." John told the two old friends.

"I think your impressions were right John, I had a look through that old copy of *Elle* magazine that Kirsty had left you when I arrived earlier and it's not only Kirsty that appears in it, there's a short article about an up-and-coming young fashion photographer called Sandy Mackenzie. There's even a small pen picture of him and even after all these years, you can see the similarities between him and Angus. I think Kirsty was definitely trying to tell you something John." Peter handed the two brothers the magazine, open at the page containing the article.

"You're right Peter, there's a remarkable likeness to Angus even after all this time." Mathew agreed and John nodded.

"Anyway, I was going to meet Kirsty," John continued, "to tell her what I'd found out about Danny Tyler and his conviction for drug smuggling. I'd been receiving some threatening phone calls for somewhile and had taken to carrying that old truncheon with me whenever I was out alone and it was dark."

"Caroline thought it might have been Scotty Perry trying to scare you." Mathew said.

"Scotty is an idiot at times and he drinks far too much, but he's not violent and threatening phone calls is not his style. No, I don't know who made the calls and there's something else, I seem to remember hearing heavy footsteps behind me when I was making my way down to the jetty. I could barely breathe at the time because of the heart attack, so I wasn't really paying attention and the pain in my chest and back was so bad that I didn't even look behind me to try and see who it was. I may never know who made the calls, as you know, during a long career in the police force putting criminals away in prison you can make a lot of enemies, there'll be a long list of suspects I would imagine. The good news is that since I've been back home there's been no more calls." John said, deliberately not mentioning his suspicions that someone may even have hit him on his way to the loch that evening. He didn't want to worry his brother or Caroline for that matter.

Both Peter and Mathew noticed that John was beginning to look tired, when the discussion was interrupted by Caroline arriving in the kitchen with two large shopping bags.

"Hello Peter, back from your travels I see, what are you three rascals plotting?" Caroline asked as she dumped the bags on the kitchen floor.

"How we could persuade you to invite me to stay for dinner this evening as well." Peter smiled.

"Yes, I thought you might want to stay so I bought an extra portion of salmon, in the meantime John, you need to rest in bed for an hour." Caroline replied.

# CHAPTER TWENTY-ONE

## A VISITOR FROM COLOMBIA

"Oh my God, what happened?" Kirsty groaned as she opened her eyes and saw Harry Steele coming out of the hotel bathroom with a towel wrapped around his waist.

"One *Campari* and soda, half a bottle of white wine and three mojitos, that's what happened!" Harry grinned at Kirsty, who had sat up in bed clutching the sheet to her chest.

"I mean, did anything happen when we got back here last night?" Kirsty asked, anxiously.

"Well, despite you attempting to undress me and get me into bed with you, I managed to get you undressed and into bed where, thankfully, you quickly dropped off to sleep and spent the night snoring like a trooper. I, on the other hand, slept on the sofa over there, top marks for booking a deluxe room Kirsty." Harry replied and came and sat on the bed next to her.

"Thank you Harry, it was so selfish of me, you must think I'm terrible." Kirsty said sadly.

"Not at all, we had a great evening out even if it did end up a bit messy, so you're flying back up to Scotland today then." Harry said, considering the breakfast menu, which he'd picked up from one of the bedside tables.

"No, I need to stay in London for one more day, I'll call Angus and tell him, not sure why, he couldn't care less. Oh, and I need your help with one more thing and then I'll be out of your hair. First of all, can you please look the other way whilst I get to the bathroom?" Kirsty asked, slipping out of bed.

"Why do you think I can help you?" Harry asked, as Kirsty returned from the bathroom wearing a white toweling bath robe, which sported the hotel's gold crest on its breast pocket.

"I need to go and see Maureen Tyler today, it's important, do you know how I can contact her?" Kirsty asked.

"She left Mackenzie, Blount donkey's years ago, it was about the time you took up with Angus. I haven't heard what happened to her, but I know someone from our days working there who might still be in touch with her. I'll tell you what, you order us some breakfast from room service and I'll make some calls, I'll have the full English." Harry replied and winked at Kirsty.

"Alright I'll order you it, though I can't face breakfast I feel awful, I noticed you only had one whiskey sour at the cocktail bar and you let me virtually drown in mojitos, you crafty devil." Kirsty said, shaking her head.

\*\*\*\*\*\*\*\*\*\*\*\*\*\*\*\*\*\*\*\*

"How did you get hold of my phone number?" Maureen asked, as the waiter brought them each a cup of coffee.

Kirsty and Maureen Tyler were sat opposite each other in a smart café within the *Westfield Shopping Centre*. It was conveniently situated within walking distance from Maureen's home in Shepherd's Bush and a short taxi ride from the hotel Kirsty was staying at in South Kensington. She had called Angus to tell him she would be staying a further night in London, before she set off to meet Maureen. He had told her that he was still in Inverness and would be staying another night. Kirsty hadn't asked why, his usual excuse was that he was still sorting out what was left of his family's estate in the area.

"I got it from an ex-colleague of yours at Mackenzie, Blount, I don't know exactly who though, a friend of mine

186

spoke to her." Kirsty explained, feeling slightly unsettled partly because of Maureen's unfriendly attitude towards her and partly because she was suffering from a monumental hangover. She had made little effort with her appearance and was wearing scruffy clothes and no make-up, whereas Maureen, who she hadn't seen for more than ten years, looked very attractive and was immaculately dressed in a navy-blue trouser suit and bottle green polo neck sweater. She looked as though she'd just had her hair done as well, it was a beautiful auburn colour and she had it tied back. For some unknown reason, Kirsty was pleased that she looked so good, it would have been awful meeting her if she had looked a mess she thought to herself.

"Well, you're obviously not going to tell me who gave you my number. So, you'd better tell me why you wanted to see me?" Maureen said, looking at her watch.

"Look Maureen, I know that I'm lucky that you've even agreed to see me because of the way I behaved when I arrived at Mackenzie, Blount all those years ago and started dating Angus. It was a horrible thing to do, so selfish and I'm sorry, but one day maybe even you will understand why I did it. Anyway, I'm sorry and now I need to ask for your help." Kirsty said and took a sip of her cappuccino.

Maureen considered her in silence for a few seconds and for a moment Kirsty felt so uncomfortable she thought she might just get up and leave. Slowly though, a smile began to appear on Maureen's face and once again Kirsty thought what a good-looking woman she was.

"If you could just see yourself Kirsty, no makeup, baggy old jumper, scruffy torn jeans and I think I can even smell alcohol on your breath, but despite all that you still look pretty good and yet, here you are sat talking to me and I'll bet it's because of that bastard Angus Mackenzie. He can marry the most beautiful woman and he'll still screw things up. So, fire away, what do you want to know?" Maureen asked, confidently.

For a moment, Kirsty felt as if she was going to be sick, but quickly took another sip of coffee and the feeling passed. How embarrassing, she suddenly thought to herself, I turn up wondering whether this glamorous woman sat opposite me is going to look a mess and here I am stinking of booze at eleven o'clock in the morning.

"Angus has received a blackmail letter from your brother Danny and I just want to know what it's all about." Kirsty said, close to tears.

"I'll tell you what it's all about Kirsty, but by the time I've finished I have a feeling you'll wish I hadn't. My brother, Daniel, spent the best years of his life in prison because he'd got mixed up with a bunch of hardened, ruthless criminals, drug smugglers. Angus Mackenzie played a big part in their crimes over a number of years, using his knowledge and influence from within the shipping industry to transport class A drugs from Colombia to the UK. For all I know, he probably made enough money to buy a luxury hotel in Scotland and he got away with it, scot-free, excuse the pun. When I first met your husband, he was flat broke after his old man went bust and had to sell his family business, as well as most of his land. Angus needed money and he made it through the illegal drugs trade and all the misery that comes with it." Maureen explained.

Kirsty sat looking horrified, whilst Maureen told her the whole story that her brother had recounted to her following his release from prison.

"Can I ask whether Angus has been in touch with your brother since he sent the letter?" Kirsty asked.

"No, he hasn't, but you can tell him from me, that if he doesn't come up with the money soon, I'll be going to the police. Things are closing in on Angus Mackenzie you know Kirsty, you're the second person who's been to see me about him in the past week, the first was a renowned investigative journalist, time is running out for him, it may already be too late." Maureen said.

"Peter Wilson?" Kirsty asked, surprised at the news.

"That's the fella Kirsty." Maureen replied and she was already getting to her feet and putting on her coat.

Kirsty watched Maureen leave the café and for the first time in ten years she didn't feel sorry for her, in fact, she was quite impressed by a woman who had shown dignity in the face of some real setbacks in her life.

Kirsty's own mood had suddenly shifted from feeling sorry for herself to a feeling of growing anger with her husband. The realisation that she had spent the past ten years married to a man who had been smuggling illegal drugs into the country, the type of drugs that had killed the true love of her life and his own younger brother was devastating. Listening to the story of how Maureen's own brother had been lured into a life of serious crime and how much she had cared for him, trooping around the country visiting him in prison whenever she could had somehow lifted her own spirits. Angus Mackenzie would not get away with this she promised herself. Kirsty paid the bill and made her way back to her hotel in Kensington.

*********************

Maureen had barely got back home and taken her coat off when her mobile phone rang again. For a moment she thought it was another one of those nuisance calls, supposedly from a call centre, but in reality from an office somewhere abroad, telling her that her broadband connection was about to be cutoff unless she paid the caller a lot of money. But strangely, she thought she heard the name Mackenzie mentioned. She started to pay attention and asked the caller to slow down and start again. The caller told her that he was a young Colombian man called Andres, his English wasn't great and he had a very strong accent but he seemed to be asking her whether they could meet. He said he was in London looking for his father and needed her help. Maureen was confused, but emboldened by the manner in which she had handled the meeting with Kirsty Mackenzie she decided on the spur of the moment that yes, perhaps she would help the young man find his father, if she possibly could. She wasn't sure why he had mentioned the name Mackenzie and she had no idea why he had rung her or even where he had found her mobile phone number. For a fleeting moment, she even wondered whether Angus had given him her number and this young man from Colombia was going to pay her the money she had asked for in the blackmail letter. The Colombian connection certainly seemed to make sense and she couldn't help herself feeling quite excited at the prospect of meeting the young man and him handing over a large sum of money.

Eventually, he said it was his first time in England and asked her again whether they could meet. She knew it was a risk she would be taking, meeting a young man that she had never met before but agreed to meet him at three o'clock in Trafalgar Square, at the foot of Nelson's Column. That should be a safe venue she thought to herself as she put the phone down and he should be able to find it easy enough as well.

*******************

Maureen took the Central Line from Shepherd's Bush, changed on to the Bakerloo Line at Oxford Circus and got off the train at Charing Cross station. When she stepped on to the Strand it was exactly three o'clock and still light, the winter solstice was approaching and within another hour it would be dark. Walking into the wind towards Trafalgar Square she realised how cold it was and wrapped her scarf more tightly around her neck.

As Maureen crossed Trafalgar Square she was almost sure she could see Andres standing next to the pedestal of Nelson's Column. He looked young, probably in his early twenties she guessed and she could detect some Latin blood when she got nearer to him and looked more closely at his features, he was also very handsome. She introduced herself and the two of them shook hands. Andres was wearing jeans and a black leather jacket and he looked freezing cold. Maureen suggested that they cross the road and head for the café in the National Gallery, where she knew it would be warm. Once she had bought coffee for them both, they found a seat. For a brief moment Maureen wondered what an earth she was doing meeting this young man of whom she knew nothing about, other than him telling her over the phone that he was looking for his father. However, for some strange reason that she couldn't quite fathom out, she knew that she was doing the right thing and it was important.

"Where did you get my phone number from Andres?" Maureen asked, amused that it was the second time she had asked that same question in the past few hours.

"First, I am sorry, my English not good." Andres apologised and she noticed that he had a very strong accent.

"Who gave you my number?" Maureen pointed at her mobile phone, which was sat on the table next to her coffee.

"Ah, my mother know your friend Linda, I phone Linda when I arrive London." Andres explained.

Maureen couldn't think who Linda was but gave Andres the benefit of the doubt. It now seemed unimportant how he'd got hold of it, he sat very quietly opposite her, seemingly waiting for the next question.

"Andres, tell me why you are in London and why you wanted to see me?" Maureen asked, intrigued by the young man.

"I am looking for my father, his name is Angus Mackenzie." Andres answered. "My mother, Valeria Alvarez, say you know him."

Maureen sat for a few seconds staring at this handsome young man, until she suddenly remembered that Valeria

Alvarez had worked in the Mackenzie, Blount office in Cartagena, she had seen her name on countless pieces of correspondence during the years that she worked for the shipping company and had even spoken with her once or twice on the telephone. Then she remembered Linda, Linda Barrett, of course from Marketing in the Bishopsgate office, they still exchange Christmas cards.

This all went through Maureen's mind in a matter of seconds as she stared at Andres and could see clearly now that the young Colombian was Angus Mackenzie's son. There was no doubt about that and surprisingly she wasn't angry, in fact she was actually interested to hear the young man's story.

"I sorry, I make you upset, you know my father, yes?" Andres asked and Maureen thought he looked sad, she felt as though she wanted to hug him.

"You have never met your father?" Maureen asked.

"No, I am in Cartagena, Colombia."

"How old are you Andres?"

"Twenty-one." He replied and Maureen nodded knowingly, it was about twenty-one years ago that Angus Mackenzie had spent six months on secondment in the Cartagena office in Colombia. It all made sense to her now.

"Yes, I know your father Andres," Maureen smiled, "and I know where he lives, it's a long way from London, he lives in Scotland."

# CHAPTER TWENTY-TWO

## FATHER AND SON

Thankfully, when Kirsty's suspicions that Angus Mackenzie had spent years smuggling drugs into the UK had been confirmed by Maureen Tyler, she was more than five hundred miles away from her home, The Sound of Sleet Country House Hotel. Had she seen her husband within a few hours of her meeting with Maureen, she is convinced that she would have tried to kill him. She was, what is often described in the mystery novels she liked to read, incandescent with rage. She had completely forgotten the humiliation she had felt during her conversation with Maureen. Arrogantly, she had arrived for their meeting half expecting Maureen to look like some dowdy, ageing woman who had let herself go since being rejected more than ten years ago by her partner. Ironically, she was the one who looked a mess and stunk of booze at eleven o'clock in the morning, whereas Maureen looked terrific. However, the intense anger she now felt towards her husband had completely blotted out her embarrassment.

Harry was waiting for her when she returned to the hotel in Kensington. She had burst into tears when she saw him and he held her tightly, he was kind and calmed her down. She wanted him to make love to her there and then, in some silly way to punish Angus, but he refused and told her that if ever she wants him when she has separated from her husband, he would be there for her.

Kirsty checked out of the hotel and took a cab with Harry to his house in Fulham, where the two of them watched television and ate take away pizza, partly in an attempt to cure her hangover. Harry made up the bed in the spare room, where she spent a restless night thinking about her return to Scotland and Angus Mackenzie.

********************

The following morning Kirsty flew back to Inverness, picked up a hire car at the airport and drove back to the hotel. By early afternoon she was in one of the rowing boats, which were moored by the concrete jetty, crossing the loch towards the Tower on the nearby island. The previous day a large Christmas tree had been delivered and taken across the loch under Morag's supervision and then erected outside the folly so that it faced the hotel.

Kirsty would spend what was left of the afternoon decorating the tree as well as the inside of the Tower and its rooftop as she had done every December for the past ten years. It was a tradition, which culminated in her raising the Scottish flag on the rooftop, which in turn, was a signal for Angus to join her on the island. Only this year, unbeknown to her husband, the reception he would receive would not be as convivial as it had been in previous years. Kirsty hadn't seen Angus since she had returned to Scotland from London, he had been away on business in Inverness, but as tradition would have it he would be back as darkness fell and would join her in the Tower, bringing with him flowers and a bottle of champagne.

By mid-afternoon, Kirsty had finished decorating the tree and had connected the lights to the power supply. She had also prepared the 'flaming' torches, using citronella oil as fuel, which sat in cradles on the interior walls of the Tower rooftop. They provided a beautiful warm light. Finally, she had raised the Saltire. As usual, as darkness began to fall, she rang Morag, who was in the hotel dining room. She told Kirsty that the decorated Christmas tree with its lights, as well as the flickering flame from the torches on the rooftop and the fluttering Scottish flag, looked stunning. Kirsty thanked Morag and went down from the rooftop, passing through the room on the second floor containing the cabinets which housed the collection of flags, to the bedroom on the first floor where she waited for Angus. She wanted him to think that everything was normal when he arrived.

********************

It was one of the most beautiful and unusual train journeys that Maureen had ever taken and it wasn't just the wonderful scenery between Glasgow and Mallaig that she enjoyed, it was also the company. The previous day, as pre-arranged, Maureen had met Andres at Heathrow Airport and the two of them had flown to Glasgow. She had booked single rooms for them at a hotel close to Glasgow's Queen Street Station and the two unlikely new friends went out for dinner at a nearby Chinese restaurant ahead of their five-hour train journey to Mallaig, which Maureen had booked for the following day.

Since meeting Andres at Trafalgar Square, something strange had happened to Maureen, she felt an affection towards this young man, it wasn't a sexual attraction he was thirty years younger than her for goodness sake and it wasn't even her maternal instinct, she simply wanted to help him find his father. She had given the subject a lot of thought over the past forty-eight hours and the fact that his father was Angus Mackenzie was immaterial, she was sure that if his father had been another man she would have still wanted to help him. Surprisingly, meeting Andres had somehow helped her own mental state, in so much that for the first time she could remember in years she no longer felt hatred towards Angus, she simply felt indifference when she thought of him. She had come to the conclusion that it was her brother Daniel who had suffered the most because

195

of Angus Mackenzie's behaviour and since her brother's release from prison, he seemed quite content to enjoy his life meeting his friends in the various watering holes situated in Shepherd's Bush. Daniel had told her, on numerous occasions, that he now wanted to forget the whole sorry episode of his time spent in prison.

Perhaps it was losing her own parents in a car accident when she was about Andres's age that resulted in her wanting to help him reunite with his father, she may never know she thought to herself as the train sped through the spectacular Scottish countryside on its journey to Mallaig.

Maureen asked Andres about his life in Colombia and was fascinated when he described how he had become a well-known figure on *YouTube* and then a popular actor in one of the country's most watched telenovelas. Knowing that they were embarking on a very long train journey, Maureen had bought them sandwiches and cakes, as well as beer for Andres and a small bottle of wine for herself at the railway station in Glasgow. Whilst they ate and drank, Andres explained why he had suddenly decided to find his father and both of them found the funny side of it when he told her about his disastrous appearance on the chat show, which had led to the 'mysterious' British father that he had never met becoming a national news story.

Maureen didn't tell him about her long relationship with his father, she knew that Andres had been in touch by phone with his mother since they had set out for Scotland and suspected she would have told him. It was common knowledge at Mackenzie, Blount, back in the day, that she was Angus's girlfriend and she would have been surprised if, at some point, the news hadn't spread to the office in Cartagena. She had decided that she would tell Andres the truth if he asked, but in all honesty she didn't really see the point of dredging up the past and anyway, it was not the driving force behind her helping him find his father. During the long journey she did tell him about her life growing up in London, the death of her parents and even her brother's imprisonment, although she didn't go into any details about the crimes he had committed. Andres's English was not that good and his delivery was very slow, but he was adept in expressing his feelings even in a foreign language and the sympathy he showed her on hearing of these tragic events touched Maureen.

The train journey was magical, from the views across Loch Lomond, the beautiful wilderness of Rannoch Moor, the viaducts on the journey towards Fort William to the stunning approach to Mallaig itself. Both Maureen and Andres were pleased they had chosen the scenic route, rather than flying direct from London to Inverness, even though the train was delayed and it was dusk as it pulled into Mallaig station. They managed to find a taxi outside the station and asked the driver to take them to the Sound of Sleet Country House Hotel, where Maureen had booked them both rooms.

******************

"It's a tradition." Morag told them.

Peter, Mathew, Caroline and John had one of the window tables in the dining room at The Sound and were enjoying a late lunch. It was the first time John had ventured out from the Lodge since he had been discharged from hospital and the staff at the hotel had been making a fuss of him.

"Yes, I remember it from previous years." Caroline said, as Morag served the four of them their pre-lunch drinks, "Each year, when the Christmas tree is in place, Kirsty rows across to the island, decorates it and lights the torches on the rooftop."

"Don't forget the flag Caroline, Kirsty raises the Saltire, which is a signal for Angus to join her in the Tower." Morag added, with a wink.

"And we've got grandstand seats, what a wonderful tradition." Mathew said.

They could see from the dining room that Kirsty had already climbed up a very tall step ladder and was draping lights over the large Christmas tree.

"Have you seen Angus yet Morag?" Caroline asked, adding some tonic water to her large glass of gin.

"He's on his way back from Inverness, but no worry, he'll be here this afternoon to row across and join Kirsty as darkness falls." Morag replied and returned to the kitchen.

"How does it feel to be out and about again John?" Peter asked.

"Marvelous, thank you Peter and I just want to take this opportunity to thank all of you for the kindness you have shown me since I was taken ill and as well as that, I have an important announcement to make." John said, looking slightly nervous.

"We're all ears John." Mathew said, smiling.

"Well, I know it's about time you and Peter returned to your homes in London, but I understand Mathew that you are loathe to be leaving me on my own in the Lodge." John said.

"You know that I'll stay here as long as you need me to." Mathew interrupted.

"Yes, I know you would and I'm really grateful for all that you've done for me, but soon there will be no need because Caroline has agreed to move into the Lodge with me." John announced, wondering what his brother's reaction would be. As it turned out, he needn't have worried.

"That's terrific news John and I'm really pleased for the two of you." Mathew said.

"Deserves a toast I would say," Peter added, "to Caroline and John!"

"I'm relieved that you two approve," Caroline said after they had raised their glasses, "you both knew me quite well all those years ago at the newspaper and I was a bit worried that my reputation may have counted against me."

"We always knew that you were an old softy under all that bravado Caroline." Peter joked and as he did Morag re-entered the dining room talking to Kirsty on her mobile phone as the finishing touches were being made to the Christmas tree in front of the Tower. When the call had ended she fetched the four diners their meals from the kitchen.

"Keep an eye on the loch in the next hour or so, Angus is back from Inverness and he'll be rowing across the loch to join Kirsty as soon as the light starts to fade. He'll turn the floodlight on over the loch, so you'll get a good view of him." Morag told them.

*******************

Kirsty sat on the chaise longue in the bedroom on the first floor waiting for Angus to arrive. A ritual she had gone through since they'd had the Tower renovated, shortly after moving into the hotel. She had thought through what she was about to tell him and had reconciled with herself that it was the only realistic course of action open to her. She was not prepared to live with someone who, according to Maureen Tyler and Harry Steele, had been heavily involved in the drug smuggling business. As far as she was concerned, their marriage was over.

She didn't have to wait long, within just a few minutes of her sitting down she heard the sound of the front door opening, she had left it on the latch because she knew Angus had a habit of forgetting his key.

"Champagne and flowers!" he announced as he came into the bedroom and left them on the dressing table, before flopping down on the bed. Kirsty sat quietly, biding her time until Angus was settled on the bed.

199

"Well, what do you say or, has the cat got your tongue?" he asked.

"I'm going to divorce you Angus, that's what I've got to say," and by the quiet but confident way in which Kirsty said it, he was left in no doubt that she was deadly serious.

"What an earth are you talking about?" Angus asked, turning onto his side and propping himself up on his elbow so he could see his wife clearly on the chaise longue.

"I'm not going to spend the rest of my life with someone who spent years of his life smuggling class A drugs into the country, you need to pack your things and leave Angus, today." Kirsty told him, still in a confident, measured tone.

"Have you gone mad?" Angus asked, raising his voice.

"Angus, I have proof, I've met Maureen Tyler and she has told me the whole sordid tale." She replied.

"She's just a jealous old woman." Angus had now sat up on the side of the bed facing Kirsty.

"Don't try and deny it Angus, it would be embarrassing and anyway it's not the only proof I have, the auditor's report you tried to hide would make interesting reading for the police I dare say and there's also the blackmail letter from Maureen's brother." Kirsty was standing now, she'd said all she had intended to say and was about to leave when Angus jumped up and violently grabbed her by the arm.

"Let go, you're hurting me!" Kirsty shouted, becoming angry herself.

"What do you know about my life?" Angus replied, by now he had pushed Kirsty against the dressing table still holding her arm and was shouting in her face. "Some young girl from the backstreets of Glasgow, what the hell do you know?"

Kirsty pulled herself out of his grip, she had never been so angry in her life and no longer cared what he thought.

"I'll tell you what I know Angus Mackenzie, I know that your brother, yes your brother Sandy, was a real man who wasn't scared to stand up to bullies like you and your father, when he was big enough to stand up to you both that is." Kirsty suddenly wanted to hurt Angus, who was staring at her open mouthed.

"Who on earth are you talking about, my brother, Alex?" Angus looked confused and frightened, but suddenly remembered the inscription on the plaque in the cemetery commemorating Sandy Mackenzie, the name some of Alex's friends had called his younger brother when they were growing up in the Highlands.

"He was Sandy when I lived happily with him before I met you and I wish he was still here with me." Kirsty had lost control by now and was in tears.

"You're lying, you're making it up!" Angus shouted, anger returning to his face, but deep down he knew it was the truth.

"Oh no I'm not, I saw you leaving flowers in the cemetery, feeling guilty were you? Well, so you should be, because it was exactly the kind of drugs that you were importing from South America that killed your brother, you wicked bastard!" Kirsty shouted.

"You never told me," Angus said quietly, almost as if he were speaking to himself, "all this time and you never told me you evil bitch."

He tried to grab Kirsty's arm again, but she stepped to one side and he momentarily lost balance and stumbled into the dressing table, knocking it over. She saw her chance to escape from him, but he was blocking the door to the staircase leading down to the ground floor kitchen, the only way was up, through the flag room to the rooftop, where she thought at least she could shout for help. She had a few seconds start and tore upstairs screaming, but by the time she had pushed open the door of the flag room and stumbled onto the rooftop he was right behind her and she suddenly went sprawling face down on the concrete floor, shouting for help.

201

She managed to roll over on to her back before Angus fell on top of her, trying to cover her mouth with his right hand. The rooftop was lit by the flickering flames of the torches that she had prepared earlier and she suddenly felt very scared. His whole bodyweight was on top of her and apart from her right arm, she could hardly move. For a split second, she was sure he was going to strangle her, he had one hand covering her mouth and the other gripping her neck. Her right hand stretched out and touched something and she realised it was the plastic container which was still half full of the citronella oil that she had used earlier that afternoon as fuel for the wall torches.

Kirsty knew she had to act quickly, the pressure on her neck and mouth was becoming unbearable, she could barely breathe. With her right hand she managed to reach out and unscrew the plastic top of the container and then grip it by the handle on its side. Angus was intent on stopping her from struggling and calling out for help and at first he didn't even notice when Kirsty lifted the plastic container and started to pour the oil over his back, starting just above his waistline and moving up to his shoulder blades. When the container was empty, she flung it across the rooftop, it made a loud clattering noise and it was at this point that Angus realised that something was wrong, his back felt wet and there was a smell of oil. He released his grip on Kirsty's mouth and neck and put one hand behind his back, touching his fuel-soaked shirt. Just for a second, Kirsty recognised the puzzled expression on his face that she had first seen in the cemetery when he'd become aware that it had started to rain and he was wet, the same expression she had seen on Sandy's face so many times before.

She took her chance whilst he was momentarily distracted and using all her strength she managed to turn Angus onto his side, it was to do with weight distribution, she remembered learning about it when taking a first aid course and putting a heavy patient into the recovery position. With her adrenalin pumping, Kirsty quickly got to her feet and removed one of the flaming torches from its cradle on the wall behind her. Angus stood up and unsteadily moved towards her again, shouting and threatening to throw her off the rooftop.

"You take one more step towards me and you'll go up like a bonfire!" Kirsty told him, gripping the flaming torch in front of her with both hands.

\*\*\*\*\*\*\*\*\*\*\*\*\*\*\*\*\*\*\*\*

Following their lunch, Peter, Mathew, Caroline and John ambled out of the dining room into the spacious reception area of the hotel. John was beginning to feel tired and Caroline had suggested that it was best if they all returned to the Lodge for coffee. Just before they left, Peter's attention was drawn to the couple browsing the tourist brochures, some of them offering trips from Mallaig to Skye and the other islands, in the stand next to the reception desk. As he moved closer he was surprised to see it was Maureen Tyler and a young man.

"Hello Maureen, we meet again." Peter said cheerfully and she seemed genuinely pleased to see him.

"It's nice to see you Peter are you staying here?" Maureen asked, curiously.

"Yes, my friend's brother has been unwell and I've been spending some time up here to lend support." Peter nodded in the direction of Mathew, Caroline and John, who had sat down on the large sofa near the entrance to the hotel. As he did, the young man who had been looking at the brochures with Maureen joined them.

"This is Andres Alvarez, he has travelled up from London with me." Maureen said and the two men shook hands. "Peter is a journalist Andres, but don't worry he's not the type of reporter who writes nasty stories about

203

celebrities. Andres is a well-known actor in Colombia Peter."

"So, what brings the two of you all the way up here Maureen?" Peter asked, struggling to understand their relationship.

"Andres is a friend and he needed help, he's come all the way from Colombia to find his father, who he's never met before." Maureen said coolly and Peter immediately grasped what she was about to tell him. "His father is Angus Mackenzie, have you seen him today Peter?"

Before Peter had the chance to answer the question the guests in the reception area were distracted by a commotion near the entrance to the hotel, when suddenly Morag dashed inside. Clearly, something was wrong.

"Someone call the police, Kirsty is screaming for help from the Tower, she's in danger!" Morag shouted.

Peter strode outside to get a better view of the Tower, quickly followed by Mathew, Maureen and Andres. They could clearly see the flames from the torches flickering on the Tower's rooftop, but there was no sign of Kirsty or Angus.

"Is there a rowing boat down at the jetty?" Peter asked Morag.

"Yes, there's one there, but be careful Peter." Morag replied, whilst Caroline phoned for the police.

Peter and Mathew quickly made their way through the gardens down towards the loch, followed by Andres.

"You should stay at the hotel with Maureen." Peter told him, as the three of them reached the concrete jetty where they were relieved to see a rowing boat tied up.

"No, I want to help." Andres told the two old friends.

The three of them lowered themselves into the boat, which Peter had untied and Mathew started to row them across Loch Morar towards the island on which the Tower stood. Fortunately, Angus had turned on the floodlight before he had set out across the loch which helped guide them and this, together with Mathew's experience of rowing from his days at Oxford and later for a rowing club in south-west London, meant they were tying up the boat on the small island in no time at all.

Fortunately, the front door had been left on the latch and Peter led the way into the kitchen diner and upstairs to the bedroom on the first floor, where they could see signs of an earlier struggle, the dressing table had been knocked over and bedding was strewn across the floor. As the three of them continued upwards towards the rooftop, they began to hear voices. Peter noticed the flags in their glass fronted cabinets as he passed through the flag room on the second floor, before opening the door on to the roof.

Angus was stood with his back to Peter and the first thing he noticed was the smell of some kind of fuel, it had a citrus, fruity aroma and then he saw that the back of Angus's shirt was wet. Kirsty was stood on the other side of the rooftop with her back to the wall facing Angus desperately gripping a flaming torch in front of her. She had clearly been in a terrible struggle, her shirt was ripped and her face cut and already badly bruised.

Whilst he took in this dreadful scene, Peter edged forward to allow Mathew and Andres to join him on the rooftop. Angus turned around to face the three of them and he looked terrifying. Peter calmly walked past him across to Kirsty, took the torch from her hands and replaced it in its cradle on the wall. As Kirsty fell sobbing into Peter's arms Angus lunged at Mathew, who deftly swung him around and pinned him to the wall next to the door. He was still struggling and cursing them until Andres put his hand on his shoulder.

"Father, stop, no more." The young man said firmly and it stopped Angus Mackenzie in his tracks. For the first time since Andres had appeared on the rooftop, Angus looked closely at the young man with that characteristically puzzled look on his face. Kirsty, who was being consoled

205

by Peter, had heard Andres speak to her husband and stood staring at the two of them, open mouthed in astonishment. By now, Mathew had released his grip on Angus and had stepped aside as the father and son faced each other. Tears started to stream down Angus's face and instinctively, the two of them hugged each other.

********************

Peter could hear the sound of a police car's siren as he told Mathew he was going to take Kirsty back across the loch to the hotel. He found a blanket for her as they passed through the bedroom and he wrapped it around her shoulders. In the kitchen, he poured her a glass of whiskey to help warm her up, she looked cold and thoroughly dishevelled after her ordeal and the sooner she was back in the hotel the better. Once outside the Tower, Peter helped her down into one of the rowing boats and then untied it from the small jetty before carefully getting into the boat himself.

"Are you ready Kirsty, it'll only take a few minutes for me to row us back across the loch and you'll be safe and warm in the hotel." Peter was deliberately making conversation, Kirsty looked very pale and was shivering despite the warm blanket wrapped around her and Peter wanted to make sure she didn't pass out during the short journey.

"I told him, after ten years, I finally told him." Kirsty whispered. They had set out across the loch and it was deadly quiet, apart from the sound of the oars on the water as Peter rowed.

"What did you tell him Kirsty?" Peter asked.

"I told him about Sandy and he said he was going to kill me." She replied, sobbing.

"It's over now, you're safe." Peter said reassuringly.

Two policemen were waiting for them when they arrived at the jetty and helped them out of the rowing boat. Peter gave them an outline of the situation in the Tower and warned them that the shirt Angus was wearing appeared to have been doused in some kind of fuel. After a few minutes, the two policemen set off across the loch in the boat that Peter and Kirsty had vacated.

Kirsty was comforted by Morag and Caroline who were also waiting by the jetty and they helped her back inside the hotel. She looked even more shocked when she saw Maureen Tyler in reception heading towards Peter. For a moment, Kirsty felt as if she was having one of those strange dreams when people you know from your past appear in the most unexpected places.

Maureen was concerned for Andres and wanted to know from Peter whether he was safe. Peter reassured her that Mathew was still in the Tower waiting for the police to arrive and he wouldn't let the young man come to any harm. A doctor soon arrived in reception and Caroline showed her up to Kirsty's apartment at the back of the hotel where Morag was looking after her.

After about an hour, the two policemen returned in one of the rowing boats with Angus and they were followed across the loch by Mathew and Andres in one of the other boats. Mathew had found a change of shirt and a blanket for Angus and his fuel-soaked shirt had been placed in a plastic carrier bag and handed to the police. On arrival at the hotel, Angus was immediately driven by the policemen to Mallaig. Before they left, one of them told Mathew that they would be back later in the evening to take statements from those involved in the 'afternoon's events'.

Maureen was relieved to see Andres return and gave him a hug on the steps of the hotel, for some reason she felt responsible for the young man whilst he was in her company. Together with Peter and Mathew, Caroline and John, who had remained sitting in the hotel reception whilst events unfolded, the six of them retired to the hotel bar, where they ordered drinks, whiskey for the men, brandy for Maureen and a large gin and tonic for Caroline. Introductions were made, apart from Andres, Maureen had only met Peter before, but all of them had one thing in common, they had experienced an afternoon that they would never forget. When the drinks arrived, it was a surprisingly calm Andres who was the first to speak.

"Salud! Is it always like this in Scotland?" the young actor asked, raising his glass as well as a few smiles.

# CHAPTER TWENTY-THREE

## PETER AND MAUREEN

A Police Officer returned to the hotel later in the evening but Kirsty was too unwell to provide a statement. She promised that she would do so tomorrow and the officer agreed to return in the morning.

After the police officer had seen Kirsty, Peter sat in the dining room with him and gave him a full statement covering what he had witnessed at the Tower, as well as all he knew about Angus Mackenzie's involvement with drug smuggling, which mainly consisted of what Maureen had told him during their conversation in the café near St. Paul's Cathedral.

Maureen refused to give a statement, but left her address with the officer should the police wish to contact her or her brother at some point in the future. Before the officer spoke with Maureen, Peter had suggested to her that she might want to get some advice from a solicitor. After all, there was the matter of a blackmail letter that may well need to be explained.

Maureen and Andres had decided that the two of them would travel back to Glasgow by train in the morning and then onwards by air to London. Andres had spoken with his mother by phone and told her that he would be travelling back to Colombia in a few days' time. He told her nothing of the events in Scotland over the phone, she would only have been worried for his safety.

Angus Mackenzie was held in custody in Mallaig, pending further investigations. The police knew that the situation would become much clearer once they had spoken with Kirsty. The doctor had told her that although she had some nasty bruising on her face, neck and arms, as well as a chipped tooth, it appeared that no bones had been broken. She said she would arrange for some X-rays to be taken in hospital, just to be on the safe side.

Mathew, Caroline and John made their way back to the Lodge later in the evening after Mathew had provided a statement to the police officer. Mathew had told his brother and Caroline that he would be travelling back to London with Peter in a couple of days' time.

*********************

"I suppose I should thank you Peter, since we first met my life has been turned upside down and completely changed, for the better I'm pleased to say." Maureen said.

The two of them were sat next to the log fire in the cosy hotel bar, Peter enjoying his second glass of whiskey and Maureen her second brandy, this time with coke. They were the last couple left in the bar and Douglas, the young barman who also worked as the night porter, had told them he'd be on the reception desk if they wanted another drink. Peter put another log on the fire. After such a traumatic day, everyone else had gone to bed.

"Thank me?" Peter replied, sounding surprised.

"Not just you, Andres as well, in fact even Kirsty helped. I'd been so unhappy and bitter for years and years, angry because I'd been dumped by Angus and more recently, furious when Daniel told me that he'd taken all the blame for the drug trafficking he'd got mixed up with. But I've learnt over the past few weeks that splitting up with Angus was a blessing in disguise, a narrow escape if today was anything to go by and Daniel is quite happy with his life, boozing with his mates in Shepherd's Bush. He doesn't need me brooding over his past misfortune." Maureen paused and took a sip of brandy and coke.

"And Andres, how has he helped you?" Peter asked. "It looks as though it's the other way around to me, you've helped him."

"Andres had kind of lost his dad, never even met him until today, me and Daniel lost our mum and dad when we were quite young and I just wanted to help him. He taught me a lot about not dwelling on the past and so on when we talked on the train journey. For such a young man, he is very wise. To be honest, when we spoke about the past I was really thinking about my relationship with Angus, rather than what happened to mum and dad. I think I came to terms with my parents death some time ago. It was a terrible accident they were involved in, that's all I'm afraid. I'm going to tell Andres the whole story about his father on the train back to Glasgow, he deserves to know the truth. I can see quite a lot of Angus in him you know, he's probably a bit of a rascal at heart but I like him, he's got spirit. As for Kirsty......"

"Before you tell me how Kirsty helped you," Peter interrupted, "there's something I discovered that I think you need to know. You deserve to know the truth as well."

"I can tell by the look on your face Peter that I might be in for a shock." Maureen smiled.

"I remember you telling me that you were puzzled that it was Kirsty chasing after Angus, rather than the other way around." Peter started to explain.

"Afterwards, I regretted saying that to you, I thought you'd think it was just me being bitter, blaming the beautiful woman for running off with Angus." Maureen said.

"If you don't mind me saying so, you need to stop putting yourself down and being so modest Maureen, I'm sat with a beautiful woman here tonight." Peter looked at Maureen and there was a slightly embarrassing silence. "The thing is, it looks like you are right about Kirsty chasing after him, it appears that before meeting Angus, she had once lived with his younger brother."

"That's incredible. Alex, the brother Angus hardly ever spoke about. He died, didn't he?" Maureen said, looking surprised.

"Yes, a drugs overdose, most people knew him as Sandy by then, he was a very talented fashion photographer." Peter explained.

"Did Angus know that Kirsty had once lived with him?" Maureen asked.

"Not until today as far as I know, it may go some way to explain what happened on the rooftop earlier." Peter said.

"I met Kirsty in London a few days ago, she had rung me and said she needed to see me urgently. She said something to me that at the time I didn't understand, she told me that one day, even I might understand why she chased after Angus." Maureen said.

"We may never know why Kirsty wanted Angus so badly, relationships can be complicated Maureen." Peter said, finishing his whiskey.

"What an amazing story and I'd have never known about it if this handsome man in a smart *Burberry* coat hadn't walked up my garden path and knocked on my door a few weeks ago." Maureen said.

"You mean you saw me. Why on earth didn't you answer the door?" Peter asked.

"I thought to myself, I wonder who that good looking man is knocking at my door, I wanted to answer but I was so bitter and twisted at the time that I just assumed it was another bloke up to no good." Maureen answered and drank the last of her brandy and coke.

"You were happy enough to meet me in the café though." Peter reminded her.

"I was curious I suppose and stupidly thought you might help me get some money out of Angus Mackenzie, fat chance of that though. Shall we walk down to the loch?" Maureen suddenly suggested.

Peter helped her on with her coat and the two of them went out into the cold night. There wasn't a cloud in the sky, which was unusual for the west coast of Scotland at this time of year Peter thought to himself, as Maureen slipped her hand inside his arm and they walked together down to the loch.

They didn't speak as they looked across the loch to the Tower, which was still lit up by the floodlight and it suddenly struck Peter how much he liked Maureen, she seemed to give him a connection to his past, growing up in Birmingham, girlfriends when he was studying at Oxford. He knew that Maureen was from Shepherd's Bush and in terms of town and gown, she was definitely a town girl.

She turned to face Peter, put her arms around his neck and they kissed.

"Shall we have one more drink?" Maureen whispered.

"I've got a bottle of Scotch in my room." Peter replied.

"I'd like that." Maureen snuggled up next to him as they made their way back to the hotel.

\*\*\*\*\*\*\*\*\*\*\*\*\*\*\*\*\*\*\*\*

The alarm sounded on Peter's mobile phone at nine o'clock and he fumbled to switch it off. He then turned over expecting to see Maureen lying next to him. For a split second he was confused, wondering whether the previous day had been a strange dream but the confusion quickly turned to disappointment because Maureen had gone, only for him to remember that she had an early train to catch with Andres to Glasgow.

He sat up in bed and drank the water that was left in the glass on his bedside table. His mouth was dry and his head was slightly fuzzy due to the whiskey he had drank the night before. After collecting his thoughts, Peter got out of bed and went into the bathroom. There was a folded note sat on top of his shaving bag. He unfolded it and read the message, it was from Maureen and simply said that she had enjoyed last night and would like to see him again and if he wanted to see her, he knew where she was. Peter smiled, he suddenly felt extremely happy.

# CHAPTER TWENTY-FOUR

## A SILVER LINING

"It was very brave of you two to go straight across to the Tower, you had no idea what to expect." Caroline told Peter and Mathew. She was helping John cook dinner for the four of them in the kitchen of the Lodge. It was their last meal together because Peter and Mathew would be returning to London the following morning.

"And Andres of course, he was with us, the really dangerous part was that somehow Kirsty had managed to douse Angus in the citronella oil, which she'd used earlier in the day as fuel for the torches. God only knows what would have happened if she'd ignited it with the torch she was holding. Anyway, Mathew had Angus out of harm's way pinned up against the wall soon after we arrived on the rooftop." Peter explained.

"It was still brave of the three of you as far as I'm concerned, do you think Kirsty would have used the torch if you hadn't turned up?" Caroline asked.

"If he'd tried to attack her again, I'm not sure what else she could have done to defend herself, trouble was, the oil had almost certainly splashed on Kirsty's clothes as well when she poured it over Angus, he was lying on top of her at the time, so it could have ended up very nasty indeed." Mathew said, opening a bottle of red wine for them to enjoy with the moussaka Caroline was cooking.

"It's a remarkable story, as if the drug smuggling wasn't enough, there's Angus's long-lost son from Colombia turning up with Maureen Tyler of all people and on top of all of that, there's Kirsty's previous relationship with

215

Angus's younger brother, extraordinary. My ex-husband would have been beside himself if you two had come up with a story like that when he owned the newspaper." Caroline said, laying the table.

"Anthony was never short of scoops when we worked for him Caroline." Peter reminded her.

"Oh, I know and he never stopped telling me, you two were the golden boys in his eyes." Caroline said.

"And to be honest, Kirsty got to the bottom of Angus's crimes on her own in the end and didn't really need any help." Peter said.

"Well, she certainly needed help when she was stuck up on that roof with that monster, that's for sure." Caroline reminded them.

"That's true Caroline. The Mackenzie family certainly had a lot of skeletons in the cupboard." John said.

"What I can't get my head around, is why didn't Kirsty tell Angus about Sandy when they first met?" Mathew asked.

"Yes, I've been giving that a lot of thought as well Matt, fear of being rejected by Angus? Perhaps if he'd known about her relationship with Sandy, he may not have wanted to have anything to do with her. According to Maureen, it was Kirsty who did all the chasing, she even got a job at the shipping company where he worked so that she could get to know him. We may never know the answer, but by all accounts her life was turned upside down when Sandy died, it had a terrible effect on her." Peter surmised.

"Andres seems like a nice young man and extremely good looking." Caroline laughed.

"Yes, he does, he's a TV star in Colombia." Peter said.

"Really? That's interesting." Caroline replied.

"Maureen told me about him last night after all the excitement had died down, it's partly because of his fame in Colombia that he decided to come here to find his father. Apparently, the media had been hounding him and his family over his parentage since a disastrous appearance on some chat show over there." Peter explained.

"Do you think there's a connection between Andres's mother and the drug racket, an accomplice in the shipping industry working in Cartagena would have been very useful for the smugglers I would think." John wondered aloud.

"You've got your policemen's helmet back on John, but I'm sure it'll be something the police will be asking Angus Mackenzie when he's interviewed.......that looks wonderful!" Mathew exclaimed, as Caroline gingerly transported the moussaka from the oven to the kitchen table.

After dinner, Peter decided to make his way back to the hotel. After saying goodbye to John, Caroline showed him out and the two of them stood on the doorstep of the Lodge for a few minutes discussing their plans for the next few days and weeks, until Peter changed the subject.

"I'm delighted you and John are getting together Caroline, I reckon you'll make a great couple, so well suited and after all, who wants to be on their own as they grow older, I don't think I do anymore." Peter said

"Thank you Peter, that's kind of you, by the way, I looked out of my bedroom window last night before I turned in," Caroline suddenly said, making eye contact with Peter, "and I saw a couple down by the loch, couldn't quite make out who they were, but it looked very romantic you know, particularly after all the unpleasantness earlier on in the day."

"Probably just some couple in love Caroline." Peter smiled and said goodnight.

"Yes, probably, goodnight Peter." Caroline replied.

*******************

The following morning, Peter checked out at the hotel reception desk before going into the dining room. After breakfast, he would drive his hire car to Fort William, where he would drop it off. Mathew would follow him in his car and the two of them would then head back to London together.

Morag had been doing a sterling job standing in for Kirsty and Angus and she brought Peter a full Scottish breakfast, he thought that a substantial meal would fortify him ahead of the long drive home. After a few minutes, Kirsty came in and joined him at his table. They were the only two in the dining room. It was the first time he had seen Kirsty since he had brought her back from the Tower in the rowing boat. The bruising on her face looked very nasty and Peter thought it must be painful.

"I've come to say thank you Peter. I don't know what would have happened if you hadn't shown up. He wanted to kill me. It was brave of the three of you to come and rescue me, I'll never forget it."

"We're all just pleased you're safe Kirsty, what will you do now?" Peter asked.

"Not sure really, my Aunty Moira is coming from Glasgow to stay with me and an old friend from London said he is coming up to stay as well, so I'll have plenty of company. Harry's a lawyer who worked with us at Mackenzie, Blount. I think the police will be interested in some information he has for them about the drug smuggling operation. Why did you go and see Maureen Tyler when you went back to London? She told me that you'd been to see her." Kirsty asked.

"At first, I was worried that someone might be trying to hurt John and I wanted to help him. By then, I'd seen the copy of the blackmail letter you'd given him and started following things up. You should know Kirsty, that whilst I was back in London, I also met Grace Garcia and Maggie Riley and I spoke to Barbara Tripp on the phone. Sorry about all that, but one thing led to another, by which time I needed to get to the bottom of things, see the whole picture, so to speak." Peter explained.

218

"Thanks for being so honest, you have been very thorough haven't you, I'll know where to come if I ever need a private detective." Kirsty tried to laugh, but because of the bruising to her face it was too painful and she grimaced.

"They all send their love and best wishes to you Kirsty, the only reason they agreed to speak with me was because they're fond of you and care about you. In fact, Grace said she would love to hear from you now that she's back in the UK and asked me to give you this." Peter said, handing her the card Grace had given him when he had visited her at her home in Belgravia.

"Thank you, I suppose what you would really like to know is why I tracked down Angus after Sandy's death and then married him." Kirsty said.

"I think I can understand why you might have wanted to find him and perhaps even have a relationship with him, but then not telling him that you had once lived with his brother, well it is a bit......"

"Weird?" Kirsty interrupted, "I've thought about that many times over the years Peter and if I knew the answer, I'd tell you, I may never know."

"You left those fashion magazines with John, I looked through them, great photos of you, must bring back a lot of memories. I spotted that one of them had a profile of Sandy in it, 'the brilliant young fashion photographer' was the heading I think, did you deliberately leave that particular magazine with John?" Peter asked.

"Because I wanted to tell someone about Sandy? Probably, it was a pretty big secret to have kept for more than ten years. On a brighter note, I'm pleased John's is making a good recovery and I understand that Caroline is moving in with him. As they say, every cloud has a silver lining." Kirsty said, changing the subject as she carefully got to her feet and left Peter to finish his breakfast.

\*\*\*\*\*\*\*\*\*\*\*\*\*\*\*\*\*\*\*\*

Peter made one telephone call before leaving Scotland, it was to Finlay Robertson. He told the elderly Scotsman the whole story. Finlay listened quietly and Peter could imagine him sat in his beautiful home in Edinburgh.

"So, money and greed were Angus Mackenzie's downfall," Finlay said, when Peter had finished, "although I must say, there's clearly a lot of the father in the son, Cameron Mackenzie was a thoroughly bad lot too. Poor Kirsty, whatever made her marry the scoundrel, I suppose you could call it brotherly love."

# CHAPTER TWENTY-FIVE

## LONDON - CHRISTMAS EVE 2015

Peter and Mathew were stood at the bar in *The Elephant and Castle*, their favourite pub in London. For Mathew, it was a short walk from his home in Kensington, whereas for Peter it was a tube journey from Marylebone. They had been frequenting the pub, which had been decorated festively, for the best part of forty years, ever since they had both moved to London from Oxford to start working for a national newspaper and had shared a rented flat in Notting Hill.

The barmaid had commented on how handsome the two regulars looked, unusually both dressed in smart suits. Peter was wearing a charcoal grey *Paul Smith* suit, one of his favourite designers, with an open neck white shirt and Mathew sported a more traditional navy-blue chalk stripe three-piece suit, with a pale blue shirt and a red and white spotted silk tie. Although it was only five o'clock, it was already dark outside and cold and they had hung their overcoats on the coat stand near the door.

"We have a date, a double date I suppose you could call it." Mathew explained with a grin.

"Two lucky ladies." The barmaid teased.

"We're the lucky ones." Mathew replied laughing and the two old friends took their pints of beer to a nearby table.

Mathew had bought four tickets for a carol service at a nearby hall, starting at six-thirty and Peter had booked a table at *Locanda Ottoemezzo*, a lovely Italian restaurant, also in Kensington, for eight o'clock.

"I've been meaning to ask you Matt, when you were left up on the rooftop with Angus and Andres did they speak to each other?" Peter asked, when the two of them were settled at their table.

"Yes, they did at first. Once I'd got Angus out of that oil-soaked shirt and changed, the three of us went into the flag room and sat down to wait for the police to arrive. I let them sit next to each and I sat opposite them, I didn't want to let Angus out of my sight for obvious reasons, but by then he had calmed down and was resigned to the fact that the game was up. He looked thoroughly deflated. Andres didn't say too much at first, he must have been shocked by what had happened, but Angus asked him about Cartagena, his home and his mother, I think he said her name is Valeria. They chatted for about ten minutes, Angus doing most of the talking. In his own way, I think he was saying how sorry he was that they had never met before now. It was all quite amicable until he asked Andres how he had found him in the Highlands of Scotland. As soon as Andres mentioned that a very kind lady called Maureen had helped him and they had travelled to Scotland from London together, Angus clammed up. I think he probably blames her for the predicament he now finds himself in." Mathew explained.

"I suppose he's right in a way, if Maureen hadn't written that blackmail letter pretending to be her brother things may have been very different." Peter said.

"Speaking of Maureen, you two seemed to be getting on very well together, before I returned to the Lodge the other night." Mathew suggested.

"I like her a lot Matt, she's had a tough time, parents died when she was young, getting mixed up with Angus Mackenzie, a pretty hopeless brother who she never gave up on, I like her spirit, amongst other things." Peter replied.

"It's not just that you feel sorry for her then?" Mathew asked.

"I wondered about that, but no it's not, there's a lot more to her than meets the eye and I find her very attractive." Peter said.

"And what about Taraneh?" Mathew asked, reading Peter's mind.

"I know, complications, it's not great timing is it, oh well, we'll see." Peter replied and as he did, Taraneh and her old friend Rita arrived at *The Elephant and Castle*.

"Taraneh, lovely to see you again," Peter stood up and they kissed on both cheeks, "and Rita, great to see you too, Taraneh, you've met Mathew before, in this very pub if I remember rightly."

"Yes, of course how could I forget, I nearly knocked you over Peter rushing in to avoid the rain, Mathew can I introduce my oldest, best friend in the world, this is Rita." Taraneh said and Mathew and Rita shook hands.

"Less of the oldest if you don't mind Tara love." Rita said with a wink and the four of them laughed.

"So, enough of the small talk, what are you two fabulous ladies having to drink, a glass of bubbly?" Mathew asked heading to the bar.

"Oh, I like you already Mathew, thank you, that would be wonderful." Rita replied and Taraneh smiled, nodding in agreement. She was already deep in conversation with Peter, so Rita joined Mathew at the bar.

The two friends couldn't have looked more different, Mathew thought as he ordered the drinks. Taraneh had dark hair and olive skin, whereas Rita was blonde, with a pale complexion and as the evening went on it also became apparent that they had very different personalities, Taraneh being the quieter, more thoughtful friend and Rita being quite loud and extrovert. They did have one thing in common though, they both looked extremely glamorous.

The carol service was a great success. The hall, which was a short walk from *The Elephant and Castle*, had been beautifully decorated in festive colours and the choir were

223

brilliant. Until the service started the other three were unaware that Rita was a long-standing member of a choir group and had once sung with a local opera company in Liverpool, her home town. She had a fabulous voice, which she used to full affect when the audience were invited to join in. Mathew loved it and his deep baritone voice, of which he was very proud, complimented Rita's mezzo-soprano. The two of them were easily the loudest voices in the audience, much to the amusement of Peter and Taraneh. After a rousing version of the final carol, Hark, the Herald Angels Sing, the four of them headed off to the restaurant.

As Peter had suspected before they met, Mathew and Rita got along famously. It had been a long-standing joke between the two old friends that whilst Mathew was the more conservative of the pair in both his outlook to life and his dress sense, favouring tweeds, pin-stripes and brogues, he had always had a much more colourful love life than the more modern minded, fashion-conscious Peter, who had been married to Gloria for the best part of thirty years, before her untimely death.

Over the years, Mathew had had a string of relationships, often with quite flamboyant, sometimes eccentric women. Peter and Gloria always found them so interesting when they met up in a foursome. His sister Judith's description of some of them was "unsuitable", which always made Peter smile. He thought of Mathew's relationship with Maggie Riley, who he'd recently caught up with and he thought that it was interesting how opposites could often attract and this appeared to be the case in both Taraneh's and Rita's friendship and now, by the look of things, Rita's and Mathew's.

The food and wine at the restaurant were wonderful and over dinner Rita entertained the others with stories about her life growing up in Liverpool. The youngest of seven children to Roman Catholic parents she'd had a tough, but loving upbringing and like Taraneh, she had always dreamt of becoming a nurse. Her dream had come true when she was accepted to train as a nurse in Oxford in the early nineteen-seventies. She started nursing on the same day as Taraneh and they had been friends ever since then.

After two failed marriages and three sons, Rita's life changed dramatically at the turn of the millennium when she was left seventy thousand pounds by a deceased uncle and with the money opened her own care home near Liverpool. Within five years, she had opened three further care homes in the North West and two years ago sold them for a large sum to one of the largest care home operators in the UK.

"She's worth millions!" Taraneh teased her old friend.

"And worth every penny Tara love." Rita replied and winked at Mathew and Peter.

"Well, it's a marvelous, heart-warming story Rita, that's for sure and what do you do with your time now that you're a lady of leisure?" Mathew asked.

"She'll never be a lady of leisure Mathew, she never stops." Taraneh interrupted.

"As a pair of experienced journalists, you'll probably laugh, but I'm writing a book about my experiences in life." Rita told them.

"Not at all Rita," Peter said, "from what you've told us this evening, it'll probably be a best seller."

"So, you two men have been very good listeners this evening, are you going to tell us about what you've been up to in Scotland, I saw a news report a few days ago about an attack on a former fashion model in a remote part of the Highlands not too far from Mallaig, wasn't that where you two have been staying?" Taraneh asked.

"Yes it was and it's a long story, perhaps for another time." Peter replied.

\*\*\*\*\*\*\*\*\*\*\*\*\*\*\*\*\*\*\*\*

225

Mathew escorted the two ladies on foot back to Taraneh's flat, which was on his way home and Peter returned to Marylebone by taxi. It had been a memorable evening and one the four of them agreed to repeat in the New Year.

Before they left the restaurant, Peter and Taraneh snatched a moment on their own whilst waiting for his taxi to arrive. She told him that she would be returning to Tehran in early January, but before leaving she would like to cook Persian food for him and invited him to her flat in Kensington for dinner on New Year's Eve. Peter accepted and the two of them embraced warmly before he left in the taxi.

It was during the short journey home that his phone pinged and he looked at his text messages. It was from Maureen Tyler and simply said, '*Happy Christmas Peter, miss you X*'

Printed in Great Britain
by Amazon

10458821R00132